WEEKEND
IN
DINLOCK

WEEKEND
IN
DINLOCK

BY
CLANCY SIGAL

HOUGHTON MIFFLIN COMPANY BOSTON
THE RIVERSIDE PRESS CAMBRIDGE
1960

The Riverside Press

Cambridge · Massachusetts

Printed in the U. S. A.

TO

DORIS

AUTHOR'S NOTE

Thank you, is all I can say to my friends, and their friends, in the north of England whose kindness to an inquisitive and often tactless stranger made this book possible. Hospitality can never be repaid. At the least, I can assure them that neither they nor their particular village will be found within these pages. Dinlock is imaginary, in that it is many places I have seen, and its people are not 'real' except in the sense that they are a sum of the total of what I wish to say about what I saw.

1

WEEKEND IN DINLOCK

It was two or three months ago that I first met Davie, the young coal miner from South Yorkshire. He was, and is, a lonely, temperamental, impulsive boy, a miner who paints under circumstances which shame me.

From the beginning we got along.

I had heard tales of Davie long before we finally met; of his sudden spurting trips down from Yorkshire to London and of the wild, drunken self-pitying, sometimes cruel ways in which he spent the rare releases he gave himself from the prison of his village, the village he has painted in his hundred completed pictures. Though they never said so in words, it was easy to see that his London friends, his art dealer and his various rescuers among the critics and patrons and fellow artists who encouraged and sheltered him on these trips, often lending him money, never repaid, looked upon Davie as a strange, frightening animal sprung out of the muck of the Midlands earth. There were stories of Davie getting drunk in a hundred different ways, Davie wading into a mob of teddy boys at Camden Town tube station, Davie having to be dragged comatose to safety by one of the miscellaneous women who somehow seemed always to be around when he exploded, Davie drunkenly flirting with a forlorn middle-aged actress and then brutally, unforgivably insulting her.

They were my friends too. And when I asked about Davie they shrugged, wearily, and made cynical compassionate remarks. Yes, Davie was a phenomenon. Yes, he had a terrible life, trying to paint what he felt while working in the mines and raising a family. Yes, at all costs he must be befriended, helped. But not by me, they said, not me any longer, I've had a bellyful of Davie, his drunks, his fists, his maunderings. All right, criticise us, they said, you don't know. Just wait. He'll do it to you too. Don't misunderstand. It's not that we don't *like* Davie, just. . . .

It was my turn.

He showed up, as I had been told he would one rainy Saturday morning, abruptly, eagerly, very young, looking sincere, talking with a bold sweetness. A slim hard-built boy, and I thought, of course, I knew he'd be just like this, he even looks like Mike Corrigan, the black-witted Irishman from Los Angeles who bored and scared and excited and borrowed money from us all, trying to prove, for ever prove —God alone knows what—until he died in a lorry drivers' free-for-all on the Cahuenga freeway.

When I opened the door of my room in Islington he was there, shyly. "They said as how tha' might be able to put me oop."

So we spent three days and three nights bumming and drinking and talking, Davie away from his village, his painting, his family and the pit, in London town, Davie talking and wondering and pitying and praising himself during the day as if his life depended on it and stinking, vicious drunk at night; only once had we to fight with our fists, inconclusively, and in that time he began to pall on me too and then I saw why he had palled on the others, because he was in the kind of pickle which would kill lesser men. Working the afternoon shift in the mine, he said simply, coming home at midnight to paint pictures of the mine and village until the morning, propping himself up with benzedrine and codeine and caring for the children while his wife was also having another, a house-proud provincial wife, he said, who hated the idea and fact of his painting and him eating himself up with guilt because he only suspected (and I thought, at

10

this distance, I knew) he didn't love her, doing all the things necessary to sustain his prestige in a mining village where nothing compares to how well a man stands in the eyes of other men. And in the same house two sullen, unforgiving elder sisters, another load he has taken on his shoulders, Davie a man who piles it on and piles it on, the only time he can short the circuit is the traditional breaking time of the Yorkshire miner, when he drinks, and all this on a miner's wage. And down in London he was alternately whipped and proud, feeling inferior but also a little proud of his art, knowing he was crude and hungry to learn, always proud of his class and of the one thing nobody could take away from him, the fact that he was a miner, a Yorkshire miner, a village miner, and the very cream at that, a collier on the coal face.

So we spent those nights and days, in Islington and in Soho, him searching for Life and Light and Women, and me telling him, Davie, this stuff is for kids, and him saying, You don't know what it's like in the village, if you don't want to stick with me then go back home and I'll do it myself and anyway I feel like a fight, I've got to smash somebody *soon*. And with us on the second night was my friend, the bearded carpenter Anthony, nineteen and a conscientious objector, whom Davie treated with a gentleness because Anthony was so young and had never dug coal in his short life; Davie even, God help us all, advised Anthony. But advise me Davie wouldn't dare. Wasn't I working class just like him, didn't I *understand* even before the words were out and didn't that prove I had worker's blood, not like the London intellectuals with their coffee bars and neuroses. And anyway, wasn't I an artist just like him? When he was drunk I never tried to disabuse him.

Three days and three nights. And the second of those nights, early dawn, sprawled under the statue of Eros with me telling him that any man who has to hit is a coward and him bridling and dealing me a test blow in the stomach, and me saying (and meaning) if you pick a fight with me I'll

11

break your skull with this bottle in my hand, and him believing it and (which tells me more about the village than all his stories) respecting me for it. So there we sit and I listen to his troubles. He wants a woman, he goes for too long without a real one, and what's he to do with the family, and one minute he loves his wife and the next she is his nightmare, and always, always coming back to that without which he feels he is nothing: he can shift a day's coal in a day's time.

Davie adores what little publicity he's received in the London and Yorkshire press, in a child's way, openly, with none of the spurious modesties. And, too, proud of his fists. He gets into fights, a lot of them, not quite as many as he says, but enough.

Taller than I, a wiry handsome body, unruly white-blond hair which he pays a village beau's attention to, and pieces of rock for hands, large slow bright eyes with long almost womanish lashes, a pliable Scots-Irish mouth with a perpetually split lip, a short wide strong neck. Vain, cocky, lugubrious, sincere, playing the young worker if there is an audience of Londoners and sobering up if there isn't (but he is a young worker), passionate in everything he does, seldom rational in our way, inconsolably emotional, quick to be hurt, quick to insult, quick to forgive, his ways the ways of the village, a story spinner, sometimes a liar, making out his background worse than it was (he's read the literature of the working-class boy) without completely understanding that what's he got is bad enough by double.

We sent Anthony home to his mother and sat under the statue of Eros and watched the Sunday night crowds in the Circus dwindle to last tubes and buses, and then Davie had to find a woman, in a dive on Frith Street. We sat there, in a dark Wurlitzerized cellar, and whores swarmed. Buy me a drinkie, honey, two bob for you, ten bob for me, and when the place closes we'll talk about it. Davie's eyes sparkled, he nudged me and wanted to know if this was the kind of place I knew about. I told him this was for the hicks. He bridled,

12

I like it here, it's interesting, it is really London. A painted moroness entwined herself around him, and bless the boy as soon as she said she was from Dundee, the birthplace of his grandfather, he was telling her the whole story, he's a collier who has made over a hundred pictures and how long now has it been she's been away from home? I said, Davie, last time I was here she told me she came from New York. You're too cynical, Davie said. The Cypriot pimps flooded in at closing time, an army not looking at us, and I got Davie out before a brawl could start.

We were broke so we walked all that night, from Soho to Islington. He wanted to get a woman, any woman, and I told him, Davie, you'll get VD. The ancient fear of the ancient curse and he subsided with his crooked, play-acting, charming, conscious grin. Oh no, he declared virtuously, he wouldn't want to catch anything to pass on to his family. I sang, "Father Dear Father Come Away with Me Now", "The Bell in the Tower", etc. Davie said, You shouldn't be making fun of us who have to work all day for a living. We chased each other around a lamp post, meaning to do one another harm, until a black police car came cruising by, near Euston, and I said, Look innocent.

And Davie secretly relieved he didn't have to go on playing the maddened bull.

The next night, his last, after a morning and afternoon of lassitude and long silences because he has temporarily talked himself out and is wise to Londoners' boredom quotient, and is sullen with himself for not being able to stop from talking, talking about what (himself, painting, himself) he can't talk about in the village, and because we had an ugly argument about who should take the empties down to the rubbish bin, he went off by himself and when he returned, on the morning he was to go back, he had a story of a rich night's wandering in Soho. A courtly and sordid experience, it was, concerning a beautiful tart and her knife-wielding protector and all the rest. I knew it was a bloody lie, most of

13

it. But Davie was not the kind to come back empty-handed, without even a story, after a dreary dull Monday night walking the streets of the West End and finding, as everybody finds, nothing. So he came back with a gory whopper appealing in its adolescent naïveté, a naïveté which it is not above him to affect but which even he had small awareness of how deeply it actually ran inside himself, a sustained disingenuousness born of the fear of insight.

Piling guilt upon guilt in order to prove he's as good as—who?

That last morning Davie kept insisting, Come up to the village. See how I live. Look at them, live with them, and then you'll see why I'm proud of them and why I'm the way I am when I come to London, and come because you're my friend.

I said, Okay, Davie, set it up.

I go, not knowing that my destination would be so distant. Up into the Midlands, then into Yorkshire. Change at Barnsley for a smaller train, and get off at Hamthorpe, the old Roman market centre crammed full of Saturday shoppers, an old grey city like all the others, and then a 20-minute bus ride to the incredible universe of Dinlock, at the edge of the world.

Not through the windows of the bus, but when I ask the conductress to let me off at the cinema, which Davie gave me as a landmark, do I get my first inkling of Dinlock. In this tiny village she did not know where the only cinema was. Yes, she had been on this run for a long time, three years. But no, she couldn't help. Ask the locals, she advised.

I walk along the wind-swept, cold streets of Dinlock without any people on them. Ugly and dreary, certainly, but no more so than many such coal towns I've visited. The usual semi-detached and back-to-back malignancies, shabby brick dwellings with unkempt gardens, the brick old and cracked and sooted. By now, I'm accustomed to the awful sameness of height, number of windows, rows and rows of cottages until they become phalanxes, solid, seemingly unending from one side of England to the other, the arid window holes and dry, obdurate people. It is like a deserted village. I walk slowly. I am cold and I wonder what lies below this taut grey skin of village. Where is everybody? It is Saturday afternoon.

The houses are below, on a downhill slope, radiating centrally from the fulcrum of the long low stone wall beside me. And then, rounding a corner, I stop stone cold. There it is, uphill, the explanation for the village, its reason for existence and non-existence. The mine.

I look across the scarred, mired field up to the pit, with its

15

familiar outline of tipples and jutting colliery wheels and machinery housing and chimneys under which at any given time one-third of the male population of Dinlock is digging coal. Though it is a quarter of a mile away, lowering dramatically in the darkening mist and emitting no sound except the clanking and chipping in my own imagination, it dominates the village. It is built on top of it. Everything—streets, people, wind—seems to point to the pit. They call it The Hill.

Two teenage girls in cloth coats come by. I ask my way, nodding dumbly. Yorkshire speech is impossible to the newcomer; broad, thickly slurring, archaic. I turn down into the 'centre' of Dinlock and walk to the main street which is main by virtue of the existence of a pub, a cinema, a row of small shops for some reason encircled by a ten-foot high unpainted wooden fence. Only children play in the empty streets. They run, as I walk, leaning to the bias, like listing passengers of a ship which is just beginning to sink. All the streets of Dinlock are laid out on a maddeningly slight incline sweeping past the stone wall up to the colliery mound and pit-head. The village is larger than I had expected; it sprawls jaggedly, the houses like brick algae clinging to the flanks of a worn-out volcano. And everything still points to the mine.

Nobody much pays attention to me. People don't rush to their windows to catch a glimpse of the visitor. What had I expected; this isn't darkest Africa. Or is it? Then I see: they are watching me, but carefully, from across the street and behind curtains, with something akin to astonishment in their careful Yorkshire eyes. At me? Then I understand. A year ago, on 14th Street in New York, for twelve dollars, I bought a white duffle coat which I'd just had cleaned in London. It is still cream-white. The colour seems to dazzle them; it is clean, without dirt or greyness, hence, I must have just come from another world, where you did not breathe coal dust and the chill winds off the Yorkshire moors which seem more a frigid gas than a breath of air. (Two hours later I look down

16

at the coat and it is lightly smudged. The next day I am one of them: grey).

Davie's house is, of course, like all the others. It's in the middle of a long street where all the houses look exactly alike except, I suppose, to the loving eye. In Davie's small uncared-for garden the wash dances on the line, sending out soft violent flaps which sound unnaturally raucous in the still, chill air. All over the village virtually the only sound is the flap of drying fabric.

Loretta, Davie's wife, comes to the door, shy and tentative, masking the anxiety provoked by Davie's work and city friends with the constraint of the miner's woman. She is young, but already, like most of the women I am to meet, beginning to look worked out. Loretta was once a beautiful and well-shaped girl, today she is—winning; in a few years she will not be attractive or pretty. She is a girl who lost the idea of beauty before it fully took hold, and now her broad, plump shoulders slope and hunch, for all the world as if she had never been a dreaming child.

Davie was on late shift last night and is still sleeping up-stairs, so Loretta and I, watching the kids, sit and make desultory conversation, or rather none at all. She is deter-mined to play the Yorkshire wife, speaking only when spoken to. I hem and haw, she says nothing, the kids stare enrap-tured in curiosity, Peter 6 and peaceful, Jenny 3 and rowdy, and pugnacious baby Michael. Their talk, and Loretta's, unintelligible because it is thickest Yorkshire without con-cessions to visitors. Note for Americans: think of a heavy Scots brogue, with the leaden lilt of the Irish countryside, substract the articles of speech, and that's Yorkshire; when it sounds like anything American it's liquored-up Boston shanty.

In our heavy silence I examine the house, near freezing outside and only the living-room-parlour heated, even though miners get their coal free, having but to pay haulage. (All the rooms in all the houses I am to visit are unheated except for the parlour. Old fear-ridden customs die hard hereabouts.) A small kitchen equipped with a half-size washing machine and dryer (these are the household appliances before which Davie swears Loretta abases herself; from what he said in London I had visualised a cottage crammed with gadgets), a parlour only slightly larger (four paces long, two paces wide), an adjoining room for the television set and two beds for Davie's sisters, two bedrooms upstairs and indoor plumbing, the kitchen sink serving also that purpose; the furniture cheap and modernistic, the house not particularly clean or neat. Where is Loretta's house-proudness? I still don't know.

The children grow restless in the silence, Loretta sits reserved and detached murmuring to baby Michael, and then Davie, sleep still in his eyes, comes in from the bedroom and roars "Sit!" and Peter and Jenny leap for the couch and are instantly silent, ram-rod stiff. With hardly a nod yet to me, he wrestles with the kids a few moments and then says, "Loretta, do tha' have to play that damn' thing for ever!" Loretta gets up, having abdicated the kids to her awakened husband, and switches off the radio set which has been on the Light Programme all the time and which, except when Davie commands otherwise, remains so tuned throughout the entire weekend of waking hours. (He permits the telly on only when the children are asleep, probably the only miner in Dinlock to do so.) Then she stands near the glazed-tile fireplace, arms folded, and watches Davie play on the floor with the kids.

Everyone in the house, I learn, is sick of one thing or another, as is true in most of the homes I visit today. Peter, the eldest, has had his piercing cough since birth. ("Doctor says twill go away in tahm," Loretta says), Jenny has an ear-ache and has had it for months, baby Michael has the croup and Loretta has had back trouble since her last confinement, and as for Davie, "'E's never too well, y'know."

The kids are awesomely obedient to Davie, ignore the mother who is cheerlessly efficient at hiding her resentments. As soon as he can, Davie runs upstairs to put on some clothes, and with an uncomfortable word or two to Loretta (he is a bit afraid of her, and her tongue, of which I have heard overmuch in London) we go out. We are hardly out the door before he starts talking about his passion, his anchor and his albatross, the village. In the house he was sternly, fiercely paternal, natural in an elder man's role, subdued, indecisive and halting with me; now he is once again the enthusiastic young gallant. It would kill him to know how much he hated, and needed, that house.

Up one wind-gusted street and down another I learn the village gossip, and also learn about Davie, and how very much a part of the village he is even when he is analysing them with the self-conscious and self-proud frankness of the young intellectual who must paint his pictures to prevent his staves from unspringing. His talk is ringed with iron assumptions I am to see acted out, above all else that a Dinlock man is judged by how good a miner he is (and exactly where in the mine, that is important), how consistent a provider, how fair a mixer, how tough.

(Later, I am to meet Will Lawson, intelligent, sober, loyal to the men and his family, steady, the model president when we can find him—and even to his vacillations and irresolutions—for an American trade union, if not the mayor of the town. Here, in Dinlock, Will is nobody. And rightly so, says Davie, who complains Will "takes a back seat". What does it mean? Will doesn't like to use his fists. He could, but won't. He will turn aside a foolish insult rather than try to prove he is as tough as the next man. Therefore, though liked, an odd man out. Will's critics would feel easier if only he were not a face worker.)

The first house Davie and I go into is down his own street, on the corner, a semi-detached, squalid, packed with quiet children including the ubiquitous new baby, Kathleen the

19

mother slightly addled and proudly showing off her new Health Service teeth, removing them from her mouth and passing them around for our inspection. We agree they are smashing. Davie talks with her about the baby who almost died prematurely, and approves the eldest son's choice of 'courting' socks, red and yellow. The boy is 14, frail, thin, a Dickens character like so many of the grey-faced oddly bumptious village kids, looks eleven, is ready to go down into the pit, no Dad around. The living-room is exactly that, where the whole squirming mass of semi-washed conservative family eats, often sleeps, always lives, quarrels and watches TV. There is a table, a soft chair, a hard chair, a picture or two on the walls papered with vivid, lunging patterns (newly purchased and shown off) and that's it. Here, criticism of worldly possessions is irrelevant to the point of sinfulness.

Telly has had a wholesale impact. Half the miners' families own a set, and the other half desperately wants one. The village librarian says reading of books has plummeted since introduction of TV. If I had to live in Dinlock I would worship at the desire to get a set. Telly is the road *out*. And if anyone worries, as he reads elsewhere about the corruption of native Yorkshire culture consequent on the fragmentation of primary societies, I want him to show me exactly what has been corrupted; life in Dinlock before, during and after telly, is dingy, narrow, primitive, with the enforced virtues of primevalness and riddled with inherent outrages. Coal mining is still what Shaw said it was, an atrocity, and village living is the accomplice to the atrocity. Dinlock, the archetype face-to-face community, is utterly a world unto itself, more accurately a fiercely warring world where the hosts of hope and the hosts of necessity clash head-on in a scaled-down holocaust of hopelessness. The New York, the big town, to Dinlock is Hamthorpe; Bagdad is Barnsley, only 35 minutes away by bus and I have spoken to mature women who have not visited Barnsley since the end of the war. Loretta, a

Barnsley factory girl, has not been back to her native city since she was married. It is this fact which hangs over the village like the shadow of the colliery; if you live in Dinlock you must make Dinlock your life, and you cannot live in Dinlock and be accepted by the core if you have a real means of escape.

It is this nucleus, this bound-up core, that I am to spend my time with. Only numerically are they a minority. For they are convinced of themselves as the real heart of the village. You can see it in the way they carry themselves, in their unvocal assurance of *themselves in place*, that if they were to leave it tomorrow Dinlock would become merely an inhabitation. This prime social fact does not go unrecognised by the other villagers, if only by the half-envious half-resentful way they keep out of this inner ring of face-men and their wives. Those others, this majority, this rest, out there in the whole village, to listen to Davie you would never know they existed.

And Barnsley is still 35 minutes away by bus.

Afterwards, out in the street, Davie emphasises that Kathleen's house is not typical. She is 'not all there', has a lazy husband and 'plays around'.

A lazy husband. In Davie's mind, and the mind of all the others, the cardinal sin for a man is not to provide. It is not an uncomplicated matter, for these miners are 'contract men', that is, legally they are independent labourers who can work as much or as little as they desire. Some men choose to work only two, three shifts a week. These are the lazy ones, and are frowned upon, even when it is said of them, In their place if I could afford to I'd do the same. Davie himself now works only three, four shifts a week so as to give himself more time to paint. Through a series of complications—a year ago in a slack time, he and a few other colliers transferred out of Dinlock—Davie finds himself working over at Beckley pit, three miles away, and it is this, more than anything else, which has caused him to, if not lose face then certainly remove himself a bit from the hearts of the villagers. Beckley is 300 miles away as far as Dinlock colliers are concerned.

I was rude in Kathleen's house. She asked me how old I thought it was. Thirty years, I reflected, fifteen I said. She looked hurt. "Nay, only four." Davie calls them the slums of the future. These are the National Coal Board houses, NCB houses, not much different in aspect than the famed Council houses, squarish, cramped affairs with the ceilings already cracking, grey inside and out in all the various disheartening shades. Yet these are the best houses in the village, queued for and fought over to get into. It is one of the big reasons why the men go into the pit and stay there, to snare a house. If they quit the pit they must leave their houses, and that is a very critical matter. It is one way the NCB has of holding a pistol to the men's heads. And let me say this at the outset. The British coal mines may be nationalised, they may be 'public property', but as far as the miners are concerned the bosses are still the bosses, NCB or no. The men would never go back to the old way, when the big mines were privately owned, but the hope of the early days of nationalisation is shot dead in its tracks, vanished, to be replaced by a militant, if unevenly loyal, cynicism. The miners are acutely, defensively aware that the national press has zeroed in on them for 'irresponsibility' in the form of absenteeism, wildcat strikes, unwillingness to accept foreign labour, 'low' productivity and all the rest, and that is one of the chief reasons why they love Davie, because in his paintings, shown in London and occasionally reproduced, he is telling their story as they want it to be told, straightforwardly and without frills and from their point of view. Davie represents them to a hostile world, and they are grateful in their own quiet, poetic way.

Davie, as a miner, speaks bitterly of the NCB and of the top National Union of Mineworkers leaders who, he says, side with the NCB. Slowly I am to discover he is speaking for all the miners in his anger and disillusionment. Not that the miners are always in the right, when it comes to the timing and spark-reason of their disputes. Sometimes, and this is obvious even to outsiders, they're off base. But the history of exploitation is far too recent, and hallowed, to allow them to drop their guard, to soften their traditional suspicion of 'upstairs', even for a moment. As only fundamentally honest men can be, they are naïvely shocked, nauseated to the point of zenophobic fury, by stories which the London newspapers print about them. Let the reporters come down and see for themselves! (That is why, at first, they like me, because I go everywhere they wish me to go, look at everything they want me to see. Later, for precisely the same reason, they start to change their minds.)

Next we go to Glenn's house. Glenn, huge and grinning, a trifle too good-looking, broad-faced and fleshy, something weak in him; a miner, and like many a 'Geordie'. He and Davie are old, close friends; for years they worked down in Dinlock pit together, on the same face team. Glenn is a talker, a charmer, a shiftless anarchist, except when his woman is around, which is today. She roams silently back and forth between kitchen and parlour, speaking once when introduced and then for ever silent. Like most Dinlock wives past a certain age (she looks 45, is 31) she appears pregnant and is not, I am informed later by Loretta, who also tells me that the major, and sometimes sole topic of gossip amongst the village women is 'who's expecting?' and by whom, frankly, among friends, now.

Like a good many Dinlock men who served in the Forces, Glenn has been places and tries feverishly to cudgel up memory, as he sprawls, tiredly or phlegmatically I cannot tell. When his kids—two boys and a girl—roar in, Glenn takes the youngest boy in his arms and rocks him lovingly, singing a soft Scottish lullaby. Everywhere I go I am a witness of this spontaneous, fierce show of quiet love between the fathers up from pit and the children, with the wives looking

23

on tolerantly (and having what thoughts?). In Dinlock, fatherhood is an ancient rite.

Later, Davie is to say that he's fed up with Glenn, who is going to pieces and won't work the number of shifts necessary to keep his family going. He doesn't, Davie avers, give a damn for the family. I don't know, it seems to me Glenn has a sweet and reasonable relationship with the kids, all except the eldest, a Modigliani boy, who stands aloof and cautious. I try talking to the boy who only draws himself farther away. Glenn's wife, Jane, walks over and says, quietly but audibly, That's the one Glenn beats regular, and then slips away into the kitchen. As he does his wife, Davie adds.

I don't know any more. The way Davie describes him, Glenn is an A-1 foul ball. Which just goes to show something. Right now, Glenn is putting on a big show (and it is a show, insists Davie) of being the hard-working trade unionist miner. We talk about—wage rates. Yes, even to a stranger, who has demonstrably never been down a mine in his life, the colliers of Dinlock cannot help but obsessively bring the talk around to—wage rates. It is what miners in Yorkshire talk about, morning, noon and evening. It is both the substance and the ploy of conversation. So now we talk about a new NCB price book. Glenn explains in detail how, whether measured in tonnage or yards, a miner has to shift a certain amount of coal in any given eight-hour period in order to feed his family, which Davie says is exactly what Glenn does not do. I am taken in by Glenn's strong, tender and sentimental handling of his children, and his reserved shrewd manner with wage rates, and Davie warns me that the Dinlockers are not above showing off their best side to a visitor. Glenn also likes to talk about international politics, and once he gets going he can sound like a Lowland Orsini. Afterwards, Davie remarks in disgust that that's Glenn's way, all talk and little action, although there was a time when things were different, when he and Glenn and Walter for a short time ran the local Labour Party branch and raised

24

Yorkshire hell, as when single-handedly they saved a Rumanian from sacking, an act of no small courage in a community which is stubbornly, even proudly set against the importation of foreign labour.

I know the miners are sensitive to this issue and I try to be tactful, but their attitudes are sufficiently two-sided to force them to talk—suspiciously too much—about it. Dinlock, they loudly declaim, has a long habit of barring foreign labour, and that's the way it's going to stay. From the way the branch union officials talk about it you would think it was a progressive tradition, and in a way it is, in the sense that importation (or the threat) of foreigners was always the owners' weapon against the miners in order, the miners say, to artificially inflate the reservoir of workers and depress living standards. The issue came to a head a while back when the NCB, which had invited Hungarian refugees to take a course in English mining customs, logically attempted to place the Hungarians in the pits. Very few were accepted.

The Yorkshire miner is not consistent in his attitude, but he feels strongly on the matter. Retrogressive, mindless anti-foreignism is mixed up in his mind with the defence of miners' rights, the irrational with the shrewd. Details aside, the miners are very much afraid the Coal Board will, at some future time as did the coal bosses before it, use foreign labour to make the indigenous miners toe the line. This fear, valid or not (and it's not easy to say: the old days may be gone but where are the new days?) co-operates easily with the clannish fear of outsiders of the Englishman, than which there is no more steel-tipped epithet in Yorkshire but which, in fact, the Yorkshireman is. Ever mindful of his vanguard position in the working class, the Yorkshire miner finds in this economically-justified prejudice a magnificently convenient outlet for illiberal and narrow-minded sentiments he would be too proud to express in another context.

Now that I have been down Dinlock pit I have to say

25

that if I had to go down again, for the duration of my working life, if I were a miner dependent for my life on perfect team-work in the shaft where the spoken word must be immediately understood, if I were a miner from Dinlock where the nagging fear of death or disabling injury still hangs, in 1959, like the presence of death itself, I would have second and third thoughts about granting welcome to Hungarians or Poles who want to take a job at my side.

Also, though few of the Dinlock men will come out and say so at first, it often comes down to the question of good old-fashioned speed-up.

Over the years, the Dinlock miner has evolved for himself a system of personal production by which he manages steadily to get out high-quality coal without killing himself in the process. Unquestionably, few miners work at top speed. If they did they would be dead men inside a few years. (As it is, pneumonocosis takes a fearful toll at Dinlock; it is the constant dread, shrugged off because there's nothing for it but acceptance as one of the occupational risks.) Each coal face collier expects to shift eight yards of coal every day in order to make his wage. He could shift more, but won't. But the foreign labourer, accustomed to more intense exploitation (whether under Rakosi, Berman or private ownership), and eager to prove himself in a new and often hostile land, Dinlock men claim, works like a demon, produces more and makes the Yorkshire lad look bad. Along comes NCB and says, if the Pole can do it you can. A familiar argument, and the Dinlock collier wants none of it.

In this situation it is natural for the collier to marshal not only intellectualised counter-arguments but also emotional ones. Over at Beckley pit, a few miles away, Poles are working in large numbers. It is, say the Dinlockers, a bad pit, bad morale, slightly higher output, a weak union, rank-and-file dissension, a sloppy village; the Poles are wild, dirty, impolite, etc. Word for word what we in America always hear when Negroes 'invade' an all-white neighbourhood.

I decide to try and point this out, and I am greeted with a reasoning which is always the clincher in any working-class community, "If tha' were down in pit with us thy tune 'ud change quick enough."

And, when all else fails, they tell you about the bad blood which exists between Dinlock and Beckley, an ever-present tautology. Harold Bolton, the king-pin of the union branch, whom I am to meet later, tells me about the famous night a busload of Poles from Beckley roared into Dinlock bent on mayhem and were met by a platoon of pit men and of the small riot which ensued and which sent the Beckley faction into retreat. I should like to hear the other side, I say. Bolton is properly shocked. How can there be another side?

All this being so, imagine what happened in Dinlock when a lone Rumanian, poor bastard, was by some administrative error in Barnsley, assigned to the Dinlock pit. Well, say the men with smug pride, we got rid of him in two shakes. But by this time he had been moved into a new NCB house, and the union demanded his expulsion from that too. Davie and Glenn and Walter, they tell you with something of the old political fire, stood up for the Rumanian, and he's still living there, just over in the next street. Nobody seems to be paying him much attention, and when I suggest he is being ostracised Davie and Glenn give me sincere, innocent looks, as if it must have been 3000 other blokes.

Why don't you paint the Rumanian, you've done just about everybody else in the village, I tell Davie. He shrugs. Painter he may be, socialist and all that, but first and foremost a proud and prejudiced Dinlock man. No, says Davie, he won't do the Rumanian, though maybe it is a good idea, he concedes. Then he admits he couldn't because, "Ah'm too much on one side, tha' can see that." He doesn't like foreigners either, and gives me his disarming crooked grin. Some socialist, I say. I'm not defending myself, he says, but that is the way it is.

In Glenn's house, and in the palpable relationship between

27

Glenn and Davie, you see at close quarters how the rigid structure of friendship creates its warmth and limitations. For make no mistake, the governing rules in Dinlock are as rigid, as unquestioned and sanctified as the rules inside a monastery or a military academy. This has to be so, given the pact Dinlockers have made with themselves and each other to make the village their whole life; otherwise the place would have erupted long ago. Miners are cordial but formal with each other, intimate but restrained, frank but never inquisitive, honouring in the breach and in the act a code of personal conduct as elaborate (and as romantic) as that of the medieval knight.

Above all, the Dinlock collier regards himself as A Man, in every single department of his life. The slightest traces of femininity, of softness (except along definite and long-prescribed lines), of sexual ambiguity, are ruthlessly rooted out, or suppressed. Homosexuality and rape do not exist in the village mind.

Davie, I say, some would have you believe that in any community which places such an overt and exaggerated emphasis upon manliness (however poetically accomplished, however much a defence of the crux of life, pit work), and in which women are so dramatically subordinated (again very much in response to the rhythm of the life of the pit) and are regarded as inherently inferior if inherently necessary, the subterraneanism of homosexuality must be around somewhere. And Davie doubles up with laughter and slaps his knee and says, "Ah, lad, that is a funny thing indeed you're saying."

I ask Davie why there's no rape. He says with a laugh, "Why should there be, when all you have to do is ask." He thinks he's making a joke. Later, I see what a complicated joke it is. Flirtation and unfaithfulness, I am enthusiastically assured, are endemic in the village—but never (hand on heart) at the risk of the family. A stranger wonders when the women, so quiet, so sullen, so dominated, can find the time, but I am so persistently, and from all sides, with a puritanical wink here and a sly dig there, *told* that they do—*and* with a vengeance—that I begin to wonder if they themselves know how to distinguish tale from deed at this late date. I use the word vengeance advisedly.

Like all Dinlock men, Davie is full of contradictory attitudes towards women. He glorifies and romanticises them, is afraid of them, domineers, insists they are inferior and says once women have equal rights they will take over the world. Woman exists, Davie says, with no backward glance at his own marriage, to keep the miner going down into the pit, to feed him and his children, to love him and his children. What about love for her? Davie skips away from the question. A Dinlock man must provide for his family, he repeats stubbornly; if he does that it is enough.

At Glenn's house, while he loftily expatiates on the Russian mine system (a surprising number of Dinlock colliers will, this weekend, contrast Soviet and Dinlock pit methods) I see what they eat, a typical Dinlock meal, kept hot in a small grated compartment next to the fireplace, chips and eggs and tea. I notice Glenn's pregnant-looking wife wears eyeshadow and lipstick in the kitchen. An act of defiance? The effect is to limn pathetically her worn and haggard features.

Another wife comes in, big beefy bluff, with a handshake that cracks and a voice like the shattering of old china, Louise, the next-door neighbour. She and Glenn's woman confer in a corner while the men talk on, but this woman clearly is unlike Glenn's; she's won her fight with men, has Louise, and just let one of them make a wrong move! But even Louise behaves within the rules, speaking only when spoken to. There are eight of us, including squalling wrestling kids, in the room (four paces by two paces) and nobody seems to remark on it, nor do I believe would they if twice our number suddenly walked in. Hospitality is, in this house as in others, instant, dignified and non-exuberant. They've been poor, bone-poor, for so many generations, these Yorkshire people (Dinlock colliery shut down in 1930, 1936 and 1937, and the memory is like hot acid) that terms like inhospitality and ungenerosity and stinginess have no real application here. They give you what they can and assume you won't ask for more than you need.

The last cottage we go to this afternoon belongs to Walter, who is, or used to be, Davie's best friend, even over and above Glenn.

Walter is a governor of a local estate school, a reader, with intellectual pretensions which Davie says do not run deep, a man who will read anything he can get his hands on and then quote authoritatively. He is a fragile inefficient miner, say the men in the pub, who should work on surface, but pride keeps Walter down at the face and it will kill him because he is not built to stand the gaff. He and Davie once shared the same girl, a shop assistant from Hamthorpe. At one point last year, when everyone concerned felt the water was getting too deep, they met in Davie's house—Davie and Loretta, Walter and his wife, and the girl—to negotiate a settlement, talking it out amongst themselves, admitting the infidelities and cuckoldries and shaking hands on it. "That naht of honest talk," says Davie, "made things even better than they had been before." And he believes it, what's more. "Somehow, all that messin' around with one another's women didn't make Walter and me enemies, but brought us closer and made us better friends," concludes Davie wonderingly.

We go into Walter's house, one of the back-to-backs, at the top of the street and facing squarely the colliery. Sally, Walter's wife, is a trim, sexy little thing with one of those dangerous withheld bitter faces which makes for trouble between men. Crouched on his haunches in front of the fire is Walter's pit-partner, a gap-toothed, guilty-looking miner with carefully waved hair and two-inch sideburns, too ingratiating. They've been alone in the house and try to conceal their displeasure at the sudden interruption but Yorkshire people are not very practised at the conversational arts in such circumstances and talk lags, falters and Davie and I are embarrassed. Walter is off at the pictures with the children and Davie mumbles we'll come around later. Walter's wife and Walter's mate breathe hardly a word to us, glaring almost against their wills, and we get out of there pursued by their stone-cold glares.

So this is what lies below the stoical, dignified skin of Dinlock village, I say. And Davie says, Yes, this is what it is like.

Davie and I cut across a field towards his house. A tall wire fence is in the way. Nimbly he scales it. I am a clumsy climber, so I rush it, the way I was taught in the Army, flinging myself over in a kind of graceless uncontrolled cartwheel because I know it's only one of the many ways Dinlockers have of testing strength. Davie, and some soccer players in the field, are impressed by what they believe is me showing off.

It is late afternoon, and Davie takes me to see the Miners' Welfare Hall, as near a city hall as Dinlock has. He is immensely proud of the newly-painted barnlike structure. It belongs to the Miners' Union. Only a year ago, Davie explains as he conducts me through the big neat auditorium dominated by a four-wall brawny slashing mural of The Miners' Progress and the various smaller rooms designed for committee meetings and band practice, the Welfare Hall had been the disgrace of the village, ramshackle, dilapidated, unpainted and unattended. Bolton, says Davie, changed all that. Thundering, cajoling, flattering, borrowing and stealing, he single-handedly brought about the transformation. Not that Davie approves Bolton's methods. "Harold, he's a bit of a gangster, y'understand." But he got things done.

About Bolton, his name is Harold Bolton, and he is *de facto* mayor of Dinlock, the big cheese full of himself and wondrous works, the Lord High Fixer and Arbitrator, the Public Figure, full-time branch union treasurer and the portrait of whom is Davie's most famous. (The Russians bought the picture and reproduced it on thousands of postcards with the title, "A British Militant".) Bolton (nobody uses his first name) was the man who befriended and encouraged Davie and made him protégé when Davie first came to Dinlock. Davie has told me much of Bolton down in London, by turns warning and praising. The relationship is simple. Bolton is the father, openly and unashamedly substituting for Davie's father killed on policeman's duties in Palestine, 1939.

Coming out of band room we meet the man himself, Bolton. He is startlingly like Davie's portrait of him. An odd-looking man with not all the parts fitting. Very thickset, very wide and bulky, a long wedge-shaped head driven deep into wide powerful shoulders, one ear torn off and the flap stitched tight against the head, completely bald, a wrinkled quizzical forehead, bushy eyebrows, cold blue appraising eyes, a thin patrician nose and set, curiously sensual lips, a face cross-hatched by razor-thin scars, a bow-legged assured stance. Bolton.

"Ah, Davie, Ah see thy visitor 'as coom. Will tha' do the introductions?"

Davie does, suddenly out of breath and awkwardly falling over himself in a kitten's cradle of outstretched, clasped hands. His Yorkshire accent noticeably thickens. It always does when he's around with the other men.

"Ah've been showin' him the hall, Bolton."

"Aye. Good. Ah'll do it properly, shall I?"

So Bolton takes me in hand and gives me a re-conducted tour of the Welfare Hall, pointedly explaining how it was all due to Bolton, which is what he calls himself. It isn't easy to defend yourself against, or even find offensive, such direct blatant self-congratulation. The thing is, as I am to hear again and again from everyone in Dinlock, the man has actually done these things, and much more, even if by the time I leave the village I have had a bellyful of Bolton stroking his own back.

Davie and Bolton are enormously proud of the new Welfare Hall. Bolton painstakingly shows me where new steps have been installed, a floor re-tiled in the kitchen, curtains put in the games room, Davie chiding Bolton for the unorthodox methods he employed in re-building the hall and simultaneously softening the impelled sharpness by urging Bolton to stand for local council. And what emerges from this afternoon is that Bolton is an extremely complex individual, hungry for plaudits and recognition, quick to sense slight, his public personna that of the sober, slow-thinking slow-talking Yorkshireman behind which lurks a good brain, a tender ego and a consuming ambition to be or do something of which I am not aware. There is a deceptive air to Bolton's terrible engine, outwardly solid, reasonable, peaceable; but he can be hard and spiteful.

With Davie tagging along, Bolton escorts me around the village whose physical face he is, literally, transfiguring. On the outer rim of the village, between one of the three pubs and the local, slaggy river, is a swampy field now pitted with tractor runways and embryonic circles and squarish outlines in the wet dirt. That's to be the sports ground, says Bolton, complete with cricket pitch, football field, cycle track and even two tennis courts. All my doing, says Bolton straight. Pushing, pushing, pushing, says Davie.

We climb the new brick wall and go over the field in the darkness of a fast-descending night as Bolton explains where everything is to be, in this, his monument. And also tells me of the new school ("Comprehensive, mind ye") he intends having built in Dinlock. Before I get through, he vows, Dinlock will be a model village. Aye that's so, assents Davie, proud of Bolton and ashamed of Bolton's naked thirst for not the limelight but that quiet recognition by his fellow villagers which Bolton seems never to get enough of. Does

33

he have other, broader ambitions? I don't know. Perhaps. He's a very cool character, Bolton.

(But I'm worried about him, says Davie. There's been a change. A new pompousness, a small shift in emphasis from representing the men to wanting to control the situation in which he represents them. Tomorrow, after a visit to the colliery up on The Hill, Bolton is to make a point of telling me that though he called the pit under-manager Mr. Tooley in front of us, in their private conversations they are on a first-name basis. Davie says to me, but not to Bolton, that's the traditional way a miners' leader begins the sell-out. But to me, not to Bolton. It nags at Davie, this hankering of Bolton's to get on first name terms with the boss. Bolton, he thinks, has begun to see himself as *the* axis of all areas of life in Dinlock. He admits that Bolton's stern enthusiasm in putting the miner's case remains constant. But the poison seeds are there, he insists.)

Meanwhile, Bolton leans on the low brick wall and gazes at the night-shrouded field. Shortly after work started, he says, seepage was found. All these years, without anyone in the village knowing about it, one of the nearby larger towns was secretly piping its drainage into and under Dinlock. Bolton spits angrily. "Tol' 'em where to put their damn' seepage."

Eager for me not to leave the village without seeing its glamorous side, Davie puts a rhetorical question to Bolton. "Hey," he says, "isn't this where tha' and Len had the mix-up?" "Aye," says Bolton, and he tells the story of the fight, relishing its details. Yorkshire men love to tell about the rows, especially the ones they've won.

"We were in Poob," says Bolton. "Saturday naht, how long ago, Davie?"

"Year, year half."

Bolton thinks about this. "Well, Len 'ud been drinking. He's a nasty 'un whun 'e drinks, 'e is." (I've yet to meet a

34

miner in Dinlock who does not describe the other guy as an unstable drinker.)

"Ye're not so bad at it th'self, Boiton," says Davie.

"Aye," replied Bolton, "Ah can hold my own," and I remember that Bolton was for ten years a Regular Navy man, veteran of police duty in Singapore and combat in the North Sea and the Pacific, torpedoed three times. War's outbreak had found him stationed in Ceylon. (Like so many other miners in Dinlock Bolton has seen something of the world; in West Club I am to meet man after man who has been a long-service soldier or seaman in the merchant navy; but always they come back to Dinlock. Why? Dunno, they say. Mining's in a man's blood, they say.)

"Ah'm sitting with boys an' Len cooms over an' says, 'Bolton, Ah'm to knock down three men tonaht. Davie'll be first, you second and Michael Griffith third, Ah'm tellin' tha' this now,'" remembers Bolton. "'So Ah leave off with boys,' an' Ah answered, 'Len, Ah'll not play second to no man, even to Davie, who Ah luv like a son. If tha're to do me tha'll do me first.' So we went outside. Remember, Davie?"

"There was a proper crowd," remembers Davie.

"We climb over this very wall," narrates Bolton. "And Len starts dancing all around me, fancy, his fists up." The memory of it all breaks Bolton and Davie up, they chuckle wildly.

"A minute or two of this and Ah says to Len, Ah'm an old man, and I cannot any longer do those things. If tha' want to fight with me Ah'll stay still and tha coom in to me."

Davie adds, "Len's 26 then, Bolton's 52."

"Finally he charges in and Ah land him a proper one side of head. Remember, Davie? Down he goes. Up he cooms and he rushes me. We go down. He butts me. It hurt Ah can tell tha'. In a couple of minutes he were a proper mess, eh Davie?"

35

"Aye," says Davie, "blood."

"In morning—tha' didn't know this, Davie—Ah go by Len's house and ask him to shake hands. He cooms out and we have another do, in garden. Enough. We go poob and drink. Len, 'e's a bad 'un 'e drinks, right Davie?"

Davie says, "Next day his head was black and big as a balloon."

Bolton says to me, "Not bad for an old man, eh?"

"You and Len still friends, Bolton?"

"Why, Davie, tha' know me. Len's got his faults, no man can say he don't, but Ah'll drink with him any time of day or naht."

I hope, Bolton says slapping my stomach, Davie don't get into too many brawls while you're among us. I slap his stomach and say, If he does I'll manage to protect him. You hear that, Davie, laughs Bolton. I think, if it's a brawl I don't want it to be with Bolton. A belly like steel.

Bolton muses, looking out at the field across the wall. It's a good village. The way you're going, Bolton says Davie, it'll be a model village. Bolton beams. Then scowls. It's a fight, Davie. The bosses and us, to see who'll rule the roost. He nudges Davie. Is it all right to speak in front of him. Davie uneasily submits my bona fides.

Fine, fine, says Bolton. And for the next quarter of an hour orates like a *dynamilero* or Hyndmanite, about the class war, and who will rule the roost, them or us, and it's the end that counts not the means. "Fook me if tha don't live to see the day when we shoot the bluidy capitalists instead of compensatin' them." As for the bloody Hungarians, they were counter-revolutionary traitors to the cause of international proletarianism in the pay and under the directions of that Papist bitch, Mindzenty, and deserved what they got.

Afterwards, Davie warns me not to take Bolton seriously when he gives out with all that Bolshevik talk. It was Bolton who moved the branch resolution supporting the revolution-

36

ary miners in November, 1956, and it was Bolton who organised the women to send food and clothes parcels to the Hungarian refugee camps in Austria. Anyway, Bolton likes to make an impression, Davie repeats, and right now he's trying to make an impression on you. The habit will be his downfall. He doesn't talk like that in the village.

"Tha understand," Bolton says, arms folded on the brick, "Ah don't talk like that in the village." Davie nudges me slyly. The visitor is being handed an accolade. The thing's got to be done slowly and surely there, in the village, Bolton says. A slow wink appears in his furrowed, care-lined American-politician's face. "See tha' at Poob later," he says, shaking the visitor's hand. "Aye, Davie, tha've brought down a raht smart lad this tahm."

We separate for tea.

After we leave Bolton, Davie warns, "Bolton will butter you on both sides and eat you for Sunday morning breakfast."

On the way back to his house Davie is greeted on all sides with a mixture of respect, affection and a queer involuntary diffidence. That's because I don't work at Dinlock pit any more, Davie says. "It bothers them but they don't know it yet. They're waiting for me to make a wrong move so they can say it wouldn't have happened if Ah hadn't of gone to Beckley pit." He tells me about the fight a couple of years ago he had with a mine foreman. On Sunday morning, Davie says, he called the man out of his cottage (a former Guardsman and twice his size) and bashed him fearfully. It is the fourth time Davie has told me of this particular fight. Countless re-tellings of fist fights are one of the ways to pass the endless time in Dinlock. A brand-new auditor is heaven-sent.

Davie tightens up as we turn into his street. He doesn't know how Loretta has taken to me; two days before I showed up I found a telegram from Davie in my room in Islington, some cock-and-bull story about there being no room at his house due to unexpected relatives from the North; a funk out, the third, in one form or another, since Davie found out I was coming to Dinlock. But now there's nothing for it. I'm here.

Aye, you're here now, Davie says with a sigh. He denies avoiding the invitation. Why press? Things haven't been going well between Loretta and Davie, and cutting down on his shift work in order to paint hasn't helped. Loretta resents his friends, his painting, anything that clearly marks him off from the normal Yorkshire coal miner, which she desperately wants him to be and only be, he says. But, on balance, it's been more peaceful in the house since a bit of money started coming in from his pictures, and Davie has succeeded in identifying friends from London with the money to her, so she will abide me temporarily. "And if not," he flares up, "hell with her. Ah'm the man in the house." His hand moves to his mouth as if to cough and I know he is taking another benzedrine pill.

Dinner of chips and eggs, Loretta equable. At the table Davie makes no attempt to draw Loretta in with us; he has so little opportunity to talk that he wants to take advantage of every small moment. So, after dinner, while Loretta curls in on the anti-macassar covered sofa with *True Romances*, Davie and I talk. On what level do Davie and Loretta get with each other? I am never to find out. I know Davie is never at ease when Loretta and I are in the same room, and he constantly cautions me to do nothing which might stir her up. Once, during dinner, relating to a minor household matter, she gave him a little bit of sarcastic tongue and his mouth flew open, he was hurt, as if stung by a slap in the face. It wasn't much of a remark, as such can go, but he's learned to take these things badly. Should he, for my benefit, show some fight? He thought better of it, subsided. Dinner was a hurried, tense business. Then Davie went upstairs to shave and he and I went out

for a Saturday night in the mining village of Dinlock,
Yorks.

For the people of Dinlock there are two nights a week,
on Saturday and Sunday, when it is permissible, nay encouraged, to relieve the accumulated fatigue and anxieties of
Monday through Friday by the simple exercise of the bended
arm in East Clu', West Clu' and Pub. (There are three pubs
in the village, and three clubs, but for the miners it's East,
West and *the* pub; the others, frequented by shopkeepers
and non-miners, might just as well not exist.) I have been
prepared for this by a thousand references, from Davie and
others, to the undiluted joys and comforts of the two clubs
and the pub which constitute the sole and supreme theatres
of recreation, rest and relaxation. When I'd left Bolton earlier
that afternoon, after he'd described the fist fight he'd had
with Len a few years ago, he had made a solemn rite
out of the invitation to join him at East Club later in the
evening.

East Clu' (referring to which side of the colliery it is on)
was for many years the only social centre of the town. It is
the drinking club of the Miners' Union, no women allowed
except on weekends at specified hours, and that concession
bitterly fought by the old-timers when it was introduced after
the war. In a poster-covered ante-room Davie signs me in at
a huge book guarded by a gnarled old trustee in a neat grey
suit. "59, and he's still on the face. I did him once, remember
the one called 'Charge Hand'?" He opens the door. "You'll
lahk it here," he promises. Davie is all slicked up for the
night, wearing his best and only suit, a sharp single-breasted
model he bought down in London, shined shoes, painstakingly combed and fluffed hair and a silk tie peacefully
knotted.

The atmosphere in East Clu' is of a miners' lodge hall in

39

any small Pennsylvania coal town. Smoky, sweaty, crowded, divided into a main hall containing a small stage and a billiard room with several oversize tables, both served by a bustling bar, placards with Club Rules tacked up all over the place. To get the visitor in is a major operation, involving suspension of some regulation or other, and when I do walk in all eyes go to me, weighing.

Pretending not to notice, Davie steers me to the bar. He says, What'll you have, you can't refuse a drink here, it'll look bad for me if you do. I dislike beer, choose Scotch, only later feel the error but by then it is compounded beyond salvage. We sit and drink sternly in the main room while the telly up front crackles, on a specially-constructed high table, then goes silent as the Club fills in anticipation of the night's official entertainment, tombola and the turns. A few women slip in, for it's the permissible Saturday night, and the women are hostile to East Club. It is the man's exclusive province, for years the only place where the men could gather to talk on top of the pit. "Heads down!" shouts a man on the stage.

The miners bend to their bingo cards. No activity in Dinlock is without its mystique and technical vocabulary, including tombola. The man drones, "Bed and breakfast 2 and 6, clickety-click 66," lining up with each drawn number a phrase, reaching back into the years, and properly read (which I cannot do) giving in its way a social history of England. How long ago was it that a hotel room and breakfast cost 30 pence?

The man calling the number is Tommy Hunter, who will get very drunk tomorrow in the Club, a tall oldish man married to a young wife, and regale me with stories of submarine warfare in the Pacific, much to everyone's embarrassment. They've heard Tommy's war stories. Davie complains, why does he have to lie, to dress it up? He never was on a submarine. The truth, says Davie, is enough. Tommy was a Narvik Commando, a veteran of Dunkirk and one of Orde

40

Wingate's jungle troopers and has a fistful of medals for valour to prove it, so why does he insist he served on submarines? I do not reply by asking Davie why he does what he does when the truth will not suffice him.

Tombola is played with amiable intensity, miners drop by our table for a chat, I've come to know several, including the branch executive at a formal meeting arranged earlier by Davie. Each in turn eventually, with deceptive casualness, gets around to asking what I think of Dinlock. A visitor must know how to handle this question; they watch you carefully for the slightest sign of insincerity. My first thought is, anything I say will dissatisfy them. But then I see that they are more innocent than I thought. For them the world outside Dinlock to Barnsley is too distant to consider, and after Barnsley simply doesn't exist. They really want to know what I think, and nobody asks what I'm waiting for. Don't give us that, we know you've lived in New York and Paris and places like that.

So I tell them, one and all, the truth, that I am properly impressed. I didn't expect Dinlock to be so large; this fails to move them. I've been treated like a friend; they like this. The Welfare Hall is a marvellous thing; that's better, they nod eagerly, each man telling me what it was like before. Life, I venture, in Dinlock can be more exciting in its way than it is in London; they nod soberly, expecting as that might very well be true, as it is true for many of them.

And hardly a man goes by who does not, as he talks to me, drop a piece of pit gossip with Davie. His position in the village is shifting and ambiguous, and one of the reasons why the men want to talk to him is to help secure him in some niche in their own minds. All of Davie's friends in East Club are to be counted among the older men.

I notice that while many people in the Club are interested in the new visitor they are trying not to stare. Especially the women. Bolton comes through the door, and Davie takes me away before Bolton can monopolise me.

41

The well-beaten route between East Club and West Club (on the opposite side of the village) requires you to head directly into the teeth of the colliery towards the main street, Theresa Road, which describes a semi-circle around the colliery until you again plunge tangentially off into the forest of houses and make for the haven of West Club on the outer rim. By now, I have a plan of the village firmly fixed in my memory, and I can see that the shortest route between the two clubs need not take you by the colliery, and in fact by any standards, except one, it is an awkward and long route which requires a man bent on enjoying the night to spend two-thirds of his walk between the clubs within naked sight of the colliery up on The Hill. The exception is if you need the colliery there, within sight to remind you of something that has to do, in some way, with your enjoyment. Significantly, the younger colliers and some of the surface men take a short cut, away from the colliery.

Davie and I take Theresa Road, the long curved way along the grey stone wall. West Clu' is at the bottom of a slope on the opposite rim of the village, near the bus route to Hamthorpe and Barnsley. It is a modernistic yellow-brick building, with a large blue neon sign advertising "West Club" (a nice gesture, that, in view of the lack of competition). Inside it is formica and swedish-style chairs, instead of the oak-hewn tables and benches in the older East Club, all done up in glossy red and pale yellows, less smoke and more women, and a brassier stage equipped with built-in amplifiers; the shopkeepers come to West Clu', and the manager wears a tuxedo. "He used to be a back ripper. Now he looks like a Brighton tout. To look at him, tha'd never think he was in our Party branch." This time, Davie is referring to a wild-cat Communist party cell which he, Alf Johnson and a few more of the boys set up during a coalfield strike several years ago (and which they immediately dismantled upon King Street assigning a functionary to Dinlock).

At the door, Davie, who has had a few pints, angrily

argues with a club official who posted his name for non-payment of dues. A serious affront, the mistake is acknowledged, Davie is mollified in not particularly good grace.

The atmosphere down here in West Clu' is more sterile, too clean, red and yellow, not enough dark browns. But the women like it, says Davie. And suddenly, for no reason at all, I think of Muirkirk, the colliery which not so long ago blew up killing 17 miners. I look at the faces of the men and women around me as they drink, talk, laugh but mainly stare. The evening quickens and not only in me, on my fifth double. In London's miserable pubs the customers sit morosely from opening to closing time like respectable mummies. Here, it begins that way, but the Yorkshire personality, acted upon by the week's labour and thousand arrows of tension, flushes and inflates and begins to make its own raw music. The older ones—those incredible middle-aged women with their dangling fags and dowdy hair-dos—laugh it up, the younger ones will come in later. I see that what Davie has told me is true. The two clubs and Pub open at 5 and shut at 10. The object is to get in as early as possible and drink as much as fast as possible before Time, Gentlemen! Davie says, let's go back down to East Clu'. At first, I think he's restless, but then I see that is the pattern on the weekends, from East to West to Pub and around again (completely ignoring the other club and two other pubs).

First, we stop off at Will Lawson's, a detour to one of those gardenless tiny stone houses set in the peat on the other side of the bus route in an alley full of grim back-to-backs, in a field which D. H. Lawrence might have grown up in. Will's upstairs sleeping from morning shift (the notorious and hotly disputed Saturday morning shift), we talk to Fay, his wife. Five children, four watching telly. Fay coyly apologises for the clutter; she's picked up mannerisms somewhere. Again no telling her age, anywhere from 30 to 45, fawning, devious and hardworking. The Lawsons are a *cause célèbre*. A few weeks ago 11-year-old Jamie was birched by his

43

schoolmaster. His father, Will, took a bus to the school, where, after a short argument, he emptied a bottle of ink on the headmaster's suit and took Jamie back home with him, and has not let him go back. Warrants were issued, the police came calling, the local education authority pronounced an assinine ultimatum, the London papers took up the story with glee and the small back-to-back was deluged with reporters.

Fay draws up a chair, and with Wyatt Earp plugging away like crazy in the background, tells Davie and me how rude the reporters were, how she deplored the excitement, how she doesn't want Jamie made much of. From first to last a palpable untruth. She loves the excitement. Davie does not see this, he falls in with her complaining over the notoriety. Obviously, since Will reluctantly delivered up a public apology, the local authorities will have to back down and re-admit Jamie, but how often does something as exciting as this happen in Dinlock? "The poor child," she says, "is almost made sick with agitation." I look over at Jamie, placidly watching telly. If he's sick I want to know what he's like well, he looks like a scaled-down version of Billy Wright in his better days.

"Aye," says Davie, "it's terrible pity. Tha' should let me handle it. Ah know how to take on those newspaper fellows." Davie, the Man of the World, tolerant, sympathetic, chockfull of *savoir-faire*, letting Fay know just how weary he is of all this outrageous, dishonest publicity. It is a movie scene directed by John Ford, with Una O'Connor and Barry Fitzgerald. Benign hypocrisy on all sides such as I have not seen since I was last in Paddy Nolan's bar on Third Avenue in New York last St. Patrick's Day.

"Tha' let me take care of it, Fay," says Davie. "Tha' don't speak to any more reporters; Ah've a friend on a Yorkshire paper who will put it all down truthfully and split the money with tha' and Will. It's a big story," he keeps repeating, "could bring in two, maybe three hundred quid."

And thus, at one stroke, revealing his gruesome, charming guilessness.

Will comes down, and when we shake hands I have the impression he is the only Dinlocker who won't ask me how I like the village, and I'm right. Soft-spoken, squarely-built, quietly confident, a man in control of himself (except, perhaps, in regard to schoolmasters and ink bottles), a man to be trusted. I wonder why Davie hasn't spoken of Will. When I ask Davie about this later he says he doesn't know, he doesn't get to see Will Lawson as often as he would like.

Will has obviously had his fill of talk about Jamie and the inkbottle and the London papers, but replies politely to all questions; he is irritated by Fay's continuing enthusiasm for the subject but says nothing to her. Then, gradually, even he gets caught up in it again, even he grows righteously indignant about the reporters, except that he means it. Leave-takings from this warm, densely-packed house only by the promise to meet them later for a drink, an invitation which is to lead directly to an incident that is to be added to Dinlock's store of legends, if it is not already there. Going away, I tell Davie that I think Lawson a fine type. Yes, agrees Davie, but prone to take a back seat. Meaning what, I ask. Meaning, says Davie, he won't get into fights.

Like any Dinlocker I'm on the round. Back to East Clu'. Packed to the rafters now, a small sea of miners and their wives, listening to a turn. An imported singer from Sheffield, female, brilliantined hair, provincial glamour, giving out when a man's in love he's on fire, a good part of the audience humming along. Davie and I join the old timers in the billiard parlour. I am introduced to more miners, half of whom seem to have been to America or have relatives there. Chicago, am I? Well, do I know the Wellingtons who live on Stoney-crest Drive? Chicago's a fairly large place, I say—dubious glances, as if perhaps I am boasting about having been born there. And again the pattern of almost instinctual ellipse

45

works itself out: many of them were regular soldiers or merchant mariners, saw the world and came back to the village of their birth. I can't ask why. But I'm told anyway. High wages, good men to work with, mining's in a man's blood. During the war miners were exempt from military service. Why did so many volunteer? Patriotism, they say. Eyewash, I tell Davie. To get out of this miserable, upstanding village. Patriotism, the miners insist. They're buying the drinks, nobody will let me buy, I don't argue. I offer to change, for reasons of economy, to ale and they are insulted. Buying drinks is the ritual of rituals, and my turn will come, they patronise me. But it never does come. We stand by the bar and drink steadily. They are drinking to drop me. Not on your nelly, you bastards.

Bolton comes by and starts sounding off, the other men look a trifle bored but try not to show it. At the far end of the billiard room there is a small black bronze statue of a near-naked miner with a pick in his hand. It was done by an invalided miner's son, commissioned by Bolton out of union funds, he proudly relates. The men pull his leg. They think the bronze is daft and obscene. "If he wanted to do a proper statue," says Ray Sweet, a branch official, "why didn't he put a decent pair of clothes on the man." "Tha' have no understanding of the arts," says Bolton. "Aye, that may be," replies Ray, "but unless that there statue be of a nigger Ah know enough to put proper clothes on him." On close examination, the sculpture proves crude and forthright. The men are ashamed of it.

Down near the bar again, a small stir, a man drinking conspicuously alone, in a mackintosh and hat. Be damned, says Ray Sweet the branch vice-chairman, it's Tooley, one of the pit under-managers. Davie drags me over for introductions. My tongue is loose, I say, Glad to meet you Mr. Tooley, heard a lot about you, the men crowd around and grin and Tooley gets an I'll-bet-you-have look in his small, porcine red eyes.

46

Though the men claim to have tamed Tooley, he is still El Diabolo. And, worst of all, from the ranks. (That's why he's a special target.) I know all there is to effectively know about Tooley. How, after years spent in the pits, he took an NCB course, worked himself up from gaffer to overman to his present eminence; how he bullied and drove the men when he first came to Dinlock colliery five years ago, how he used to kick over his desk in fits of rage. The man was obviously insecure, not overloaded with brains and sent in to squeeze production out of one of England's most trouble-some and strike-ridden pits. Davie has told me countless stories about him, how Tooley's initial stupidities bound the miners closer than ever together. But now he's tamed, they insist. Six months ago, they say, he wouldn't have dared walk into East Clu', *our* Clu'.

We crowd around Tooley. They needle him, but not too hard. He turns to me, I'm from America, am I! He loudly quotes figures about the superiority of American tonnage per man hour. And it's not all due to machinery either, he declaims defiantly. The men having won their victory, just smile. Tooley, a man with rings on both fingers, a mouthful of gold and silver teeth, a head over which the freckled skin is drawn in an unhealthily tight fit, perpetually reared back as if at any moment anticipating a physical assault by an angry miner, a plodding unimaginative dullard who has all the earmarks, I think, of having quite possibly licked his job.

In the adjacent village of Beckley there is a 15-year-old girl, and this girl is Tooley's illegitimate daughter, whom he has never seen. The girl, villagers tell you, hates Tooley. And though the entire village knows about this girl, and Tooley's affair with one of the miner's wives, they do not criticise or condemn. Their tolerance has nothing to do with his being pit under-manager. "Tooley does his things quietly, and just so long as he does we'll not find it in us to use our tongues on him," says Ray Sweet, the rhino-bellied vice-chairman.

I tell Tooley I don't know much about American coal

47

mining, but he tramples on, pointedly praising American productivity, apparently on the principle that he might as well get the jump on the union men in their permanent battle. Then he surprises everyone, most of all Davie, by inviting Davie to come back to work at Dinlock. (When Davie worked at Dinlock pit, on Tooley's shift, they were, to hear both tell it, almost constantly on the point of locking the office door and having it out.)

Suddenly everyone is friendly, the ice is broken, Tooley isn't a pit man again, it's just that it's tonight, with plenty of liquor under their buckles, Tooley happy for some private reason and me with countless whiskies in him and happy for the public reason of still being on his feet. Tooley thereupon double-ploys everyone by asking me to come on a conducted tour of the colliery, tomorrow morning. Bolton and Davie eagerly assent for me before I can find my tongue. Conviviality reigns. The sheen-haired podge-faced girl singer on the stage gargles a Christmas carol. Davie and I leave for West Clu', walking half-way around the colliery, and in West Clu' we come upon another singer, an Italian in short sleeves and open-throat shirt, Lanza-like, and the proprietor in his tuxedo and mannequin smile who used to be in Davie's Party branch, and a general air of formica respectability. The new gleaming reds and yellows have bleached something out. I suppose it's good to have a nice new club to come to, but the temptation is to scratch the furniture and daub the walls with oak and mud, to shake the place down. Ah, well, the uses of literacy.

Davie wants to talk but it's not easy; too many people come by. We are invited to sit with Ed Stopp and his wife, heavily powdered and wise-cracking, I like her, in her late 40's, but who can tell? Ed is secretary of the Union in Dinlock; he looks American, a fedora hat, bright necktie, small and wiry, square-jawed, he could be president of UAW-CIO local 887. Something of a politician, a bit of a fence-mender, but a miner. His wife, Jane, and Davie exchange ribaldries. They are flirting, pretending to have had an affair when Davie did a sketch of her inscribed, 'in memory of that night in Rome'. We are joined by Greta and Arthur, who used to be a valet and is now a pit worker. Greta is Dinlock's glamour girl, black sequins, expertly lipsticked and rouged, a good bosom. The men all around us in West Clu' know their wives expect them to stare at Greta but are saving it up for more private moments.

I look around the big, crowded, not-yet-noisy room where men and women are hunched at tables and waiting for tombola to start up, and I tell Davie that the only way you can discover who is sleeping with whom, or planning to, is by the way they don't look at each other, and he says, proud of my brainwave, you've caught on. Later on, the next night, when I ask Davie to explain the mechanics to me, he does and it's enough to make the flesh crawl. A popular village game, which Davie avidly plays, is Whose Baby Is It? I am sitting in the vortex of the weekend whirlpool of release and most of it whips around me uncomprehended. Greta, for instance, does not look at me once. Not interested or flirting passionately? See, already I'm playing the Dinlock game.

And for the tenth time I am subjected to The Test. Needling, to see if and how I take it. (Stranger, take warning.) Back at East Clu', I got it left and right, here the women join in, too, with some deftness. It's one of the ways they find out about you in Dinlock. The formula is simplicity itself: probe for the most obvious vulnerability and chew at it until you get a jump, and chew at that response to produce another one, and so on until the hapless victim is at your mercy. I'm a Yank, am I? They pour it on, with a friendly smile, cracking wise about Americans and America, always open season in working-class England. Where's your Cadillac, Yank, parked outside? What's wrong, Yank, our beer too strong for you? You one of those Chicago gangsters we hear about?

A lot of envy and no spite and no mention of the fact that

49

I'm not a miner, that would be making it unfunny. I've played this game before many times, in army barracks and factories and small Ohio towns, in America, I know the rules, and in West Clu' I play it, giving as good as I get in walking that thin line between over-heartiness and the sudden helpless access of humiliating anger which can only invite contempt. Up at the old Club, East Clu', I got it in massive doses and from all sides; down at West Clu' the women change the rules slightly and covertly ask to be flirted with, but skilfully, under the noses of their husbands to show that you are an equal of their husbands. All as evidence of no weakness. Several times I am almost drawn into a lazily prepared trap by the women, especially Greta and Ed's wife, who shuck off their resentments with unbelievable subtlety and indirection by provoking quarrels between the men. Interestingly, the men themselves often join in, unconsciously, though I am convinced that in their hearts they know it can lead to no good end. I suddenly get a vision of the women, the miners' wives, crouching with cat smiles on the mantelpiece while below them on the floor the toms rip each other to death. I can't blame the women, at least not when I think about it. Theirs is not a happy or enviable predicament. Some may have won, but which ones is impossible for an outsider, and perhaps even an insider, to detect. As much, that is, as it is possible to win in Dinlock.

Tombola, which Davie cannot bear, starts up, and we excuse ourselves. The women do not look at us as we go out, back up to East Clu', where, more drinks, I've lost count. A glaze falls over Davie's eyes, his thick blond hair seems windblown; I recognise the signs. He has clicked with the liquor, it has hit him like a truck. Now anything can happen. And will. An hour ago he said, I feel like smashing something. Someone, he means. Now, he makes a fist, confiding, as he forgets he's confided before in London, *sometimes I feel like smashing it all up*. He's spoiling. The odds are that he will swing on me before the evening is over.

Inside East Clu', where it is important for him not to disgrace himself before the older men, Davie is more controlled. I look at the miners and their wives, not as young nor as gay as in West Club, and there is a patriarchal, brownish tinge of relic to the proceedings, as of old, good leather. Tough, grizzled pit-wise miners and their village-wise wives back up the imported singer on "Love Letters in the Sand".

> While precious tear drops fall
> Your memory I recall
> And days that used to be . . .
> And days that used to be
> The skies were blue above
> It was the dawn of love
> But you've forgotten me . . .

Davie and I join the union men in the adjoining billiard parlour. Tooley, the pit under-manager, is gone. We talk about him. A dense discussion of pit practises swirls around me.

I meet Carl Fish, the new Home Coal Chairman, a short stupid-looking man whose arms are too long and who looks to be in a perpetual friendly fog. Carl is taking over from the renowned Alf Jackson, who had to quit for personal reasons. The union men talk it over when Carl is out of earshot; there's more to it than that but I don't know what. A noisy row starts in the other room and the men rush to the doorway to observe critically or join in, whatever is called for. Quickly sidling among the packed tables, Carl, tonight's duty steward is on the spot with a brisk, sombre warning to a big mouth drunkenly disputing a tombola decision. Davie tells me Carl is famous for his lightning punches, that he is a masterly brawler when provoked. The wide-mouth simmers down, the men in the doorway, disappointed, apologise to me. Thought tha' maht see summat there, they mourn. Davie looks at the clock on the wall. Almost nine. Have to get to Pub to meet Loretta, he says. How about his two sisters? Oh, he replies uneasily, they're off at the cinema.

51

Pub stands on the outer edge of the village. Being the only pub in town where the miners go it is unusually large, fitted out with the customary private saloon and public bar sections plus the inevitable central, outsize room with, again, a small raised platform in the corner. The owner is a collier whose back was broken in a cave-in years ago. He stands upright behind the bar and pulls beer with stiff jerky motions, patrons know he wears a steel brace from hip to chest. By nine o'clock of a Saturday night it is crowded, smoky and very noisy, on the platform a brawny apple-cheeked drummer in a blood-red cardigan and a slumped indifferent piano basher in a collapsed tuxedo supplying a kind of rhythm section. Entering the Pub, I spot Will Lawson and Fay and their friend Frank, a husky hawk-nosed dark young miner who, Davie tells me is a carnival strong man every summer. He is wearing a riotously-coloured Hawaiian shirt sent him by a brother in Philadelphia. We wrestle for a moment in the Pub's vestibule just to make friends, and then Davie drags me away to his table.

It is quite a table. Walter's mother is there, neatly dressed, apparently sipping but actually guzzling her gin. I plop myself down on a chair between Walter, Davie's erstwhile (or is it still?) best friend, and Walter's side-burned pit-mate, and because time is of the essence the round of drinking commences without undue flourish or ceremony. Frank joins us; we get along fine; he's a good-natured giant. The recognisable, thumping music grows louder, the air smokier, Davie's eyes more glazed. Up front, the night is in full swing, with one after another of the miners, or their wives, climbing up in front of the mike to do a turn. Davie, a star turn, he boasts, threatens to do likewise. He is fairly far gone under the bitter, penetrating gaze of Walter's mother whose bulky, grey-haired Scottish maternal charm rapidly corrodes under the influence.

I talk to the son, Walter, the famous Walter, whose favourite girl-friend Davie says he seduced and showed the path to paradise. And, as I talk to Walter, I suddenly, out of no logical sequence, realise something which is to become firmer tomorrow. I look over the miners and their women along the wall drinking and singing and talking, and I think that one of the reasons why I should hate a place like Dinlock to wither away, or rather, one of the reasons why I should regret its disappearance when it does finally go, is that here there still exists a genuine *public*, in the nineteenth-century meaning of the word, and not an inert, apathetic mass. The basis for this is probably reactionary, in the sense that it exists on an obsolete and decaying fundament, but the phenomenon is unique and stirring. Note how well Dinlock fits the classic definition: virtually as many villagers express opinions as receive them (thus far); personally and though the union branch there is an opportunity to immediately and effectively answer back; opinion finds ready outlet in action (the Beckley near-riot, the constant outbreak of pit strikes) and authoritative institutions have not (yet) destroyed the autonomy of the village. Progress, as we call it, will change all this; at this very moment coal-cutting machinery below the ground and telly above it are doing the job. But even if I cannot prove, I suspect that Dinlock, as public, will turn out a hardier organism than the rootless communities of my own country.

Walter, through a haze of drink and smoke, appears a thin and grey-faced young man, a sardonic mouth and under-bright eyes, much too tall for the sparse muscle stretched on him. He wants to know if I am a Socialist, and if so what brand, his form of Yank-baiting, and he tells me he wants to go to Oxford and, as Davie predicted, quotes wildly from Gorki to J. B. Priestley. Davie is busy conversing with droppers-by, while on the platform singers come and go, less and less inhibited. Walter's mother is staring at us all glassily. I tell Walter that I met his wife earlier on, and someone at the table, which now includes a couple of elderly pit men I do not know, says Walter never takes his wife anywhere;

Walter's gap-toothed pit-mate keeps a straight face except to smile at all and sundry with dogged friendliness from time to time. Walter nods at Davie and asks, "Do tha' think our Davie's a good artist?" It's a loaded question; he wants me to join him in some attitude. I say, Davie is a fine painter. Walter sits back, glares darkly at Davie, passes his right hand under his left armpit and shakes his head. "Naw, naw," he disagrees. Presumably this is a Yorkshire, or local, gesture of brushing someone off.

Walter detests and envies Davie, Davie rankles in him, it's as though the very sight of Davie rakes him with spurs of envy, jealousy, God alone knows what else. So Walter nibbles and scratches at me, trying to get me to say that Davie isn't all he's stacked up to be by the London art critics. I wish Walter wouldn't. His imagination is hot with resentment, he is not as soberly balanced as he makes out, especially if you believe the stories in the village about Walter scrabbling for so many years at East Clu', at branch meetings and down in pit to win the men's respect as their leader only (and I see it work out before my eyes) to bedevil himself with what I suppose could be called a character flaw. Walter tries too hard to impress, his hunger for recognition impels him into attitudes of fatuous superiority which make him something of a fool in the eyes of the men, I can see that as I watch the others at the table glance at him with a jocose, half-disguised contempt. Somewhere, at some other time, my guess is that Walter might have made somebody a first-rate back-room operator, and in the right cause too. But now, here, in Dinlock, he's a frustrated unpleasant boy, Walter is; I pity him because I think he will never find the key, as Bolton has done.

At our table, Frank, the young chesty one, is smiling all the time; he's got a secret.

Drinking, talking, laughing higher and faster all over Pub now, near to closing time. Walter's bitter, clumsy efforts to win me away from Davie I shut off abruptly when Davie lurches away from the table and Walter's mother's restraining, grasping hands (middle-aged women love Davie) to do a turn on the platform stage. For a moment he is stricken with shyness, he turns deferentially and asks the drummer to back him up; then he pulls the microphone up to his mouth and bellows out,

> Puttin' on the agony, puttin' on the style,
> That's what all the young folks
> Are doing all the while, . . .

the audience beating time with him, his voice roaring all over the jam-packed Pub and thickening the haze. Frank and Walter and Walter's grey-haired mother and Walter's grinning pit-mate and I join in, *don't you rock me daddy-o*, and Walter sits back with an artificial smile of cool derision for the inferiors at his table. Davie can do everything he can do better and he can't even do this, and he swills viciously from two glasses as Davie's vocal chords fill him with misery and loathing under the pretence of indifference. Davie is pushed off the platform and Walter's pit-mate has suddenly taken over with a boogie-woogie number; Walter pays no attention. In the vortex of the roar and drink he asks me how I like Dinlock and I know better than to try and answer.

Davie staggers into his chair and Walter's mother presses him to her, half with affection half with a curious blend of hatred and repulsion. (When Walter came running to Davie's house after his girl friend left him, Davie used to go for advice and companionship to Walter's mother who lived in Walter's house with the pit-mate and the wife and the two children.) She's sozzled. Davie is sozzled. They fondle each other, she in full knowledge, he in a moment of lapse. Someone keeps putting whiskies in my hand. I wave to various miners in Pub as to old friends. Time was declared fifteen minutes ago, but most patrons remain. At a signal from the proprietor behind the bar the drummer bawls into the mike the opening words of the closing song, "Auf Wiedersehen". Before he is through the second bar everyone, but everyone, miners and their women, old sick pensioners and surface men and colliers and branch officials, all around me, have stopped talking to sway sentimentally and join in, these Yorkshire people, saying off veederzane to each other, to themselves and to all the things which I won't be around to find out about. At our table even Walter has his arms around someone, me, and I have my arm on him and Frank, and we all have our arms around someone else as we sing good night in a foreign language, hard tired brutalised and soft-hearted men, many of whom will go down into the pit within 24 hours to shift their yards, and the women, for this moment only not in league with each other against the enemy man but with the men, all singing with sweet, drunken loudness, off veederzane, into the fumes and sweat, up and over the stale crust of their trapped and tangled lives, simply off veederzane, and suddenly there I am crying like a goddam screwball but I shove another whisky to hide my face and then somehow we're outside on the road where Bolton once laid a boy named Len low.

We are part of the reluctant flow down the cool, windy road, the people drifting off into smaller, silent groups. Davie is walking with the crazy limp of the drunk. Somewhere on the road we happen on to Glenn, Davie's former pit-mate, and his wife, Jane, coming back from West Clu'. They invite us to their house for a nightcap, and a small argument ensues between Jane and Fay, who says she has prior claim to the visitor. Fay says sweetly she wouldn't want to wake up Jane's children, and Jane bluntly reminds Fay that Fay has more children than she. The men—Glenn and Davie, Will, Frank and myself—stand in the middle of the dark road, more or less enjoying the show. For a change, it's the women at it, with the men as onlookers. Nobody is particularly sober. When it is apparent that neither woman intends giving way, Will Lawson places a firm hand around his wife's waist and says, sternly, "It's been a long tahm since we've been to their house, luv." We straggle down the road in a happy procession, and then we are in Glenn's house, and Fay and Jane are preparing sandwiches.

It is a friendly wind-up to a friendly evening. Frank and Will and I are sobering up, Davie and Walter are quiet. Glenn is sitting morosely in a corner studying an NCB wage list. We all know something will break, but nobody makes a move to go. Will and I talk about Burma, where he fought in the war; in the kitchen Jane is making tea and Fay is putting raw strips of bacon between layers of store-bought white bread and looking at Frank as he lounges with a grin against one wall, Walter sitting in front of the small fireplace facing us, Davie is wandering around the room.

An argument starts, at first I'm not even sure between who and who. It has to do, I think, with Bolton. Walter is saying he doesn't think Bolton is all that good, and Davie is telling Walter he is wrong, that Bolton has done wonders for Dinlock, that Bolton is the salt of the earth. The more Davie talks the more grandiose his words until he and Walter have manœuvred themselves, by some concealed but inexorable alchemy to where Davie is fiercely defending Bolton and Walter is claiming that in addition to his other faults Bolton is not a man to be trusted. Like two dancers whirling each other closer and closer to an abyss, they make their moves with their mouths.

Glenn has fallen asleep in his corner.

How dare Walter say that about the village benefactor? demands Davie.

Walter has a right to his opinion, someone says.

Ferociously now, Davie pleads with Walter to take it back, Walter stiffly sits back and with a fixed humourless smile says there's nothing to take back.

Meanwhile, in the parlour, we others gossip on, with an eye on the two men in front of the fireplace. Walter, Davie

57

almost whines, why do you say things like that, you know Bolton is my best friend. He's my friend too, retorts Walter, and I have a different opinion from you, Davie.

From time to time Will or Frank put their oar in, gently advising Davie to ease up, which Davie does for a moment or two, wandering drunkenly but with purpose around the room and then coming to stand in front of Walter again, to glare at him, while Walter coolly sips his bottled ale and uneasily grins at me, determined not to move away, to show the white feather. Frank and Will Lawson and I speak of many things in that room, but Fay the wife chimes in, now agreeing with Davie, now allowing as how Walter might have a point, remembering a long-forgotten incident showing up Bolton's weakness for adulation, dropping a word here and a hint there, the drunken bitch-cat on the mantelpiece sprinkling oil with dainty drunkeness on the rising flames.

Davie stands over Walter who is half a head taller but pounds lighter and very likely no fighter. Davie grabs Walter's lapels. Take it back, Walter. Walter rears his head back. Go away, Davie, he says softly. The others in the room are accustomed to the origins of brawls, keep talking on in the hope it will die out. A couple of Glenn's kids, awakened by the noise, trot in and Will Lawson grabs up the youngest boy with a whoop and kisses him and calls him "Little Flower", while Frank swings the other child around the room, and Davie and Walter quietly argue while Fay watches from atop the telly set, carefully gauging the temperature and tossing in a few well-chosen but seemingly innocent words when it seems to be cooling off. Once or twice Will says, shut up Fay, and she does. Jane on a stool drawn up next to her quietly snoring husband, stirs the tea in her cup and watches, avidly. Having provided the site, they are now out of it.

It looks as if Davie and Walter will be at it all night without resolve, and Fay and Will join in to tell me just why Will had to march to that school and give the headmaster what-for, and how the inkbottle was spilled, and their shock when their boy came back from school the next day and said that he had been refused admittance, and how on the day the story came out the house was crammed with reporters, one of them even from London; they have not told the story to a newcomer for a long time and they derive pleasure from it. For a moment even Fay forgets what's happening in the corner of the parlour. Take it back! Frank and Will step between Davie and the still seated Walter, whose face is greyer, stonier. He is scared. They are two small boys, one knowing he is bigger but physically inferior and unable and unwilling to back out of this small boy's station so mixed up with adult complexities; but there is something else. Not only does Walter not back out but in the way he answers back Davie, in each sentence there is a goading word. Any man who wants to get out of a fight with dignity, but truly avoid it, will not use such words. Twice, three times Davie is pushed away by Frank or Will or me, Walter nodding and shaking his head in an attempt to find his proper role and the appropriate gestures. For the tenth time Davie asks Walter to take back what he said, and now nobody, including Davie and Walter, remembers what Walter originally said about Harold Bolton, one hand of Davie's on Walter's lapel, with the rest of us gobbling up raw bacon sandwiches and drinking tea and pretending Davie and Walter don't exist.

I wonder if I should do something. Will, for the first time, is growing somewhat embarrassed, and Fay pretends to be, Frank is relaxed, knowing that he can knock everybody's heads together if it comes to that. He must weigh 16 stone.

Will knows what I am thinking, he leans across the tea table, "It's not thy place to do anything, keep out of it," his tone firm and friendly, "it's been blowing up a long tahm," and calmly sips his tea.

Take it back, Walter, or I'll knock you silly.

If you do, Davie, I'll break your hands.

As soon as he says it Walter knows he has made a bad mistake, but even if he wanted to, which I think he does, there is no way to take back something like that in Dinlock village.

Break my hands . . . *break my hands!* Davie is triumphant, he has finally forced Walter into the position of having physically threatened him. Now why do you want to talk like that, Walter? You know you can't break my hands, why are you threatening me, Walter, I'm sorry you're talking like that. Glenn sleeps on, Jane watches. Will surveys the scene, rubs his eyes and draws a sigh. "Aye, socialism. Will it ever come to a village like Dinlock?"

Come away, Davie, calls Will. Leave it alone, calls Frank. Fay rambles on, with point, about Harold Bolton. Shut up woman, says Will through his teeth. Break my hands, whispers Davie to himself, roaming the room, working himself up while Walter grows more frightened as he sees he has, as on so many other occasions, cut himself off from retreat.

Davie seems to calm down, bends over Walter, lectures him with a wagging finger. Will and Frank and I bend to our tea. The sound of Walter's face being slapped, backhanded, is like a loud shot in the still, warm small room.

Before I can look up, Frank and Will have dragged Davie away, I sit foolishly, Walter's face is an ugly red blotch, Fay cooes, "Ah ye shouldn't 'a done 'at, Davie," and Will shouts, "Shut *up*, woman." Glenn, the host, is still slumped in a chair, but now his eyes are wide open. Was he really sleeping? Through none of this has the expression on Jane's eye-shadowed, haggard face changed. I feel a little sick, convinced that it would never have happened if I had not been there. Frank holds Davie against the wall. Davie pleads to one and all. Why did he have to say he would break my hands? Walter, his foolish bluff having been called, and perhaps in some odd way satisfied, sits motionless, a study in control, the hand holding the glass of ale in exactly the same position it was before he was struck. Only his eyes are uncontrolled; he does not know where to fix them. For a long moment he stares at the floor, as the red splotch dies away in his tight sallow face.

Walter rises to his moment of humiliation. With great and impressive dignity, as Davie is restrained from approaching him ostensibly to continue arguing and actually to take another poke, Walter gets up from his chair and goes to the sandwich-laden table. Suddenly Glenn and Jane are up on their feet and murmuring a string of formalised apologies. So also Fay and Will. Fay once more refers to the subject of the quarrel. Will gives her one heavy meaningful look and this time she shuts up for good. The children, who have been standing in the open doorway all this time, are shooed out.

Walter is making a test for himself, pouring ale into his glass with the steadiest of hands, holding himself with miserable tautness as he begins to ponder how this incident will affect his status in the village.

Davie is loud with pitisome self-justification. Why did Walter have to threaten him, why did he say those things about that fine man Bolton? He slumps down in a chair and holds his head in his hands. There is silence; bashful grins appear on the faces of Will and Fay and Frank, apologetic grins to me and yet somehow exhibitionistic. Glenn and Jane have disappeared upstairs, ostensibly to tuck the children in. Will says to Walter, I'm sorry this had to happen to you in Glenn's house, Walter. It was the wrong thing to do. I apologise for Davie.

Davie shouts, no need to apologise for me, why did Walter, etc. Almost grunting with the inaudible effort required to keep the quaver out of his voice, Walter says every man has a right to his opinion. He's right, Davie, says Will, what are you, a Nazi gangster? Davie, crooked in his chair, doggedly shakes his head. Break my hands . . . Bolton . . . why did. Walter goes back to his chair by the fireplace, lowers himself into it with deliberation and, arms folded, shakes his head with grinning sadness at me as if to say now look what's gone and happened.

61

There is a dip of inconsequentiality; gossip resumes; the visitor can actually hear the various minds probing for the correct and applicable level of tone for this situation. Davie is talking to himself, then he goes to hover near Fay and Will Lawson, while Frank and Walter and I talk of nothing. I hear, but don't believe either Walter or Frank hears, Davie blurt out something about his affair with the shopgirl Diane; he says Walter's behaviour tonight was offensive to him and that Walter tried to pick a fight because he, Davie, was a better man to Diane than Walter. That, he says, is the root of the quarrel. He is muttering. Does Walter hear? Will Lawson shuts up Davie with a sharp word, and Fay apologises all round for Davie's conduct. Davie moves over to Walter, offers to apologise. Walter says, tha've gone too far this tahm, Davie, an' Ah'll not shake hands with tha'.

This angers Davie. Again, Frank and Will separate them in a scuffling test of strength. Davie wails that all he wants to do is to apologise to Walter. While Frank and I hold Davie, Will, now the host of the house, and Walter go to the door, and we all hear Will quietly saying how sorry he is and Walter telling Will he doesn't hold anything against him. Will closes the door after Walter and returns to say, Davie I'm ashamed of you. Another round of self-justification by Davie, as Frank and Fay, Will's wife, discuss quietly something private near the fireplace.

Later, tomorrow, in West Club, Fay is to tell me, without prompting, that there is utterly no truth to the terrible lying rumour that she and Frank—"han'soom yoong Frank"—are having an affair, no truth whatsoever.

Meanwhile, Will Lawson tries to reason with Davie, to point out to Davie his folly. Every man, he insists, has a right to his opinion. It is a drunken, reasonless colloquy. Will, rises up Davie, if someone came up to me and said you were a rat, or that your wife was having an affair with a good friend of yours, what would you expect me to do? Davie, says Will quietly, I hope you'd stand up for me. There, says Davie triumphantly. But, Will insists, Harold Bolton is a public figure and a public figure can be criticised. Not in front of me says Davie, self-righteously pulling himself together on his chair; Bolton is my friend. Then you're no better than a fascist, says Will. I expect Davie to leap at this, but he is too weighed down by drink. He slumps again, shakes his head and says weakly, piteously, no Will, I'm no fascist, Walter had it coming. Whether he did or not, Davie, you should not have done it in front of your guest.

Davie looks up at me, blearily, as though he'd forgotten I was there. Yeah, yeah, he agrees, 'twas a bad thing to do. He gets up. I'll find Walter and apologise, he says. For the next five minutes in the house we all engage in grappling with Davie to keep him from following and beating the hell out of Walter. Then it starts up again, Davie explaining why he did what he did, insisting it was on the spur of an impulse that he hit Walter, with Will Lawson and Frank telling Davie he ought to be ashamed because even though Walter is the taller man he is no fighter and there was a guest in the house; suddenly I am disgusted and I stand up. Let's all get some sleep, I say. Instant agreement. I realise that is what they were waiting for, for me to say something, to end the night for them. For any of them to have done so first would have amounted in their eyes to unjustified rudeness.

Much shaking of hands and lugubrious farewells on the threshold; Davie is sullen with me. Much inexplicable winking by Fay and Frank at me. At the open doorway leading out to the dark alley Will Lawson puts his hand on my shoulder and earnestly hopes to see me tomorrow. The door shuts quietly in our faces, and Davie and I stumble across a pitch-black field. Davie almost falls on his face half a dozen times (and when we get to his house we discover that his thumb is blue and swollen). The village behind us is dark and asleep. Davie says, "Well why don't you say something?" I tell Davie I'm sleepy and I'm not thinking any more tonight. All the way home he mutters that he knows what I'm thinking

63

and I'm wrong, Walter asked for it; he is preparing an excuse for himself for the morning. He is in the kind of rough, troubled shape I have seen him in in London after he has, in one way or another, relieved his anxieties by hitting out and now is saddled with still another guilt.

In the dark, Davie raps out sharply, Come on now, tell me what you think. I tell him that I am sleepy, that it is his business and I want no part of it. He is furious with me. Before this, we had no barrier between us; now we are strangers. He knows I disapprove and I am full of disgust at him. Once before I explained, in patient detail, how this sort of stunt was more a revelation of cowardice than a display of manliness; and he wants me to go through it all again. But I have a lot of whiskies inside me, and I'm in no mood for Davie. The longer I stay silent, and now the silence between us in the dark field is very tense, the more he feels my disavowal of him. He feels lonely and drunk, betrayed by himself and now by his new friend. I almost feel sorry for him, but I am sorrier for Walter, and anyway I have had a bellyful of Dinlock for tonight. Davie lurches against me and says if I had acted the way Walter did he would have punched me too. I say that Davie did not punch Walter, he slapped him with his open hand, and that if Davie has any more ideas about his hands on people he'd better forget them. He stoops and picks up a rock from the field and weighs it from hand to hand; I pick up a rock which I have to carry in both hands. For a quarter of a mile we go across the night-shrouded field carrying rocks, and then he throws his away into the darkness, and so do I. We walk to his house in silence.

Inside, a small fire burning in the grate lights up the parlour and I fix up the short couch and a chair with blankets, undress and fit myself in. Davie wants to talk but I don't. I tell him good night and shut my eyes determinedly. I shift around on the improvised bed to make myself more comfortable. I hear him making all sorts of unnecessary noise, rattling a newspaper, filling his pipe and knocking it against

64

the mantelpiece, boiling and pouring himself some tea in the kitchen. He settles down on a chair near my head and puffs loudly on his pipe. I do not respond. Then I sleep. I wake up for a moment in the middle of the night and the dark room is empty and I think, I don't have it so bad, and then I am asleep.

I awaken to a busy living-room. Davie is combing his hair, morning-bright and sober, in front of the cracked mirror above the fireplace. Loretta who never did show up at the pub last night, and the children, are presences to whom neither Davie nor I speak more than necessary. I lumber out of the couch, dress and cook breakfast for Davie and myself.

Outside it is, as usual, cold and grey, early morning winds sweeping across the silent cottages. Half-way up his street Davie says, jauntily, you haven't told me yet what you think. I say, you know what I think, and then we round a corner and meet Bolton coming to get us. We go past Pub, past the field, up towards the colliery, Bolton and Davie formalising themselves and wary before meeting Tooley, the under-manager, the scent of the ancient struggle thickening in their nostrils.

Davie says, Bolton, I might as well tell you before you hear it, I clipped Walter last night for saying things about you. I think, so that's to be the official version. It does not particularly interest Bolton, or at least that is the way he is playing it. All he says is, "No need to have done 'at, Davie, Ah'm bound to be criticised time to time." " 'Twas more than 'at," asserts Davie, and then we are past Theresa Road and the low grey stone wall and the field and at the colliery, huge, dirty, engrossing. We are still climbing the steep, walled path up from the village when we pass two large terraced homes set aside in isolation from the village. Bolton says the pit manager and the pit engineer live there, where the owners used to live. It is a placid, grimy Victorian landscape.

Tooley greets us in the manager's office, and the tour begins. At first Bolton tries to do some of the explaining but I attach myself to Tooley; this is his show. Davie is vastly interested. He has gone down and come up from this pit more than a thousand times, but he confesses that he has never seen the colliery as a whole. Bolton rapidly loses interest. We leave the office. There are not many men around; this is Sunday. Somewhere below us Frank, on a special and controversial shift, is doing his eight yards. A man passes, on his way out of the pit, black with coal dust and fatigue; I cannot connect him with anyone I saw last night at the clubs. Davie says it is Tommy Hunter, the ex-Commando. He did not say hello because he saw the manager with us.

For the next two hours we go all over the topside of the pit, inspect the machinery, wander into the various stages of coal production on the surface. Huge dynamos, lift engines dated 1880 and gleaming, shaft cables an arm's thickness, the suction rooms at shaft entrance where my ears pop, coal dust everywhere, the tipple where the coal is graded, sifted, labelled, washed. All along the way Tooley relentlessly comments on the miner's lack of responsibility, his ignorance of his own welfare. Bolton smiles, Davie smiles. Several times we come across maintenance workers dawdling on the job, and Tooley does not have to say it. In some embarrassment, Davie says, They don't seem to be wearing themselves out. When the men see Tooley they stop their tea drinking to look at the visitors and then wait glumly for us to leave; no one moves to work. Davie says weakly, they're maintenance men; Tooley looks at him as if to say, what's that got to do with anything. Even Bolton is constrained to an apologetic grin, like a small boy caught with the jam.

Tooley turns out to be, as I thought, not very intelligent but very much up on his job. He knows coal, how to dig it out and carry it out. For a while, as we examine close-up the romance of coal, for that is what it is just so long as you are not working down in the pit, the bitter disputes between management and labour are forgotten as Tooley and Bolton and Davie counterpoint each other explaining how Dinlock colliery works. Tooley doesn't give an inch, defers in no way; how he keeps on top of his job, no doubt, and I don't blame him. The men would chew his guts out if he gave them a chance. From almost any point in the pit-yard we can look down on the village, sprawling old and inert and somnolent.

Now Tooley forgets to use his lecture to beat Bolton over the head with the alleged laziness and incompetence of the work force, and he becomes interested in my questions. Bolton and Davie are proud of the mine, but I am not sure yet what Tooley is proud of, possibly of having arrived in his relations with the men where the knives are not flourished at first sight, and on a Sunday. Once, out of Tooley's hearing, I say to Davie and Bolton that I am impressed by the fact that malingerers do not jump to their job at Tooley's approach. I tell them about the American practice. Bolton looks smug. "Aye, we've a union here, we 'ave. It's all the union," says Davie.

Tooley has several different types of engines turned on for my benefit, and even Bolton is fascinated, though he tries hard not to show it. Half the equipment I see is designed for safety. In his little shed, the Red Cross man tells me that in a normal day half a shift can report in with injuries. Bolton says this is so because no man wants to go unreported in the event he can sue the NCB later. Two giant air-pumps at pit-head cut our laughter short; if one fails the other is switched on; if both fail the men below die. The men I am with discuss only the bizarre or unusual possibilities for disaster. I have to ask about the mundane ways in which the miners work and injure themselves to death, it is so much taken for granted that they have long ago ceased to think consciously about it, and for a time they do not even see the point of my questions.

67

When Tooley takes me up to the tipple, only Davie accompanies, Bolton says he is too old to be climbing stairs. Davie confides that Bolton is bored, and perhaps even irritated. For a fat man, Tooley is surprisingly agile.

The coal-washing process, now stationary and unmanned this Sunday morning, endlessly fascinates me. Tooley says that the slag stones are removed by hand from the moving belt of coal up out of the pit. The work is done in a big draughty building whose interior is slashed and criss-crossed with belts of varying accelerations, and done by the old men too injured or pneumonocosis-ridden for pit-work. I look at the slag stones, lean over from the metal staircase to pick one up. This is work for old, sick men?

Among the blackened belts and pipes I dirty my nice white coat, sorrow for it and am ashamed. We leave the pit-head and go over to the wash room which, bereft of inhabitants, looks like the shower room of a less fatal Auschwitz, and Davie asks Tooley, with surprising deference and cordiality, Is it true that in the old days (your days, Tooley) a miner could leave his gold watch behind and not have it stolen. Tooley says maybe. Together they bemoan the loss of integrity among miners, as we talk of the gods tumbling.

All morning Davie has been unsure of himself because the surface men see him touristing in clean, Sunday clothes; then the tour is over. A final drink in the manager's office, some detailed discussion of pit problems (but not one mention of the perennial subject, wages) and Bolton leaves for a branch meeting to which I am invited if I promise not to make notes for the British newspapers. In his office, surrounded by graphs and telephones, Tooley looks stupid again.

Davie and I wander down to the Welfare Hall where the union meeting is scheduled. We wait outside the room where the union executive committee is mulling over grievances, too sacred a session for newcomers, even now Davie. Davie tells me he has not been to a branch meeting in over a year. One of the men from East Clu' comes by and says casually,

"When're tha' coomin' back to pit, Davie?" "Hello, Jack," says Davie. He turns to me and says he toys with the idea of going back to Dinlock pit, but must decide against it because his painting would allow him to work only three shifts a week, and Tooley and the pit manager would use that against the union. He asks me if I think it is the right decision.

Outside the committee room, in the newly painted hall, I talk with several miners, waiting stolidly to take up their cases. I meet Alf Johnson, the Home Coal Chairman who has just resigned for 'personal reasons', and I sense a storm blowing up at the general meeting in a few minutes. Johnson is obviously primed. A pasty-faced giant 6 foot 2 or so who knows his way around a dance hall; a boxer's face, body and stance, battered ears and nose, a sweet almost girlish voice as if the thorax alone had never taken one too many beatings. Davie says that the fight at a branch meeting many years ago between Johnson and Bolton was epic, a fight in which both men broke their noses, and Bolton a hand besides.

The committee files out and marches across the hall to a larger, lighter room for the general meeting. About twenty present, including the branch executive, a large purple NUM banner behind the President's chair. General apologies to me on all sides for lack of attendance. The secretary, Ed Stopp, leaves his chair to explain to me that the hall is always filled during crises. I tell him American unions are the same. But, I had expected more at this meeting; the pit had a walk-out a few days ago.

The branch secretary, Ed Stopp, reads the minutes of the previous meeting in machine-gun Yorkshire incomprehensible to me, and I suspect most others. Davie says nobody ever understands the way he reads the minutes. Apparently Alf Johnson does. He's on his feet, protesting. The petals open, revealing the controversy. A couple of weeks ago, in a fit of something or other, Alf quit as Chairman (unpaid) of the Home Coal Committee. An interim delegate, Carl Fish, the rocky phlegmatic man from East Clu', has already been appointed to replace him. But now Alf says that he did not mean to also resign from one of the corollary jobs traditionally linked (in Dinlock but not anywhere else) with the delegateship, that of alternate checking man (a paid job). There is a long, involved discussion about what Alf did and did not mean to do, repeated references to the union constitution, considerable argumentation.

The meeting is officially overseen by the President of the Branch. This is a very old, white-haired man whose frailness is the collapsed vigour of advancing age. He has been branch President for some years now, and is annually saluted for his services to the union and the village by re-election to what has now become an almost purely honorary position. But he is out of it, managing the meeting as a sort of guru-like umpire, saying little and referring repeatedly, with a kind of distant quietness, to the union rule book and precedent. I am never to see one of his decisions disputed even when, as will happen, several of the men are in obvious and sometimes disgusted disagreement. He is the closest to a Speaker of the House that I have seen outside Westminster, and his name is John Kilmartin. He does not, of course, work down in pit any longer (where the legends have already taken root about his prowess on the coal face); nor does he attend pub or club. He has withdrawn, though not completely, into a wise and private region of himself, and is calmly waiting for death. It is known by Dinlock that the doctors down in London have not given him long. Today as he fulfills his duties, he neither smiles nor frowns, but he has that rare quality of casting over his smallest act an unanswerable, flint-like serenity. He knows what is happening. He knows that next year if not this, one of the younger union officials will step forth boldly to offer himself for the Presidency. Village talk is that the hungriest is Ed Stopp, the union secretary. This is of some concern to the old man in the chair this Sunday (he has spent too many partisan years not to feel it), and more than anything else,

70

in the way in which he renders an *importance* to the least little utterance or procedural detail, you can see how passionately he desires that a worthy man assume his mantle. And yet, how apparent is also his belief that none who presently sit on the union executive board has the full stature to inherit the legacy of the past fifty years of miners' struggles. I wonder what he thinks of Bolton. Does he respect Bolton for not putting himself in the line of succession for the presidency, or does he sense just how cunning and aware of his own limitations Bolton is? Not once during the time I am in Dinlock— and though we cover a wide range of subjects—is Bolton to refer to the existence of his union president.

Today, this Sunday, the world of men in whose midst he is a dying monument, intrigue, envy, scramble, far far below him. A good deal of subsurface politicking; I recognise all the signs of pre-election fever. From what I can see, one clique is determined to keep Alf moving out now that he has made the first mistake, others are equally determined to ameliorate the effects of Alf's move. There is intense rivalry here. Ed Stopp, already seeing himself in the chair, is transparent; he wants Alf out, possibly sees him as a claimant to the local union presidency. Bolton is studiedly neutral. Sleepy-eyed Carl Fish, the new Home Coal Chairman, is caught in the middle; he has no ambitions, and so rises to extoll Alf's merits. Alf keeps protesting until general agreement is reached to review the question of the alternate checkweighmanship in a fortnight. There is some sentiment to settle it now in favour of Alf, but Ed Stopp insists the union by-laws will not permit it; either believing this or hoping to use the interval to his own advantage. More and more Ed sounds familiar, like a UAW-CIO local officer who likes his job too much, the job which keeps him off the belt-line; but he has not Bolton's talent for fixing the limelight on himself while seemingly refusing it. The old man, Kilmartin, sets his face impassively and rules favourably on Stopp's objection. More talk. A show of hands. The issue is compromised

71

temporarily; Alf Johnson settles back with a broad, victorious smile. I look over at Davie, and discover he's something of a stranger here too. I should have thought the tension would abate, but it's still there, and then I hear the word 'gas' and I know it won't until that word is disposed of.

Gas. Tooley and Davie told me Dinlock pit was relatively free of it, but the differences between relative and absolute can mean dead men. A rank-and-file miner behind us gets up and says his shift walked off the job last week when 2 per cent. gas was found in his seam. Immediately, though formally and in friendly terms, a battle starts. Ed Stopp's authority is being challenged. He gives a long, defensive report which even a stranger can see through. I doubt if any one of the twenty men present buys it. Ed says that he went straightaway to the gas pocket on being informed, talked to the deputy (foreman) who had already ordered the men off the job. Any other deputy would have kept the men working and left the problem to the next shift, says Ed. He makes other assertions, including his belief that under certain circumstances (clearing of gas) it is permissible for miners to work in even 5 per cent. polluted air. A wizened old miner in a trilby leans over to tap my knee and whisper, "Ah'd lakh to see 'im rippin' at 5 per cent."

It's a tortuous dispute. How much gas was there in the seam, did the men walk off before the deputy told them to, was it all right to work at either end of the gas pocket. Clearly a matter of life and death to them all, and they drone on as monotonously as though deciding on the decorations for the annual Christmas dance. Alf Johnson, the former Home Coal Chairman, rises to insert a gratuitous needle into Ed Stopp, leaving everybody with the impression that he would have handled the situation far more competently and with greater dispatch. When it appears as if the matter will become another episode in the personal quarrel between Stopp and Johnson, John Kilmartin intervenes with a few words to silence the rivals. Stopp shuts up, and Alf Johnson retreats to his seat.

I still can't figure what Ed did wrong. Finally, it emerges. He failed to storm down into the seam, bawl out the deputy and without waiting for administrative niceties tell the men to go home. And now he has to defend himself. As the discussion continues, I can see how very much for granted the men take their solidarity with the union and with the first principles of unity, and also why Dinlock ranks high in unauthorised strikes and absenteeism.

I ask Alf when he sits down, how often do you ask the NUM national office to condone a walk-out? He smiles, never. There it is. For any union official above the local level (and even some here) the Dinlock miner entertains unbounded, if tolerant and humorous, contempt, the measure being that a man loses worth according to the distance he puts between himself and the coal face. Also there is a severe, deeply embedded status gauge. At work, the top dog is the coal-face collier, the hand-getter, the man who works with pick and shovel on the actual wall of coal. This is what Davie does, and Bolton and Alf and Ed and Glenn and most of their set, the occupation classication from which spring all (note, all) the branch leaders. They are the acknowledged aristocracy, these hand-getters, for theirs is the toughest, meanest and best paid job. Ranking below them, but still within hailing distance, are the rippers, haulage men, shot firers. In another world completely are the workers on the surface. Bolton says, and I believe him, that when he can no longer work on the actual coal face he will leave the mine, that he will never accept softer work topside.

In this discussion about gas, I learn one of the anomalies. Shot-firers, the miners who work with dynamite, are on the lowest rung of the status ladder of officialdom down in the pit, but their word is law when it comes to gas. Even if all the instruments deny gas, and one shot-firer says he 'feels' it, he can, and often does, order everyone off the job, and they obey. After the meeting, when I talk to the men, I learn that most of them have had people die in mine accidents. Bolton's

73

father and brother died in cave-ins, Ed Stopp's father was killed in a Scottish mine explosion, Alf Johnson has been in two explosions and Carl Fish the man who replaces him as Home Coal Chairman was once sealed off for two days.

Bolton, incidentally, plays an exceedingly clever game about this gas business. I will bet dollars to doughnuts he had a little something to do with the delay in getting the men out of the gas-infiltrated seam, but he has covered skilfully for himself—the first union official to submit a written report and the first to put himself down on record verbally. Perhaps I'm being unfair; American instincts may not be good in a Yorkshire union meeting. The discussion concludes with everybody in agreement that next time gas is reported the union officials must move more promptly. From my vantage I still don't see how they could have done so, but Ed Stopp's long and circuitous report put my wind up. Davie tells me it is commonly assumed in the village that Ed will go for the Union presidency later this year, and that Ed is a careerist. A careerist in Dinlock.

The meeting closes as soon as the gas dispute is dealt with. The union is the principal instrument of protection, even life on the job, and at the moment they are not too interested in its ancillary functions. There is some desultory discussion of contributions to the Labour Party, a polite thank-you letter to the delegation of Soviet miners that passed through the area and gave out lapel buttons, and a canvassing of present members to see who might be available to attend the funeral in Leeds of an old miner who used to work in Dinlock pit. The sun comes out, abruptly, and the meeting is bathed in sudden light which disappears as quickly as it came. The men stir in their chairs and tamp down their pipes. Ed Stopp makes a pretty speech, thanking Davie and the visitor for their presence. (I'm not sure Davie likes being classified with the outsider.) I avoid Walter's eye. He walked in early in the meeting and sat down in a chair away from Davie, with Alf Johnson in between. They said nothing to each other, of course. Then, a moment after his arrival, Walter was on his feet explaining some of the details of the gas incident, since he was involved. Earlier in the morning I asked Davie if he was going over to Walter's to apologise, as he said he would do. No, Davie said, he would wait for Walter to apologise to him.

Now, as soon as the meeting formally, and with a pre-liminary flourish consisting of a stately decceleration of the proceedings, adjourns, Walter scoots out ahead of Davie. John Kilmartin wanders out of a side door by himself. I am told it is his custom no longer to join the men for a pint but instead to walk along the moors after the union meeting. He is not, I am assured, regarded queerly for doing this. I cannot but help wonder which ghosts he talks to then. We all adjourn, too, to East Clu'.

We start drinking. The men want to know what I think of the meeting. I tell them. I tell them about American union meetings. I tell them about the United Mine Workers of America and John L. Lewis of whom they've heard. I tell them that in the 1930's men from the Yorkshire coal-fields were in the forefront of the CIO organisation drive, men like Alan Heywood. They know this name, they tell me excitedly that there is an Alan Heywood memorial home for the aged in Yorkshire. I tell them how Lewis ruled the UMW with an iron fist, habitually sending in thugs with machine-guns to break up branch meetings which weren't going his way. Ed, Carl, Alf, Davie, Bolton, Ray, they look disbelievingly at me, as if I were going to too many films. Carl Fish says, What kind of miners ye have in America anyhow? Davie rubs his hands together and says, Oh boy I'd sure like to see Ernest Jones come down to one of our meetings. The men tell me they kicked a big union leader out of one of their meetings last year when he peremptorily tried to dissolve it prior to a strike vote. " 'E us lucky tuhve escape with 'is lahf, 'e uz," says Alf Johnson, the ex-Home Coal Chairman. I believe it.

Half an hour of Yank-baiting, I slap Ray Sweet's beer-stomach and he slaps mine, and we're getting liquored up, after noon on a Sunday. Tombola starts up. Sixty-six, clickety-click, number four open the door. Bolton and Davie and I play a game, lose, Davie and I go home for dinner. Back at East Clu' the men talked about the pit and I listened. How often they must stand in muck up to their knees, how most of them in the seams work naked to the loins because of the oppressive, moist heat, how a single dislodged rock can cause a spark to ignite the methane gas; I learn how rippers and haulers work alongside the four coal-cutting machines so far installed, how a constant stream of water must be played on the coal dust spewed up by the machines, and on the way home Davie tells me that at Beckley pit he must walk doubled-over for a mile along the roadway, to the coal face, sometimes lying on his side for hours at a time to chip at the coal, a miner's eye-view of nationalisation.

Dinner at Davie's, hot roast beef and chips and Yorkshire pudding, Loretta present, everyone including the children tense. Where are Davie's two sisters? I clear out to sleep in the cold upstairs bedroom, and when I go down the dust has settled a little. I play with the kids, and then Davie and I go out again, for still another round of East, West and Pub. Loretta will meet us later. I say, Davie, why don't you tell Loretta where we'll be. Loretta says, it won't be difficult finding you. Of course it won't, only three places in Dinlock for a miner to go to, a rendezvous never has to be definite. In the kitchen, away from the children, Davie tells Loretta he slugged Walter last night. With an open hand, with an open hand, I feel like reminding him. Loretta smiles thinly; Davie must have come home to tell her about just one fight too many in these past few years.

Early Sunday afternoon. We walk along the grey arc of Theresa Road and don't look up at the colliery, along to West Clu'. Ed Stopp and his wife, Arthur and Greta are at the tables where I saw them last night. Have they been stuck there for the past 18 hours?

Davie and I take a table apart. Davie starts seriously to talk to me. For the first time since I came he makes sense. He drinks slowly, I drink fast. Two miners come over to join us. Pit talk. Five per cent. gas, my arse! Again I am asked what part of the States I am from, by now I've given up trying to explain, I say California, Davie gets a kick out of insisting Chicago. These men, most of them born here and ready to die here, do not understand how anybody can be unsure of where they are from and I do not press the point. The umpteenth joke about Chicago gangsters. They should only know. The pall of going down to pit tomorrow, Monday morning, hangs over us all, dulling tongues. Davie mentions I used to work in Hollywood, but the miners are only politely interested. What is a visitor from Venus compared to the prospect of Monday shift, to twenty years and more of Monday shifts and East Clu', West Clu' and Pub? Some more miners come over and ask how I liked the union meeting. Each one insists on buying me a drink. Whisky oh whisky I know you of old. I tell them I felt at home in the Welfare Hall, it was like an American union meeting. Davie says, You know what Yank tells me (not my name, or 'he', but Yank), that in the American miners' union gangsters walk in and break up meetings. The men drink up smugly, one of them allows as how something like that would liven up Dinlock pit meetings. They laugh. The idea of a dishonest union official, or a physical dictator like John L. Lewis, is comprehensible but not very.

Then, somehow, in West Clu' it is much later.

Loretta joins us, prettied up, ear-rings, a trifle more animated. The ghost of the gay little Barnsley girl is not yet laid. She is standoffish with the men and their wives, not superior but distant. If she is ever like this with Davie, and he says she is, I feel sorry for him. One by one the miners get up and drift away with their wives and their drinks. The three

77

of us remain. Loretta starts drinking Babycham. Are the kids all right, Davie asks sullenly. Yes, what would be wrong with them? replies Loretta. A pretty girl in an electric blue sweater stares at me across tables, steadily unblinking. In Dinlock I do not know what that means and I drop my eyes. West Clu' fills up, tombola. We have promised to meet Bolton at East Clu' at nine o'clock. Bolton wants to come by the house later. Davie thinks I will be bored and says he will find a way out; I think he wants to talk to me.

We pass by Pub without Davie wanting to go in and then I know, for some reason, he will stay sober tonight.

How short a space of time I have been in Dinlock, and already I am swept up in its familiar, demanding routine, and already I have come face to face with the daily, semi-conscious dread of the unceasing dreariness, and semi-consciously I have come to accept that there is only Dinlock, only the two clubs and pub, only these people, and my mind's eye no longer turns outward from them. It's as if I had been coming to East Clu' for many years; I nod my head at familiar faces and forms and they greet me the same way.

In East Clu' Davie and Loretta and I take seats amongst the miners while a wavy-haired over-fed singer from Sheffield croons with stylised gesture that he's gonna sit right down and write himself a letter and make believe it came from you. We buy some tombola tickets. A procession of miners drops by the table before the game starts, to pay their respects and not to bait the Yank any more. One of the soccer players comes by and says he saw me vault the wire fence yesterday and says to Davie, " 'E's a bit of a showoff, Yank is, ain't 'e." We all laugh. I leave Davie with Loretta and walk into the billiard room to talk to Ray Sweet and Bolton and Carl and Alf Johnson who still looks grimly victorious. Ray, the bluff, bespectacled branch vice-chairman, tells me how proud he is of Ernie Bevin and how proud he is that Dinlock will never see foreign labourers, and Bolton tries to ease Ray off his perch by having it both ways (the solidarity of the international working class will win the day for us yet, lad . . . but those Hoongarians fouled their own nest), Carl keeps out of it and sticks close to Alf Johnson, hoping that Alf, and everybody else, won't think ill of him for having taken on the Home Coal job. Suddenly I like Carl and don't think he's so stupid.

I try to taper off on the whiskys, they all look insulted, Ray hands me a pineapple juice as a joke, and it's back on whisky oh whisky. Davie comes over and looks uncomfortable; he is getting ready to tell Bolton not to come by the house later. I return to the table and Loretta and I hem and haw and discover our first common ground in repetitious jokes about her greediness with potato chips and how she won't give me any. Davie comes back and sits down and says nothing. Loretta looks at him and he says he didn't have the heart to tell Bolton. Loretta says, We'll be up all night then. Tombola begins. We lose. A broken-nosed young man at the next table loudly jokes with the tombola caller, Tommy Hunter, ex-Commando and ex-submarine S.O. man in his dreams, and nobody seems to mind. Davie says his name is Dick and he had to stop work in the mine for six months when doctors located pneumonocosis in him, which here in Dinlock is more widespread than silicosis. The men all treat Dick very tenderly now, a strapping cleft-chinned lad who now has to work on the surface. Davie says, "For six months he lived in East Clu' an' we wouldn't let him buy his own drinks." Dick leans over and jokes with Loretta, hands Davie the latest wage list in case he hadn't seen it. A few minutes to closing time Davie and I ceremoniously enter the billiard parlour and have a last round with the branch union old guard, and everybody hopes I will be up to Dinlock again soon, and next time they'll take me down to the pit, I won't really understand Dinlock until I've been to pit. When we leave Bolton is with us.

All the way home (going out of our way, it seems, to begin at Theresa Road and swing slowly under the colliery) Davie and Loretta do things with their eyes to convey their regret at Bolton monopolising my time. Loretta and I walk on ahead, but she won't unbutton. The women, and the lives they lead, what they talk about and think about, are still an impenetrable mystery. As soon as I touch on one of the thousand rawly sensitive subjects coveted and nourished by Dinlock females Loretta clams up; when I mention, as lightly as possible, family matters, she burrows as far back into herself as politeness allows, and further questions are useless. You LSE firsts in sociology, come on up here and find out what these women are thinking. Where are you?

At home, Bolton settles in with a reminder from Davie that I have to catch an early bus in the morning. For some reason he flushes uncomfortably. We talk. Bolton does the routine, enumerating his list of projects for the village, telling of his war experiences, buttering me up and generally playing the bluff Yorkshireman which Davie says is pure act by now. Bolton makes boasts for the union which Davie is at pains to diminish later. Then, for some inexplicable reason, Bolton launches into a turbid panegyric on Crown, Flag and Empah. Davie closes his eyes miserably and slumps down further in his chair; Loretta begins leafing through *True Romances* only to put it away on a warning finger from her husband. A moment later she is up and making her excuses. She goes to bed. Bolton stays on. We talk, mainly repeating what I've already learned, from Bolton and others. A lull, two lulls, Davie is impatient to see Bolton go.

Slowly and grandly, at his own speed, Bolton puts on his coat and makes a long, theatrical speech to me about the world, the working class, the revolution and Harold Bolton. When he leaves I am sorry to see him go. Davie spends the next half-hour making apologies for Bolton, and the next four hours by the dying coal fire we spend talking about Davie, the trap he's in and how he can only get out of a small part of it. The house is absolutely still. Where are the two sisters? Davie looks away. Upstairs, sleeping, he says and for the first time since I've known him Davie is sober at night and talking sensibly, not so rationally that he will ever admit what he did to Walter was shameful and premeditated, but quite coolly about some levels of his life. Then, suddenly, we are all talked out. A final drink together and for no reason he could explain he comes over to shake my hand. He goes upstairs. I put my bed together in the dark room and watch the fire from under the blankets. For a long time I listen to Davie and Loretta, two not one murmur in their bed upstairs. I think for a while, about Davie and Dinlock, and then I go to sleep.

Loretta's hand on my shoulder and I wake up; she has brought the kids down and tells me to go to sleep in the kids' cold bedroom, it's six o'clock. I do not think, I sleep. Late in the morning Davie wakes me for breakfast. He and I eat it together, while Loretta, done with the children, watches us from the fireplace. The radio is on, but Davie doesn't say anything, and we eat a quick silent meal to Max Jaffa and "Roses of Picardy". I am given to understand the two sisters have already had their breakfast and are on their way to work in Hamthorpe. Davie has managed it so that I haven't met them. I pack up and say goodbye to Loretta. She does not say it was a pleasure to have me. I tell her how much I am taken with her children, and I believe she likes that. Davie does not like me talking to Loretta, and he gets me out of there. As we go down the street Loretta comes out of the house, unexpectedly, and with Peter, 6, and Jenny, 3, holding baby Michael, she waves for a long time.

Davie and I go to West Clu' for a last drink. It is Monday morning and the village is empty. I am leaving his world, and Davie is going back into it. At the bar, deserted except for a woman behind it who is sleepily polishing glasses, in an empty club, Davie and I sip our drinks and both wish for the bus to come soon.

Outside, on the cold windy corner across the street from the cinema, with the colliery looming on The Hill above us, and somewhere deep inside our friends, the naked men probing and chipping and gouging the coal, Davie says he cannot bear farewells. Neither can I. Luckily, the bus for Hamthorpe comes. I swing aboard and wave out of the window. Davie waves once and then turns down a lane and begins jogging back to his house, and Loretta, to his pictures.

I need a big city now, so I take a train to Sheffield, and see Sheffield as a Dinlocker. It must be *the* city of the world. I stay with my university friends, the Hopkinses and their friend, Murdoch, the Scot Stalinist back from Prague, whose political soul we spend the evening praying for. And in the morning I walk among the small black tenements fringing the river, Attercliffe, world famous as slums, and justly, and walk Brightside Lane, along the river, listening to the animal sounds of Firth Brown, the pounding and clanging and I feel I have come a long way. I am, at last, comfortable here. I see an open door and kid around with the workers in a drop forge. Suddenly I feel an expert on life. But Dinlock has got its hook into me, and I decide not to stay in Sheffield. I take the train to Peniston. Thinking about Dinlock, I almost miss my connection, jump on the goods wagon, fall off, jump in and tell the man in the goods wagon all about Dinlock after he brings out a bottle.

Halifax in a light drizzle. The hills and wind-swept grey-green grass above Hollygate. I need instruction in what I have seen, and so I stay with Charles, who is writing a book on miners and who teaches them, and his wife, who is writing a book on the peasant revolts, and their two boys who want to know how Los Angeles gets its water and if American desk sergeants approve when policemen shoot unarmed people. I walk with them through the old graveyard on the hill to school, which I visit. Good morning sir, hum the children, while the two boys point proudly. And in his study on my last night in Halifax, Charles clears away the eighteenth-century newspapers on his desk and listens carefully to what I say about Dinlock and thinks about it and decides, "It is a backward place, you know."

2

AND AGAIN, LATER, IN THE SUMMER

This time I need no directions to find Davie's house. I remember. After I get off the bus from Barnsley, down the hill to Theresa Road, left up the hill, and left again, and there it is, still there.

On the way I pass two women in their early thirties helping each other carry a bulky cardboard suitcase. They have flat hard bony faces and are wearing identical rabbit-fur coats and spike heels. They stare at me as I go by, and say nothing. And I think, these must be Davie's sisters, going away because I am coming. He never told me they were twins. Unmarried twins.

Kitbag in one hand, small satchel in another, I unlock the 'garden' gate, go in at the side door and call out. No reply. The house is quiet. Everything is as it was. It is a hot summer's day but a fire burns in the grate. In the hallway I cry, Davie! A sudden movement upstairs and he comes to the foot of the stairs. It is then that he looks good and vigorous, like a young lion. He comes bounding down and throws his arms around me. Shyly, we embrace.

But he is still living by a hair's-breadth. At first glance he looks the same, just as young, the handsome lad. But when he talks there is a difference. He has crossed some sort of dividing line. His talk is dryer, calmer, still alternating between romantic fantasies and black despair—but lacking the whiplash. I watch him prepare the tea and cannot help noticing the difference. He has lost weight, there are deep permanent shadows under his eyes, eyes which have lost their lunge and lustre, and the hard blond face is haggard and beginning, for the first time I have known Davie, to be lined. He has grown older.

In the parlour, even before he starts to prepare the tea, he must talk about his troubles. There have been some misunderstandings about money in letters to his friends in London, he does not want them to think he was evading or lying. He is in hock for seventy quid, or at least that's the seventy he will tell me about. His advances are all used up: he is living on loans from London. The slack has hit Hamthorpe and there are no jobs to be had outside the pit. He saves the important news for the last. He wants to find work outside the pit. "You see, Ah'm not fit any more to work coal face."

Shortly after I left, Davie says, he had an accident down Beckley pit. "It was after shift, we were coming up by paddy wagon, and I fell off. Just fell off. I hit my head on the rock and was asleep for the next day." And then, for a month, while his head healed, he lay in his bedroom upstairs with the shades drawn, neither working nor going out.

He is back at his easel now but cannot, he says, go down to the pit. "Ah'm finished with coal, once and for all." Now he stays in the house, takes care of the kids and paints. Loretta isn't working either. "It's not like London," he says, his speech not yet broadest Yorkshire because we aren't among the men. "A man doesn't let his wife go to work if he's still got legs to stand on. Not that I mind doing housework. Dishes and all that. But you must remember, in Dinlock a man'd sooner see his wife sleeping with another man than be caught doing the dishes."

It is a big weight on him, this having to stay home while all the men he knows go down to pit. But he is determined, at even this cost, to finish a new cycle of paintings, and to do many more after that.

It is the measure of how Davie has changed.

You've made a choice there, Davie, I say.

Aye, he says, you don't have to tell me. I took my painting over the pit. Do you think I need you to tell me that?

He is miserable.

We sip our tea and it all comes out in a rush, everything that Davie has been saving up. The seventy-pound debt turns out on closer inspection to be 150, and "Loretta and Ah are getting on better than ever." And I know that before I leave I will find out the truth of this too. Davie restlessly prowls the small living-room, insisting that he does not mind washing the dishes, that he is determined to stay out of pit while he paints. Then he collapses in the single soft chair in the room and covers his face in his hands. He rubs his eyes. He looks drawn and obscenely fatigued. "I don't know. I don't know." Then he bounces up with a false, cheery, "But that's not what you came up for, is it? You came up for a good time."

We discuss the details of procedure of my going down to pit, and I do not think he is aware of the non-commitalness to his voice. Nor, at the time, am I. Because, in another moment, we are, obsessed, juggling finances. At first I tell Davie he must be realistic. But then, as I remember just exactly what kind of trap he is in, I too begin to blend fact and fantasy, wondering not whether money will come in, which unless in the event of a miracle it won't, but which money will come in first. Except that I know it is a game. I look around the room, and at Davie, and I remember walking up Theresa Road as if I had lived in Dinlock for years. No, nothing has changed. A telly set next door where six months ago there wasn't. That's all.

The kids. Peter and Jenny, troop in from school, half a year larger. They come up to me for kisses as though I had been gone only a day, and then Davie is the father. He undresses them, and orders them about, and feeds them, but not with the same commanding stridency I remember. His voice, like his body, seems slack. The kids begin to rampage around. For just a moment, the moment before he assumes

86

absolute control, Davie shifts me a glance of tired irresolution. Then: "Now . . . stop it!" And they do. But they test him more this time. Peter, the eldest, white-blond and furiously strong, punches Davie in the stomach. He punches him again and again. Davie says, "Peter, how many times Ah tell thee tha' never get anywhere hittin' me there. Go on. Till tha're tired. Because tha' know what's goin' to happen when tha' finish." Davie is serious. And so is his son. Peter is a little scared. He punches his father again as Davie stands there, his small hard fists ricocheting against Davie's flat belly and making hard smacking sounds. The blows come slower, the frightened glances upward at Da' more frequent; then Peter stops altogether and waits for his punishment. Father and son look at each other, mutely. Peter bunches himself up, his chin quivers and eyes water, but he stands firm. Davie starts to unbuckle his strap. Little Jenny, 3, starts to giggle but leaves off on a look from Da'. Davie lets the strap dangle so Peter can have a good look at it, then swoops Peter off his feet and swings him around the room, up-ending him on the floor and tickling the life out of him. Suddenly they are having a fine time. Davie spraddles his son and whoops. Aside from his first sign of greeting, it is the first time I've heard him laugh. Jenny waddles over to get into the act, can't and comes over to me for a kiss. Loretta walks in.

"Well, an' what's goin' on here!" Loretta smiles at the havoc and horseplay, pretending not to see me in the corner near the radio which is on Light and for ever.

Hello, Loretta.

"Oh, Ah didn' see tha'." We shake hands, gravely. I ask how she's been keeping. "O, just fine. Everything is fine." And ten minutes before Davie telling me how they owed the grocer twenty quid. Davie stands up, pulling Peter with him, and makes a large business out of smoothing Peter's clothes while waiting to see if Loretta and I will 'take'. It's real good to be back here, I say to Loretta. It's nice to have you, she says.

Apparently, it's all right, because Davie falls back in a chair and makes a joke. We all laugh. Things do indeed seem easier between everybody, the floating easiness of the abyss. Loretta is pleasant, and sweet, and gentle, and I suddenly realise that perhaps she too has been looking forward to a visitor. This thought makes me happy. Outside, through the window, over the moor beyond the village, a Saturday dusk settles.

Davie, searching for conversation, tells Loretta I am to go down to pit this time. "Oh, tha's nice," she says. And with both of them, whenever pit is mentioned, I notice a straightening up, a swift prudence, almost an involuntary coolness. "Y'know," says Loretta, semi-confidentially, thus making me feel more at home than anything else she might do or say, "Ah never been down to pit. None of women 'ave been." Davie hurriedly interjects, "Well, you know, if you were a miner you wouldn't want to have your wife see you in the muck, would you?" It is a question. I suppose not, Davie, I say. He cannot let it go. "I mean, the women have a hard enough job without the pain of seein' how the men work." It is one of the few times I am to hear any of the men refer to the difficulties of the women. Maybe, I say. Davie doesn't want too much discussion on this point. "Uh, Loretta," he says, "we'll be goin' out." Ah, there it is, with a tip of the lip we're back in the old groove. Loretta picks up *True Romances* and flops down in the chair. Davie has got in first. She is left out. Perhaps later in the weekend, if there is time Davie will share me with her. But for the moment she has been put in her place. "Ah, all right," she says vaguely, wearily. Davie is up and rushing about to find his jacket and comb. Even though he is in a hurry to get out from under Loretta's look, he stops to arrange his hair in the cracked mirror above the mantel, carefully. Just before we go out he hesitates. "Uh, we'll be back . . . a little later."

"Yes," says Loretta without expression.

Just outside his gate Davie asks me to wait a minute. He runs back into the house, I suppose it is to make his peace with Loretta. But when I see the more tranquil expression on his face when he comes out I know what he went back for. How much of that stuff you on? I ask. "Eight, ten a day. I get these splitting headaches," Davie says, "you know, down the whole right side. Migraines or something the doctor calls 'em."

We start walking.

Up Theresa Road, as I give Davie the news of London, and then to where I knew we would start out. Behind us is the south part of the village. In front of us, beyond the low wall, across the fields and up a steep slope on which cows now graze, is Dinlock colliery. The grim square buildings, the smoke stacks and spinning carriage wheel; Davie and I stand and gaze at the mine silently, paying our respects, our voices lowered as though we stand before some grime-eaten Moloch.

Are you also on benzedrine, I ask Davie. Sure, he says, some of that. Just to get me going in the morning. And sleeping pills at night? Yes, he says, sleeping pills at night, three or four.

The chug! chug! of the colliery engines float down the dying light of the hill. But I don't ask Davie any questions. With his chin resting on his arm, leaning on the wall, he is completely submerged in his vision of the pit where he worked for so many years, out of which he made his art, where at this moment his mates are labouring and he is not.

I ask Davie if hard times have come to Dinlock. He snaps out of it as if from a dream. "Well," he says almost aggressively, "not yet, not so we'd know it in Dinlock. NCB isn't hirin' but at least we don't have much of a stockpile.

We shift the best coal in the world." He turns and gestures contemptuously. "Look over there. Beckley." He spits. "Look at it. A mountain." Some miles away, across level wooded ground, a huge mound lifts itself up. Coal. "There's your real stockpiles. Poles, slaves, bad union, bad coal. Can't sell it. But not at Dinlock." Davie is proud. It is his pit. Then he remembers he doesn't work there any more. He spits again. "Ah, what's the difference anyway, huh kid?"

We do the village. Davie is restless and gloomy. Passing Will Lawson's, I inquire if the local authority ever let Will's boy back into school. Davie says, oh, sure, that's all smoothed out now. Then he lapses into silence. The playing field, I say, looks great. Is there still a seepage problem? Don't know, mumbles Davie, have to ask Bolton. Davie is a thousand miles away. Suddenly he blurts out, "I want to write a play. But there are so many books I haven't read. Man, I've only *seen* a play twice in my whole life. I'm so uneducated." I tell Davie what Chekhov said about people like us, that the working-class writer purchases with his youth that which a more genteel writer is born with. He grabs on to this for dear life, as I once did myself. "Aye, it's true, it's true. Monday. I don't know what I'll do. Bank manager is supposed to tell me Monday if I can have some money." Then back into silence.

Slowly, he comes out of it, and briefs me on the village. We pass Glenn in the street and stop and talk. Glenn is his usual blarney self. He and Davie discuss price lists. Davie is impatient to get away. All through this weekend he is to show this same blank-eyed impatience, as though eager to get me away for a private talk between us, and yet, except for rare moments, when we are together neither of us know where to begin. Glenn passes on, and Davie says that Glenn's wife is ill, had another child, and that Glenn is working more regular shifts now. Shifts, the number of them, is a more sensitive subject than it was a year ago. Dinlock colliery, with only a small stockpile, is still quietly recruiting, but the men are back to a five-day shift, no extra days, no Saturday, no overtime. Even now, there is a union conference in Durham discussing this, but in Dinlock it is not yet a fear, only a kind of blustery gingerliness when handling the subject.

We wander up and down the wide unpeopled streets and I catch up on what's been happening. Most of the old quarrels seem to have been tranquillised, new wounds opened, and as Davie talks about it he is diffident, almost embarrassed, and in this most important way I see that he is preparing to leave the village. I wonder if he knows it yet. For the first time since I have known Davie it is with some shame when he speaks of Dinlock. Then suddenly he says, "Miners live for their weekends, kid. Let's start ours." So we do.

We dive into East Clu', the former Miners' Lodge Meeting Hall, no women allowed except between the hours of 7.30 and 10.30 Saturday nights. Too early, not many around, an ale and a whisky, Davie and I start our weekend around the snooker table. His head is like to coming apart, his eyes fuzz when focussing on the ball. I ask him if he wants to stop and he says, doggedly, no. Every few moments Davie straightens up to look around the club for Bolton. He's worried about Bolton, he says. Too cocksure of himself, too close to the pit manager, he mumbles.

The club begins to fill up. Tommy Hunter comes over to say hello, the tall toothless ex-commando, or so he says. "How be tha', lad?" Fine, George, fine. "They tell me tha' art goin' down to pit?" That's right, George.

91

"Ah, well," George says and drifts off, munching in disapproval.

Davie and I are the only ones at the snooker tables this afternoon. Then in floats Walter, the boy whom Davie slapped the last time I was here. "Hi, Davie," Walter calls. "Walter," says Davie. Both smile. I look at Davie. He says, "Oh, we made it up months ago. At a meetin' of the branch." And that is that. Walter comes over and says hello, carefuly I don't know if he remembers I was there that night at Will Lawson's. In the way he casually picks up a cue to share the game with us, without asking for an invitation, I know that it is really made up between them. And I also know, from the way Walter avoids my eyes, that he does remember I was there.

Businesslike, we shoot snooker. Davie, who has been uncommunicative through our four games, livens up to exchange the elaborate parry and thrust of gibes which passes for communication in Dinlock. For the better part of an hour Davie and Walter approach, teeter on and then withdraw from that brink of insult which must produce serious words. Davie miscues. "Aye, Davie," says Walter, "losing thy grip, man. Old, that's what it is. Old and weak." Walter shoots, Davie snookers him, and stands upright, beaming slyly. "Ah allays know how to snooker thee, Walter, don't Ah?"

"Sometimes, Davie, but not allays," says Walter.

And that's how it goes.

"Ah'm told," says Walter, "tha'll be goin' down to pit." That's right, I say. Mmmm, says Walter.

They laugh and cue balls together, and then Walter floats out the way he floated in. Odd. Six months ago he was putting himself in my way so that I would notice him; now he doesn't seem to care one way or the other. It is the same with many others, later. And the question is: is it because I'm going down to pit? Finally, during our last game that afternoon, I put the question to Davie, who says, "Oh, no, you've got the boys all wrong. They want tha' to see what it's lahk down there. Ah swear. They respect tha' for it." And he keeps his official, wide-eyed face. End of game. Snookered.

For Dinlock the night has begun.

It is still daylight but the streets, so empty and without expression during the day, are now peopled with miners in their going-out clothes. They greet you, not as on a work day with a tired quick little shake of the head, but head upright and smiling and a few words. "Hello, Yank! Thought we chased tha out of Dinlock!" Slapping of backs, and Davie takes me to Pub.

We're too early and Pub is dead. Whisky for me, ale for Davie, we sit around the gloom. Four or five men walk in and sit down at the next table. They are young, handsome and well-behaved. They give Davie a special hello. He says they are the young ones he's been telling me about, and that I will like them, they are the ones who will understand why he cannot go back down to pit. Shifting of chairs and introductions all round. They're all under 20, one is 17, all down in pit. Each one affects a soft-voiced constraint that is a direct copy of the manner of the older miners.

I ask them if they are going to stay down in pit like their fathers. "Not bloody lahkly," says Johnny quietly. Johnny is built like a young bull, or a scholarship tackle for UCLA, square rugged face, a truck-like body, a neck all thick muscle. Like the older miners his hands are oversize, calloused instruments more than human limbs, and stained almost black with nicotine. Come to think of it, I haven't met any miners whose hands don't look burned.

Johnny is easy to talk to, very sure of himself, so soft-spoken I have to lean forward to catch his words. Andy, next to him, is taller, slimmer, good-looking in a sun-filled sort of way, full of little city tricks, and I wonder what he's doing here. The other two are slope-shouldered husky young boys in dark suits and sweaters who keep their own counsel.

Sun-burned Andy drinks steadily and smiles knowingly and without the slightest offence, enjoying all of us. "No," says Johnny, "we're gettin' out. Ah've it figured out." Davie says, "Tha've had it figured out for two years, Johnny." "Never tha' mind, Ah'll get out," says Johnny, stung. He wants it known that he may lose the battles in getting out of Dinlock but not the war. A few ales, a bit of whisky, and the talk flows smoother. One of the boys who hasn't spoken says, "No other way, then the Forces." His friend nods. "We'll be gettin' out, don't tha worry," assures Johnny, more to himself than me. Davie grins. "Tha' almos' did it las' time, Johnny. Perhaps tha' can try again." Johnny laughs softly. "Perhaps Ah can, Davie. Ah'm still young." Davie, sotto voce, says, "Johnny 'uz fooking th' big shopkeeper's daughter." Johnny adds proudly, "Almos' made it too." We all laugh.

Andy, so far, has said nothing, but has sat, pouring pints down his throat with extreme, quiet good humour. While Johnny tries to work out a Chinese puzzle handed him by Andy, Davie tells me that the reason Andy stays out of the conversation is that he is the only one at the table to have done it, to actually have got out of Dinlock. He's a centre-half for a North Country League football team. He has seen the world, is rather famous in these parts, and the boys and the men go out of their way to give him plenty of chances to pull off a big head which he never does, and so, in their eyes, his skill and fame at footballing cancels out the very negative fact that he no longer works as a hand-getting collier in Dinlock pit. Andy likes to come back whenever he can to drink with his mates, but he is not one of them any more, and because neither of them tries to think otherwise everything is all right.

Andy has been listening with a beery, intent smile to Davie's recitation of his history, his eyes slightly glazed.

94

Davie says, "Andy could be a fine player, a lot of us around here say an International star, if he'd only lay off the booze." Andy smiles a wide blank smile. "Trouble is," comes in Jimmy, "he only wants to be a *good* footballer and left alone. Prefers his booze to anything better."

We sit around Andy and discuss whether Andy should sacrifice the life which is gratifying and natural to him for the greater glory of his club and England's Cup Final. Andy listens with the air of a man who hasn't the faintest intention of changing his way of life and who, in fact, is hearing something said about a rather well-meaning but comparative stranger. He's a good lad, is Andy. Is it training you're in? I ask him. He thinks about this slowly, and slowly nods his sun-burnt head. I suggest he shouldn't be drinking now. I mean, it's against the team rules. Andy slowly looks up at me and smiles that white-toothed, innocent charming smile, and just as sweetly puts a finger to his lips, admonishing me silently, gently, not to tell his manager, please. And lifts his beer.

Pub is invaded. Ten, twenty, thirty men, more coming through the door, working-class men on holiday pour in and assume command of the tables, most of which are vacant Andy says lazily, "Oh sleepin' Jesus, Barnsley men." Johnny says, "They've brought their buses with 'em. A fishin' holiday." Davie says, "Fish and chippers, we call 'em." "Once a year," says Johnny disdainfully, "they get away from their wahves." I look the strangers over. They seem a tame lot.

Just wait an hour, promises Davie. But there are seldom fights, he explains. The only thing a Dinlock man would field a Barnsley man over is a woman, and a Barnsley man knows better, he says, than to try and make time with a miner's woman.

The Barnsley men are quiet, they haven't begun to drink yet. "Oh, they've had it," says Johnny, "Robinson, pub-keeper, keeps his worst beer for these occasions. Piss." Everybody at our table laughs at what the Barnsley men are letting themselves in for. I look over at the burly, bald-pated pub-keeper, and he does indeed look happy, the only time I have ever seen him so, as he dispenses beer to the thick queue of Barnsley men. "Makes money hand over fist when they coom in," says Johnny. One of the quiet boys says, "Piss."

Nobody stiffens or becomes impolite at our table when a thin well-groomed boy comes in and sits down with us. But nobody looks his way either, after a preliminary nodding of heads. His name is Irving and he has known Johnny and Andy and the other two boys all his life, he is from the village. He has a pint and disappears. After he goes, Johnny shakes his head. Davie says, Irving doesn't work down in pit. Johnny purses up his mouth and shuts his eyes. End of Irving. He has been relegated to that sub-world of Dinlock which, in the eyes of the coal face men, includes dead-beats, surface workers and clerks.

When the piano player and drummer stroll in and take their places at the microphone up on the small platform at the far end of the room, the Barnsley men begin to liven things up a bit. They are drinking faster, and if I had no other way of knowing this I would see it in the way the young miners at our table lay back in their chairs with a kind of restive, controlled malevolence. They don't like Pub being taken over on their Saturday night, but they are silent and correct about it. There is strictly no fraternisation between the Barnsley men and the Dinlock miners; they drink in two colonies side by side without acknowledging the other's existence. As far as I can see, they aren't even looking at each other. Perhaps they aren't interested. Perhaps. All I do see is that the Barnsley men who wend their way through the pub carrying pints for their friends are very, very careful not to spill any while assiduously not looking at the miners who, when the Barnsley men pass by, do not, as with their own mates, move that slightest fraction of a polite inch to give way.

A dwarf, in Sunday-best, with a man's full-sized work gnarled face, approaches our table. Together with a fat, mustachioed Pakistani he has been the liveliest of this holiday outing, dashing backwards and forwards, emitting snatches of popular song, his beaten, rather handsome face shining with sweat. "Drink up, drink up! Fine day!" says the dwarf. Thick-set Johnny gazes stonily at him. As do the others at our table. The dwarf freezes his laugh and retreats. "Fine day for fishing!" he shouts and is swallowed up amongst the tables. The rest of us sit around and drink steadily until Davie says to me, "Coom on."

Outside Pub Davie says, "Please let's get out of Dinlock for a few minutes." He says his head is driving him crazy. We wait on the corner for a bus and look over the tops of the houses at the colliery which is silent in the fading dusk, as the streets behind us begin to fill up with miners. The bus comes.

The Queen Anne's Arms is bigger than Dinlock Pub, bigger and sleeker, situated at the crossroads on the way to Barnsley, with many cars in the parking lot. As Davie and I walk inside he says, "Johnny almost did make it, too. Fookt himself blahnd on shopkeeper's daughter. Says he'll join Navy if he can't fook himself out of village. Johnny will stay. They always do. Coal is in their bluid."

I tell Davie I'm not sure they will stay. Almost furiously, Davie replies, "Ah know, Ah tell tha'. They'll never get out." I look carefully at his eyes. On only five or six pints they are beginning to be glazed. He must be in bad shape. Last time, it took twice that number to get him to even climb up to the Yorkshire dialect. I know what will happen. Any minute now he's going to start looking for a fight. I wonder if that's why we came out of Dinlock to the Queen Anne's Arms.

The inside is a large, bare, well-polished dance floor. Davie and I take a table on the edge of the floor, next to one occupied by three unescorted girls. I ask Davie if this is the place Dinlock men come to pick up girls and he says yes. It is the official battleground.

The four-piece band picks up the beat, and several couples glide out on to the floor. It is long, swooping, conservative ballroom dancing. Half the couples are both girls. Davie and I sit morosely with our drinks and watch the young men stroll into the room. "Clerks, surface men," says Davie contemptuously. Then we sit and don't say anything for quarter of an hour. The couples dip and glide by. "See her," Davie points to a big-busted, freckle face, "she lahks me," and relapses into another long silence, emerging to observe, "It's livelier here, isn't it? That's why we coom."

The longer Davie sits and drinks the angrier, at something, he becomes. "See him. He's lookin' for a faht wi' me." I say the boy on the dance floor is not looking for a fight, he isn't even looking at us. "Don't tell me," snaps Davie. "Ah know this place. Signals. He's lookin' for one all raht," glaring at the innocent chap who is nervously becoming aware that Davie is spoiling for him. Okay, hero, I say, the shape you're in all he has to do is whistle and you'll fall apart. Davie turns his glare on me. Then he shrugs. The effort of making a grin causes him to wince. "Lad," he says, "he wouldn't even have to do that," and slumps dejectedly in his chair. An old lady in a coloured frock whirls by in the arms of a tall young man, samba'ing. "Sixty-one and enjoys fookin' lahk a rabbit," says Davie. "Hello Davie!" the old woman cries. Davie turns and says to me, lamely, "Ah just thought tha' maht lahk to see a place that was fancy instead of, you know, Dinlock."

I say, let's go back.

It is drizzling and night-time when we get off the bus. Davie sighs, "Well, no use not goin' down to Clu'. They'll all be waitin' for tha'."

98

Old East Club is in full blast as Davie signs me in, through the old oak doors and into the billiard room. Smoke, a buzz of tongues and ale smells. East Clu'. Down near the bar Bolton, surrounded by several miners, is holding court. For a moment it looks like a painting done in cigarette smoke and deep shades of clay-brown. Bolton, and the men grouped around him, with slow, canny dignity turn out to watch me approach. Formally, Bolton shakes my hand. I say hello to Carl Fish, Ray Sweet, Tommy Hunter and another man I don't know. Everybody is cautious. They treat me as though I had never been to the village. They want to see if I remember.

"Ah heard tha' were in Dinlock. We are happy to see tha' again," Bolton says with a sidelong, accusatory glance at Davie. Davie immediately apologises for not having brought me along sooner. "That's all right, Davie, Ah understand," says Bolton expansively, affably.

"Ah well," blusters in the union vice-president, fat Ray Sweet, "an' how do tha' lahk our village?"

The same question, in the same tone, as six months ago. But no, they aren't taking the micky. As much as Ray, and the others meant it the first time, he means it now.

So I give the same answers.

It is our way of bowing ceremonially to each other, un-horsed knights raising the visors.

I notice that Bolton, Carl and Ray are wearing small red badges in their lapels. The badges say, "CCCP". Ray says, "Ah, the Rooshians been to Barnsley again a few weeks ago." "Fine lads they were too," says Bolton quickly, "and the salt of the earth." All around the smoky billiard room, miners are wearing the small red CCCP badges in their lapels.

Something clicks. At first I think it is the sound from the television set in the main room. Then I know it is the scene, the whole thing, the mesh and conjunction of monotonous, unruffled talk and club noises and cue ball snicks and soft

99

clink of glasses: it is all as it was six months ago. You are there. Except, except for one thing. The composition of the various cliques, sets, groups, call them what you will, has with unbelievable subtlety and discretion, changed. These men in East Clu' are searching all the time. No, not search; that's too conscious. Rather, they are like some agglutinously moving organism, like the elements in a cell which, when seen under a powerful microscope, ceaselessly come together, swirl about in a new friction, and snail off to join and make new groups. The wrong metaphor here would be the molecules of a social atom, for when the molecular structure is rearranged the atom becomes substantially different, whereas in Dinlock the whole point, as I see it, for the men changing partners, is to preserve the village as an organic entity, as is. The last time I was here Ray Sweet was not really part of Bolton's special group, but now, for some reason, quite possibly having to do with a shrewd desire to consolidate his position in the union branch, he is holding on for dear life. Six months ago Tommy Hunter, the ex-commando, did not hang about with Bolton and Carl Fish; now he does. Perhaps these are bad examples. Tommy is growing old and is having difficulty securing a proper job at the colliery; his sudden attachment to Bolton may have more the motive of simple self-interest than I think most such liaisons have.

So, wherever I look, particularly in East Clu', I see that the bonds are as fierce—but not necessarily with the same people. Allan, for example, is part of Bolton's group now. Six months ago I did not even meet him. He is a smallish, wiry Monmouthshire man, neatly dressed, and keeps his hat on all the time. He is very knowledgeable, very respected, speaks seldom and not with a soft voice. It is unusual for anyone not of the union committees to go around with Bolton, but Allan is special. He came to Dinlock a few years ago after a long history of union activity and blacklisting out of coalfields in several parts of England.

100

John Kilmartin, the branch president, I am told, is down in a London hospital. He may not be coming back. When the men say this you can see they do not truly believe it, for they have never known a time when John Kilmartin was not here.

As usual, there is a great flap about who buys the drinks, and after Davie whispers a caution to me about the etiquette involved, I take my place in the uncharmed circle. Davie's head is splitting so painfully he can hardly bear our talk; perhaps it is just as well. For, far more than on my first visit, the men are excluding Davie. Their affection for him is openly laced with condescension. I recognise the distant tone in the way they speak to Davie. I had thought it reserved only for people, outsiders, like myself. Now I hear it used on him.

Even when there is plenty of opportunity to do so, none of the men mentions that I am to go down to pit until, with an intake of breath and a setting down of his drink, Bolton says, "Ah hear tha' art wantin' to go down to pit, lad." On cue, I say yes, will he arrange it. Bolton appears to give this careful consideration, weighing the pros and cons. Then he says, "Ah, we'll try, we'll try." Bolton is the man to arrange it, Davie loudly assures me. And I wonder who is kidding who around here.

But first Bolton, in the circle of men, must get something off his chest. "Lad, how are things in London?" I tell him. "Ay," he says, "but tha've got to leave the big city every now and again to see real lahf, isn't that raht lad?"

So, it is starting approximately when and where I thought it would. Davie gives me a quick, cautionary glance. He moves in nervously. "Ah Bolton, what are tha' talkin' like tha' for. They may live different down in London but it's lahf still." Davie is hoping Bolton will leave it at that. Perhaps at another time he could. But it is this time that I'm going down to pit. Bolton laughs. I get angry and tell him we can't all be coal miners. Bolton says evenly, "And a good thing it is too. Or the coal would be shifted poorly." "Ah Bolton," says Davie, "coal mining isn't everything." The other men turn a slow, studied look on Davie who licks his lips and runs his hand through his thick blond hair.

"Don't get me wrong, Davie," says Bolton, "Ah'm not sayin' it is." The hell you're not, I say. Some of the other men put down their glasses on the bar. Davie cries, "Ah what do we want to stand around arguin' for?" Bolton takes a while to finish up his drink, leaving us all hanging on whether or not he chooses to make trouble over this one, and when he puts down his glass he announces that he has to walk up to Pub to see a man and will I come along.

On the way to the Pub we pause at the top of Theresa Road, cross over and lean on the low brick wall and gaze across the night-strewn field to the now quiet colliery. Bolton is oddly uncommunicative, waiting for questions which I dutifully ask. Then he points up towards the colliery, whose tipple lights are indistinctly visible. "There it is, lad. The place tha'll be goin' down into. Monday we'll make it, in two days' time."

Davie says, "Where will tha' be takin' him, Bolton? Sleythorpe seam or Edgeweal or Brierly?"

Bolton says it all depends on what I want to see, mechanical or manual digging. "The mechanised seams, now they're the coomin' thing, lad. Fine new machines." I listen and say nothing. "The thing is, too, Davie, it's easier for a visitor to watch the coal mining operation in a mechanised pit." Davie knows what's going on all right. He says he thinks I might want to see the 'real' pit men at work. "Oh true, true," says Bolton, "that's how coal is *really* dug. But mechanisation is the thing, and if thy friend is here for only a short tahm perhaps it would be better to show him something, tha know, scientific and progressive. And also, as Ah say, it's easier to get around." We lean our chins on the wall at the bottom of the colliery hill and gaze up.

Well, you know, Bolton, I say, there isn't too much

question of what I want to see. You know what I want to see. Bolton says, with an almost rude finality, "All raht, then, Ah'll take tha down to see where the real men mine coal. Down Sleythorpe."

"Sleythorpe?" asks Davie.

"Sleythorpe" replies Bolton.

I nod at the sign posted above our heads asking for a total of twenty-five new workers and ask Bolton what about it, I thought the problem was over-employment. "Aye," Bolton says, "there's no redundancy at this pit. Nor need there ever be. We shift coal that gets sold." Davie says, "Not lahk over at Beckley, eh Bolton?" Bolton spits over the wall. "That's raht, not lahk fookin' Beckley." He spits again. "We'll have nowt to worry about just so long as good men stay down in pit," he adds. He puts his arm around Davie. "Ah, he's just lahk a son to me, did tha' know that, lad?"

Davie says, just as though I had never heard the story, and on this exact spot, that this is where Bolton and Len had it out that legendary night. Bolton nods agreeably. "Half tha' age too, wasn't he, Bolton?" And so, again, I hear the story, in detail, of how a man named Len picked a fight with Bolton, danced around him in the field and was finally floored.

"Aye," pronounces Bolton, "we may bash each other around but our unity cannot be cracked." He stoutly maintains, as all the Dinlock miners do, at least publicly, that he is not in the least worried about stockpiles, lay-offs and threats of a mining recession. "Conditions at Dinlock are what we made 'em, and because we made 'em lahk that the coal is better and so it will always be sold," firmly, stubbornly. So far I have met nobody in the village who feels like talking about the possible effects of a recession, of reports of growing stockpiles in the mining fields. I ask Bolton if Dinlock is on a five-day week. "Bluidy damn well it is," he replies. "And so it should be. Five days down there is enough for any man. Tha'll see."

Our talk is interrupted by a man with a red scarf around

his neck who runs towards us. He is as excited as any man I have seen in Dinlock. "Bolton," he says, "there's been an explosion over at Beckley."

Bolton turns around and starts back slowly down Theresa Road towards East Clu'. Davie, myself and the man with the red neckerchief fall in beside him. The first thing Bolton says is, "Today?" The man says yes, the accident was today. "The bluidy bastards," Bolton spits bitterly. "That's what cooms of workin' Saturdays."

Davie asks what kind of explosion, and I remember the union meeting six months ago on the question of gas percentiles. The man says nobody knows, it was not a disaster. "Anybody hurt?" asks Davie, while Bolton strides on moodily. "No tellin' yet," says the man, "we hear five or six." Bolton mutters, "They'd no raht to be workin' Saturdays."

Outside East Clu', at the bottom of a muddy hill, Bolton says, "Ah'll be goin' inside, Davie, to be tellin' some of the men." It is like a slap in the face to Davie. He is not to share even in the bearing of bad news, because it has to do with the pit and he is not of the pit any longer. When Bolton and the other man go inside the Club, Davie says with a tight mouth, "Tha've got to be partly cruel to have got as far as Bolton."

For a moment or two, outside East Clu', Davie stands around lost. Then, without a word, he heads into the village to West Clu' where he goes in directly to find Johnny, the square-set, muscular young miner. In the middle of the Saturday night crowd Johnny is sitting with a tallish, quiet Barnsley girl. Johnny has told me he doesn't belong in Dinlock and that the old ways aren't for him. But in the formal, reserved way in which he is sitting with his girl he could be any Dinlock miner thirty years older.

Davie says softly, "Johnny, Beckley's had an accident."

"Gas, fire?" asks Johnny.

"Don't know."

"Anybody hurt?"

"Pat says five or six maybe."

"Thanks, Davie. Ah have mates at Beckley." Johnny glances at the girl, his way of asking her to wait for him, she does not change expression, and then he walks out of the club. Davie leans down to the girl. "Tha' know how it is," he says. She nods.

Outside the club I say she is well on her way to becoming a miner's wife. Davie says, "Poor bluidy lass."

Down in East Clu' we stand in a large circle, seven or eight men, solemnly drinking and listening to the tombola and turns in the other room. As though he has never said it before, Ray Sweet says, "So tha're goin' down to pit, eh lad? That's a good lad." But nobody else, at this juncture, wants to pick up the ball and run with it. There is some talk about the explosion at Beckley, however. Nobody, surprisingly, expresses sorrow for the miners involved. By now it is known the injuries were few and minor. What wells up, instead, is talk laced with bitter resentment, even hatred, the Dinlocker feels towards the Beckley miner, his inept branch union, Poles in specific and foreigners in general.

Half pie-eyed, Davie turns to me and says, "And after this, what do tha' now say of us formin' a wall against the Hoongary miners. Zenophobia now, is it?" Ray is eager to jump in. "Ah guess that settles our old argument, eh lad? Tha' and thy Hoongarians. Look at what the Poles did at Beckley!" The men, led by Bolton, nod general agreement. There it is, the jingoism and the narrowness, and behind it the anxiety that Beckley, and places like Beckley, represent a real threat to them. "That kind of pit," says the branch secretary Ed

Stopp, "right on our doorstep, it's lahk the NCB havin' an extra negotiator on their side in wage sessions." I say I wonder what they would be saying about Poles and foreigners if Beckley was a well-run pit. "Impossible!" explode Ray, Carl Fish and Tommy Hunter simultaneously. "Tha' cannot work a Yorkshire pit with Warsaw miners," concludes Ray Sweet. Davie looks worried. "Don't argue with them, boy," he whispers. But it's all right. The men are satisfied they have put their point, they take no umbrage. It's just as well that I acknowledge the hostility in the air. If I don't start an argument, they will. Of that I am sure. Sooner or later.

An interesting thing here. Because I am going down to pit in two days no one touches me. Literally. Now there is none of the customary back-slapping, rib nudging hand-on-shoulder aids to conversation. In the most physical sense, I am let alone.

We all go into the next room and buy tombola cards and all lose. Tommy Hunter tells us how he was depth-charged in the Suma Straits when he was a commando, and the men needle Bolton about a grey-faced gap-toothed woman on a nearby bench who is supposed to be one of Bolton's part-time mistresses. Then, automatically, it is time to leave East Clu'.

Outside, on the dark muddy ground, the very involved, deliberate business of saying good night must be gone through. One by one the men, Ray and Ed, Tommy and Carl, peel off and disappear. Davie and I stand and talk with Bolton and Allan, the blacklisted Monmouthshire miner, about this and that, but always about the pit. They never talk about anything but the pit, and most of the talk is about wages, and after that safety, and after that the competence on the face of their various mates. I ask them about the NUM conference in Durham but it is not of much interest to them, except in so far as the issues and personalities, the union machinations and log-rolling, specifically touch on the pit and the village. Nothing that does not deal directly and conclusively with coal interests them. The Russian miners fascinated them. Yorkshire footballers do not. About all that Bolton and Allan will own up to is that they could be persuaded to support their own area president for higher union office. But they are as suspicious of him as of all trade union office holders above the branch level. From the way they talk about the area officials I suppose that they feel Dinlock pit is adequately represented, possibly even better than that, but since it is not form in Dinlock to praise higher than "Aye, seems he does his job," it's difficult to tell. Amongst the branch members there is a feeling that the higher union echelons are quite remote and out of touch, not so much because of the personalities involved but simply because losing touch with the rank and file is an inevitable occupational hazard of the trade union careerist, and the branch men hold no special rancour for the individual that does so. Or as Allan says, "Man has to get up in the world, and someone has to pay the cost." Towards the Coal Board, of course, both branch officials and men feel not only remoteness but active (if differentiated) hostility. Dinlock pit is a bellwether; the men have made it one. In some mysterious way, although Dinlock pit does not have many windows on the world or lines of communication open to other communities it is extraordinarily sensitive to shifting winds of the miners' temper. Bolton says with pride, "More bluidy strikes here than anywhere else. And all for good reason."

And we all have another good laugh over the story which Davie likes to tell, and he tells it again, in the dark field outside East Clu', about the day during the 1957 strike when a national newspaper sent a reporter into Dinlock. In this particular strike all the pits in the Barnsley area had gone back to work except Dinlock where the branch union refused until such time as a number of outstanding issues between it and the Coal Board were resolved. Finally, when the pit had been shut down tight for more than a fortnight, and the men

107

didn't have much to do except hang around Pub, Club and house, this reporter from the Daily X drove into the village in a spanking new Sunbeam, and to make matters worse brought along a woman photographer. (Still today in Dinlock there are miners who, in their hearts, believe in the ancient superstition that women are omens of bad luck, and it is only the good-natured joshing of their younger mates which prevents them from returning home if they happen to see a woman on their way to shift work.)

Bolton takes up the story. "So, lad, the union committee was meeting in the Welfare Hall to try and decide whether it wanted to recommend a go-back temporary. When we broke up without deciding anything we found this coont waitin' outside the hall. 'And what mah't thou be wantin'?' Ah asks. And he says, 'Are tha going to stay out on strahk and why?' He had a picture girl with him. So Ah turn to Ray and Alf Johnson—he was delegate then—and Ah says, 'Well, the issues are a bit too complicated for us rank-and-file miners to understand. And as for us stayin' out on strahk, we're joost on the point of decidin' that. Say, Alf, which way do tha' think the wind is blowin'?' So Alf gives me the big wink and says the wind is from the south. Ah sticks up mah wet finger up into the air and Ah say, you know, loud lahk, 'Well, then, it's more strahk. The wind is from the south. Go and announce it to the men.'" Davie and Allan can bear it no longer and, although they have heard and told the story scores of times, they hold their sides laughing. Bolton finishes.

"And tha know what that bluidy foolish coont did? He asked me if Ah would stick mah finger up in th' air again so as to have mah picture in the newspaper. So Ah did. And it was put in a couple of days later."

Davie says, "The headline on the photograph said York-shire Miners Decide on Strike by Direction of Wind."

It is a good laugh. They have several other stories about journalists which Bolton and Allan pointedly add, most of which I heard on my first trip. Dinlockers distrust, and

108

Bolton detests, newspapermen. Allan puts in, "Why do they have to lie about us, lad? Tell us that." This is not one of your Bolton's rhetorical inquiries. Allan really wants to know. He says, "All my life I've been a miner, and I haven't read the truth about us once. Not once."

Suddenly, and without any warning, the direction of conversation swerves. It is Davie who makes the first fatal slip. He says, "Aye, it was men lahk Bolton and Allan here who made Dinlock pit one of the finest in Europe." Bolton turns a steady gaze on Davie. "And thou also, Davie," he says quietly. It is a direct, savage attack.

"Ah, Bolton, that's unfair," Davie says. "Tha' know why Ah'm not at pit any more. Ah'm not fit."

"Tha' could be," says Bolton.

"Aye," says Allan, "you're young, lad, you're fit. Look at me. Fifty-three and still shifting at the face. You should come back and stand for union office."

"Ah tell tha' Ah'm not fit. Bolton, why do tha' go on? Tha' *know* Ah'm not fit!"

Bolton scrunches up his knobby, scarred face and scrutinises the night sky. He belches. "Tha' could be. And where did tha' work when tha' were fit?"

"But we've been over that. Tha' *know*," says Davie, agitated. Last year, Davie, with several other miners, transferred from Dinlock pit to try and make a little more money. "Ah couldn't go in to Tooley and ask for mah old job back."

"We would have supported thee," says Bolton.

Davie protests, "But it would have hurt the union, Bolton. Ah c'n only work a few shifts a week because o' mah paintin'. It would have given Tooley a perfect reason to hit at the union by sayin' it was tryin' to introduce a slacker into pit."

Allan says, "Then you should work a full shift, Davie, like we all do."

"But Ah'm a *painter*, man!" says Davie, almost in a roar.

We are all quiet. Davie's plea that he is also a painter dies away into the night. Around us the shadowy figures of

109

miners slip in and out of East Club. Whether or not Davie is an artist is something he will have to battle with himself, say Bolton and Allan with their silence, and let it not be said that they ever deflected a man from his true work. But their silence also judges: if true work it is.

"Ah will not make the union vulnerable because o' me," says Davie slowly. "Need not be," says Bolton complacently, "if tha' coom back to Dinlock and shift thy week. Tha' know Ah will get the union to support tha'. We can get tha' in."

"That's not the point, Bolton," cries Davie.

Allan says, "The point is, Davie, you're young, you're fit and you're not down in pit. What other point is there?'

"Oh Christ," says Davie.

Bolton and Allan crowd up to Davie, surrounding him. Allan takes Davie by the shoulders. "Davie, boy, listen. Your friends, they're all down in pit. You come down. Full shifts. It's where you belong. We can fix you up proper. Come on, Davie. Don't be like that." Davie shakes his head woozily. He cannot really believe that it's happening, and in front of me too.

Bolton breathes in expansively. "Ah," he says, "Allan, don't put pressure on the boy. He's got to make up his own mahnd. He's an artist, mahnd. Each man must make his own decisions. Let it not be said that the boy's friends ever tried to keep him down."

Davie clenches and unclenches his fists, and for a moment he appears on the verge of tears. I have never seen him in such travail. "Bolton," he pleads, "tha' know all the reasons. We talked about them naht after naht. Tha' agreed. And now, *Ah'm not fit.*"

Bolton claps his hands behind his back and stares at Davie. Allan says, "Davie, come on back down to pit. It's where you belong. Coal is in your blood, boy."

Davie, poised on the balls of his feet, his eyes watery, peers alternately at Bolton and at Allan, to see just how serious they are. And they are dead serious. They don't say a word.

110

Then Davie rares back and whoops out a laugh. He claps them both on the shoulder. "Now what do we want to be talkin' so serious for, just when we have someone from London, eh? Coom on, no more takin' out the micky. Ah know you boys. And so does the lad by now."

"Well, Davie, good night," says Allan. He walks off. Bolton coughs and spits. He says to me, "Ah'll take tha' to see pit manager tomorrow. Meet me at top of Theresa Road at 12 o'clock. Good night, Davie."

Davie watches Bolton disappear into the night. He puts his arm around me and giggles. "Ah, those boys. Tha' musn't mahnd. They want me back down in pit. They don't know what it is to be a painter, an artist, not lahk tha' and me, us, eh? But they're good boys. Tha' mustn't mahnd them. They mean well. Let's forget it."

Even by a Londoner's effete standard Davie hasn't drunk much tonight. But he can hardly carry himself as we half-walk half-stagger back up Theresa Road to West Club. Just inside, he halts and leans against the wall, for a short jagged second he seems lanced to the wall by the sudden blast of fluorescent light and club drone and piano organ banging away at "I Love Paris in the Spring". He holds up his hands as though to shield himself against the blaze of light and noise. Then he slips towards the crowd mumbling, "Och, it's these headaches."

At the bar he introduces me to a brawny, dough-faced miner. "This is Len Foot. He works at Beckley. He was at the explosion." Len is all beef, with small beady eyes very suspicious, phlegmatic, the one Bolton fought outside the pub that famous night. Davie makes a date for me to talk to Len at Len's house, tomorrow morning, to find out about the explosion. They talk at the bar.

"Were tha' hurt, Len?"

"Aye. My arm. Sahd of body." Len rolls up the sleeve of his jacket and shows us a darkish bruise. He doesn't like having me around and keeps staring at me while Davie talks to him. He nods. "Aye, it was terrible. Sheet of flame, explosion. Number 14 seam." Davie asks if anyone else was hurt, and Len says he doesn't know yet. Davie assures Len we'll be at his house in the morning. Then we leave.

Outside, something doesn't sit right. I ask Davie why Len isn't down at East Clu' talking to the men about the explosion. "The men don't lahk him," Davie says. "He's very unpopular." Because he works at Beckley? "No, other reasons. But Ah'm stickin' to Len. His wahf sat with our kids when Loretta went to hospital las' year. It's not the kahnd of thing a man wants to forget now. Coom. We promised to meet Loretta at Pub." We walk on. Davie, says "It really is other things besides Beckley, his workin' there. He's a bully. Always tryin' to faht men smaller than himself. A bully. And tha' know how miners hate a bully."

Saturday night in Pub. Roaring. Packed to the doors and windows. Andy, the reserve centre-half, and two of the young miners wave us to their table. By now, Pub has been cleared of Barnsley fish-and-chippers, the Dinlockers are here in force. The joint is really jumping. Davie and I pick our way through the crowd, laughing aside the proffered drinks. Up on the raised platform the piano player and the plump, cherubic drummer in the blood-red cardigan are having a good time bawling out, "Three Little Words". The audience joins in. Davie orders a round for us at Andy's table. They've been here since afternoon. Then Andy gets up to go. He grins down. "Bed tahm. In training," and leaves. "Good boy," says Davie. "No big head."

The evening is duplicated from the one I spent here six months ago. Soon we are singing and swaying, "Avalon". The entire room sings. The drummer has his eye on a cute little miner's wife in the corner near us, and she has more than her eye on him. She is sitting with her back to the wall on a rousing bench-full. She cannot take her eyes off the smiling drummer as she matches her words to his. Davie says, "Never know where her husban' is."

We wave Will Lawson to our table. Will, his wife Fay and a cadaverous-eyed, pinch-chested friend join us. Greetings all around, and congratulations on Will's victory over the local school board. Fay ducks her head with studied demureness. Who's she kidding? Just as soon as they sit down Will presses on his face that pained, frozen grin which is one of the ways he deals with his wife. You can just hear that grin saying back to him, Just let her do things right for once. They do not introduce their ill-natured friend who is either all drunk or half crazy.

Tonight, there is a lighter quality to the evening, the singing is more with the lips and less from the throat, but that too soon changes by the pressure of the clock. Forty-five minutes to closing time. Chorus after chorus of sentimental song washes over the tired noisy Saturday night crowd. A very fat and rather beautiful woman on a teeming bench along the wall near us chimes in, "Yes Sir That's My Baby," loudest and clearest, knife-sharp. She's Louise, I remember meeting her at Glenn's, a bouncy, rouged-up baby, full of rage and fun and get to hell out of the way anyone who tries to damp her down, and when she bursts into "Some of These Days" the crowd of miners and their wives roars approval of her note-for-note imitation of Sophie Tucker. She needs no urging to heave herself on to the platform and take the microphone away from the piano man. We're all a little tight by now. Davie and I stand up on our chairs and shout, "Go, go, go!" And she does, her plangent voice arching truly. Pub shivers with whistles and table-pounding. Out of nowhere, the thought occurs to me: Dinlock is indestructible. The people will live for ever. They will go on and on when everyone else is long dead. Balls. I'm drunk.

Hands on mike, she begins to sing slowly, *Don't know why, There's no sun up in the sky,* and the crowd quietens respectfully and there is very little talking. On the bench her miner-husband sits sullen and disapproving. A rock and roll trio of staggering young miners try to clamber up to the platform but the fat woman refuses to give way. Her husband looks away steadfastly.

. . . *You're gonna miss me, Honey.* The miners and their wives try to join in, but the fat, red-cheeked woman is too much for them and their massed voices tumble raggedly after hers until she finishes in muscular and unruffled triumph. I whistle shrilly through my fingers and clasp my hands over my head in a boxer's salute, and she loudly kisses her fingers at me. Only then does she step down, half drunk on applause, and squeezes back into place on the bench. She and another miner's wife spontaneously embrace, kissing each other in a flushed, exultant explosion. All the wives around throw back their heads and rip out defiant laughter. In hollow, uneasy dignity the husbands cheer. The other woman's husband reaches over to restrain his wife and is pushed off. Davie laughs and says, "He's a Stalinist. Only one in village."

Loretta comes in and a place at the table is made by Will and myself for her. Davie, though high by now, is extremely attentive. He goes to get her a Champale with a cherry in it. Loretta and I smile at each other. We talk, not about very much, but for the first time she does not sprinkle her responses sulkily with "Ah, weel, Ah don't know now" and "Ah suppose so, never thought about it quite that way." Straight out, she asks me if I am lonely when I come to Dinlock and nods her head knowingly, almost approvingly, when I say yes.

When Davie comes back he puts his arm around her and says, "How are tha', luv?"

"Oh, Ah'm fahn, Davie. Really." Davie presses her hand, to reassure him and her of the utterly unreassurable. And just for a short moment a sliver of light shines through on the thing that must have brought them together a hundred years

114

ago in the city of Barnsley: youth, hope and a stubborn refusal to face the fact of the world.

Cautiously, unsurely, but with pleasure, Loretta responds to Davie. And I find myself praying for them. And perhaps because I am a drunken stranger in their midst, I find myself hating, directly and unobscurely, that which has risen around all of us to cause a young husband and a young wife to make connection only by chance.

After everybody sings "I'll Be With You In Apple Blossom Time", the wife of the Stalinist miner rises from the bench to take the microphone and warble "Scotland, My Glory", a thin, grey-haired woman whose scrawny throat vibrates violently. Her husband sits sullen and dour. As the woman refuses to relinquish the mike her husband, too, steadfastly looks away. He is furious. When she finally does step down she is tipsy on applause and squeezes back into place where she and the fat woman embrace again, kissing each other. The men around them laugh uproariously but also are disturbed. At our table Will Lawson's wife, Fay, shouts, "There's a girl, Maggie!" and Will glowers and tries to shush her. He glances an apology at me for her intemperateness. I wonder what happened to Frank, the brawny miner who was around six months ago. Later, when I ask, Loretta says, "Oh, he's around. Not at the Lawsons any more. But he's around."

Now we all have our arms around each other, swaying and singing, "The Street I Live On". The entire place is moving with half-shut eyes, tranquilly, all together now. Davie jumps up and pushes two miners off the platform. He takes hold of the microphone, goes into a crouch as he has seen other singers do, and lets go with "Stupid Cupid", a crowd pleaser. His mouth is too close to the mike, and the sound roars out, thrusting and strangled and rich. Then he grips the slim metallic stem with both hands, murmuring hugely, "One o'clock, two o'clock three o'clock—*rock*!" his large bright eyes watered over with pain and alcohol and the memory of two old men making impossible demands of him in a muddy field, his unruly blond hair swept over his eyes, flicking the hair out of his eyes while he turns to face Loretta, at our table, his eyes openly, boldly, intimately on her. Loretta blushes, and Davie sways his hips erotically in time to the drum-and-piano accompaniment behind him. Loretta looks away, she looks at me and giggles. Fay Lawson lowers her head and makes an approving face at Loretta who says, "Shush now wi' that sort of thing," and she is happier than I have ever seen her, her large, sculptured head moving in all directions, except towards Davie, and in all directions drinking from Davie's voice, "We're gonna rock, rock, *rock* all night . . .!"

A final turn from the miner-painter. "I Want to Grow Old With You". Softly, his eyes shut, Davie caresses the mike frankly, and nobody in Pub makes fun or even smiles, except as he sings, softly. His eyelids flutter open, and this time Loretta looks up at him, her wide full lips slightly parted, very conscious of herself and looking at Davie's eyes, not searching because she has never been taught to search. ". . . and when we die, up to heaven we'll fly . . . together". Davie ends his song, a naked sincerity blended with self-conscious dash. He leaps down from the stage and takes his place at the table, with all of us, head rather high, pride rather restored, what Bolton and Allan earlier did to him forgotten—no, not forgotten, its spread through his system temporarily arrested.

"That was great, Davie," says Fay. Loretta is silent a moment, then reaches over and smooths back Davie's hair. "That hair, Ah don't know why tha' don't get it cut shorter," is all she says. Davie takes her hand and kisses it. Everyone at our table looks away, all in various degrees shocked. Even, I think, in Will Lawson's case, offended. The Lawsons' friend, the haunted man, emits a scarecrow glare and looks as though he were getting ready to knock Davie down.

But all that is over. It's closing time. Just like that. No

"Time, gentlemen!" Just the chuckling, chubby drummer pulling the mike over to him, giving a farewell wink to the cute little woman who is dying for him, and bawling out, steadily, unemotionally, "Auf Wiedersehen", and the audience joining in, "Ow weederzane . . . ow weederzane . . ." our arms around each other, swaying, crooning, all of us, Time, gentlemen. This time my eyes, six months later and older, are very dry. I just want to get out of Pub and into the air. Maybe out of Dinlock altogether.

A last drink, and outside, amidst a stream of miners and miners' wives going home in the night, Davie walks up to the disapproving Stalinist husband and needles, "Ernest, thy wahf did ver' well tonaht. Congratulate her for me." The village Stalinist grunts and turns away. "Oh, Davie, leave him be," says Loretta, with her arm tightly in her husband's, smiling happily. We say good night to the Lawsons and their sinister friend who simply wanders away without a word. Will steers his wife away quickly before she can say anything incriminating.

On the way home Loretta slips one arm in Davie's, and one arm in mine. Arm in arm we follow the narrow back alleys and fields under what is now a clear, starry night. Davie and Loretta are husband and wife, talking madly between themselves of nothing in particular, avoiding the general to renew the particular and in this way saluting the widening gulf. But now, at this moment, they touch.

In the house the children are asleep, the fire has gone out and Davie carefully combs his hair in the small cracked mirror hanging from a nail above the fireplace. He picks up a piece of coal and holds it up. "That's Dinlock coal, lad." He is coming down to that half-sober state which is his most deceptive, when he can talk straight bilge for an entire evening with the mien of a parson. Loretta, who has been making

117

tea, comes out of the kitchen unexpectedly to say, "But mah trouble is that Ah simply don't have the education to understand the things tha' an' Davie are interested in. Ah wish Ah did soomtahm, but Ah don't." She lays the table and we sit around, close to midnight, drinking tea and slicing pieces of a tenpenny jelly roll. Davie is feeling pretty good, and so is Loretta, whose hope is that Davie will not, as he usually does, mumble something about how it's all right for her to go to bed early because he and I want to talk. But tonight, cockeyed as he is, Davie wants to placate Loretta and stubbornly keeps the conversation on the level which Loretta can participate in.

"Ah luv," scoffs Davie, "no such thing. The lad here lahks tha' the way tha' are."

"Davie," says Loretta, not as a complaint but straight, "Ah know what Ah say. Ah'm so busy with the kids, and Ah've no trainin', tha' and he maht joos' as well be talkin' of the moon for all Ah know of intellectual and those scientific things."

Loretta, I say, the measure of a woman is how much of a woman she is, how capable she is of love and understanding and building life around her from the materials she has at hand. Soon I am even convincing myself. Loretta puts down the tea and searches my face soberly. "But what about Karen?" she asks. Karen is my friend down in London. "Ah sure would lahk to meet Karen soomtahm." Next time I come to Dinlock I'll bring her, I lie. "Please do, Ah would so lahk to meet her. Ah don't meet too many of Davie's friends."

On an impulse, they tell me how they met. It was in Barnsley. There was a riot at a dance. Davie against a mob which threw him downstairs. Loretta had come down to the street outside and they had sat on a kerbstone while she used her jacket to wipe the blood from Davie's face. "It was a yellow jacket, wi' little bits of fur on it, y'know, and Ah never could properly clean it after that," says Loretta. "There were about twenty of 'em," says Davie.

118

"Oh Davie, how can you tell such stories."

"Well, ten."

"That's better."

Together, they reminisce. With only slight objections from Davie, Loretta brings out their wedding photographs from under a pile of towels and work clothes in the big bureau. There they are, in front of the church on a dismal side street in Barnsley, Loretta in a newly-bought dress ("Sky blue it was, first one mah girl friend and Ah saw we took, omen of good luck, that") with a round hat and a veil, Davie in his one and only suit, pressed yesterday and badly fitting, with bell-bottom trousers. In the photograph Davie is proud and calm, Loretta unruffled and hasn't learned the habitual stoop of the Dinlock wife. "It was a smashin' weddin' ", they say, and laugh together when they realise they have said it in unison.

Out come other photographs, other memories. Blackpool, the honeymoon, Loretta and the pigeons on the pier, Davie and Loretta on a merry-go-round. Nine years ago. The one and only time Loretta has been further from Dinlock than Barnsley. She has never been to London. Photographs of the last days of their honeymoon, Margate. Loretta in a bathing suit, slim, full of youth. "Aye," says Davie, "look at that figure, wasn't she somethin' ". Loretta is quiet. "That bosom, aye it was a bosom," says Davie. He looks over at Loretta and puts his arm around her. "But she's still a knock-out," he adds carefully. Loretta takes one of the snapshots from Davie and studies it steadily. Then she says, "Ah was a pretty girl."

For a couple of hours, into the night, they weave about us a caul of warm, selective nostalgia. I have never heard

119

Loretta so open. Which means, for her, two sentences at a time. We are sitting on the small couch, huddled together, with Loretta at my side and Davie on the arm-rest holding her hand and one arm around my shoulder, and our voices are unnaturally loud, and we are ready to laugh at anything. Remembrance, and momentary contact with his wife, has its natural effect on Davie, and he begins to draw a fantastically sentimentalised version of his marriage, on the spot, so totally at variance with the truth that even a stranger can see, and I wonder why Loretta is not made uneasy. She acquiesces in this picture partly because she wants to believe in it, partly because she actually does. If, as Davie says, "Marriage is the only thing", then it must be so and her confused hungers and child-bride blunderings must be only the inevitable and to-be-expected 'working out'. In Dinlock, and in places like it, I have seen husbands and wives tearing each other's hearts out and ascribing it to, "Well, tha' know, lad, it takes some workin' out."

It overpowers me. This one time I must go along. I tell them both I envy them their happiness and their family. And perhaps with some part of me I believe it. "And what about tha'?" asks Loretta, hypnotised by a mirage of connubial richness she has never experienced. "Lad," says Davie, completely bulldogged by his own propaganda, "isn't it about tahm tha' settled down." They are too full of themselves, of the alchemic substitution of what might have been for what is, not to want to share it with me. They urge marriage on me like a love offering. "Tha're a bluidy fool if tha' don't marry Karen, Ah mean it," says Davie. "Ah've never met 'er," says Loretta, "but from all Davie says, Ah couldn't be more in agreement." Loretta, the contented matron. I dodge with the usual bachelor's evasions, play the fool which is exactly what they want. I think of the kids asleep upstairs, of the two spinster sisters sent away for the weekend, of the wedding photographs and us in the parlour, of the talks Davie and I have had under the statue of Eros, of *True*

120

Romances folded on the washrack in the kitchen, and I say, "I'm crazy, I guess."

Davie says, "Well, tha' said it, not us." And he and Loretta laugh together, holding hands. Tonight I am Keenan Wynn, the lonely bachelor uncle who by his sheer existence proves the validity of all marriages. I keep them laughing, harder and harder, into the night, because it is laughter in opposition to the way I live, to the way Davie would like to be free, to the ways Loretta has yet to learn she would like to be flying high. Laughter, for them, now, is cement.

"Davie," says Loretta softly, "it's three in the morning." Davie looks quickly at me. Oh Jesus, Davie, just this once have a sense of the moment. "All raht, luv," he says, taking her hand and walking to the door with her. He turns to me, almost apologetically. "We'll have plenty of tahm to talk tomorrow." They shut the door quietly behind them, and I can hear them walk up to their bedroom. I wash in the kitchen sink, smother the fire and arrange the soft chair and small couch into a bed. I turn off the light and open the curtains. I stare out into the night of Dinlock. Upstairs, there is no sound. I shrug helplessly.

"Tahm, lad."

Loretta's gentle voice, waking me, Sunday morning. It is the house of the day again. Davie is the last to get up. Loretta makes a breakfast for us. Davie goes into the kitchen. I go in with him. How many of those things do you take anyway? I ask. His voice is thin and far away as he feeds himself white tablets. "Six in the morning," he says. A dozen more during the day.

After breakfast, I take the kids out to play. Peter punches me while Jenny crawls all over me. There are lots of kids on the street this morning, and they come over and ask Peter if his dad has painted any more pictures, which is more than

121

I have ever heard Loretta ask. When I take the kids back in Loretta is washing the dishes. Davie goes into the kitchen and says something. Her back stiffens. Davie comes into the parlour and says briskly that we're going out for a walk. We put on our jackets.

"We'll be back," says Davie, avoiding his wife's eyes.

"Aye," she says without expression.

Davie and I walk around the village in the late morning drizzle and don't say very much. When the rain comes down harder we duck into the doorway of a small store. For a while we stand there, staring at the line of NCB brick cottages across the street, every one like every other one, except that some don't have TV antennae, yet. There doesn't seem much to say. The streets are peaceful and deserted. Then Davie sighs.

"Ah've outgrown the village. Ah've got to leave."

I turn to watch him. He nods. "Aye, Ah've been thinkin'." A small chill begins to spread inside me, the kind of sick coldness that must have come to Davie the first time he realised that he had outgrown Dinlock. All the things we had argued about are not arguable any more.

He says, "If Ah don't get out of village it'll strangle me. Lahk it does them. But where to? Where?"

Now that he is finally talking this way, I have a small, terrifying guilt. To take him out of village, this could also be death for him. I say so. Yes, he knows. "But the death here is sumthin' Ah'm sure about; maybe the other one won't happen." He turns to me. "But where can Ah go? What can Ah do? Ah'm a coal face worker. Ah know no other trade. It's been my lahf, lad. Lad, Ah really do need help."

I have never heard Davie talk like this. He is not excited, and he is not playing to a gallery. I tell Davie he's not talked like this before; I've got to have time to think. When I get back down to London I'll talk to friends about an art

122

scholarship, anything. Davie says simply, "Please, lad." He's breaking me up. That old dread returns, the possibility that he can only produce his paintings as an act of escape. Dinlock is his shroud, but it may also be his motor, charging him up with a creative desperation which sends him to the easel as the only way to mark himself live. He knows this. But he says he must get out at all costs.

It is with a feeling of bursting lungs, as though shot to the surface of a lake in which I was drowning, that I hear Davie say, "It's tahm tha' went and met Bolton."

Bolton is waiting for me at the bottom of Theresa Road. The rain has stopped. "Tha'rt late," he says shortly and starts off up the street. He sees me looking at the left side of his head where a square white bandage conceals his missing ear. "Started pussin' again," he says.

Bolton and I don't talk much as we climb the steep cobbled hill to the colliery. He says not a word about my going down, just chews his gum with a set face. I can't tell whether he likes the idea or not. Maybe he doesn't know himself.

In the yellow-tiled colliery office a change occurs in Bolton. As he tells an assistant he wants to see the under-manager, he becomes the union official, taking the gum out of his mouth, the hat off his head and sticking his chest out just a little more than usual; almost as though compensating for a first instinct to go hat in hand to the guv'nor.

We're ushered into Tooley's office, and I am surprised. I had remembered him as a fat, red-faced, stupid-looking man of painfully obvious ineptitude. Now he is sitting on his desk, cross-legged, poring over a sheaf of reports on a clipboard. He is in miner's clothes, an old jacket and torn pants, boots and helmet. His face is black with coal dust. Bolton later tells me Tooley goes down into the pit and roams around checking production every day. Tooley is busy this morning;

the interview doesn't last long. I can go down to pit tomorrow morning. Politely, Bolton asks if he can go with me—"Mr. Tooley". Tooley nods. The interview is ended. Bolton jerks his head at me and we start to go out, dismissed. Tooley says, "We're not so bad as we're made out. You'll see." And just before I shut the door he says, again, "We're painted in bad colours. We're all right."

On the walk back down to the village I remark on how amenable Tooley seemed. "We *made* him polite," says Bolton. "The union. Us. Oh, tha' should 'ave seen him when he first coom. Was going to run pit his way—or so he thought." He chuckles as he recounts some of the long bitter history of the union branch in Dinlock. There were, he says, suicides in the village when the pit shut down in the 30's. His own older brother died of fever in Singapore after leaving the destitute village to join the Forces. His father was killed in a mine cave-in near Barnsley, and his only sister's husband is permanently disabled with pneumonocosis. Bolton speaks of incidents 25 years ago as though they occurred very recently. "A man should not have to watch his children starve," he says. What chance is there of it ever happening again? I ask. "Every chance," he replies angrily, "and that's why we need the union." He spits his gum out on the road. "Anyway, there's different ways for children to starve."

He continues. "The union, it's all that's ever stood between us and the old days. Raht here in Dinlock, the branch. Not the union politicians, or the area officials, or the Labour Party. Our own union. Always was, always will be. We made the pit a place for decent men to work." He saddens.

"Aye, that's when Davie was here, at pit, where he belonged." I remain silent. "Ah, tha' should've seen him in those days, lad. He was a young eagle. He'd learnt his lessons and his fists were lahk hammers poundin' the capitalists to

124

bits. A hell-raiser was our Davie. Before he took up that paintin' and all. Not that Ah begrudge it him. In '55 strahk, before all the pits had voted to go back to work, there were reasons why Dinlock pit was not the strategic one. Tolthorpe was. They had a big mass meeting. Union officials came up, all the way from London, to tell the men to go back to work. Well, the opposition, the men who wanted to stay on strahk, weren't organised. But Davie went to the mass meeting in Tolthorpe and he didn't tell any of us what he was to do. The minute Davie trahd to speak he got chucked out of meetin' hall. So he set himself up on top of a motorcar for when the boys at the meetin' broke. And he started to speak. Aye, Ah wish tha' could've been there to hear Davie speak. An eagle. Flashing eyes. He looved those men. He pleaded with them not to go back. At first nobody listened. Then a few. More and more came out until maybe there were 2000 men gathered around that motorcar; most couldn't hear but passed it on. When soom of the Tolthorpe union boys tried to shove Davie off there was a bit of a roughhouse. The men demanded Davie have the raht to speak. And speak he did. 'Tolthorpe speaks in the name of whole British working class tonight' says Davie. Aye, it was beautiful, mark me. He finished by sayin', Ah still remember, 'Don't vote on the money. Vote on the principle'."

We turn off into Theresa Road and take the short cut to Pub. What happened? I ask. Bolton laughs and spits. "Oh, the men listened very respectfully, an' that's somthin' when tha' remember Davie was in the eyes of a great many veteran miners only a child. They listened, they did, and then they trooped back into that hall and voted near almost to unanimous to go back to work. The strahk ended next morning."

Davie is waiting for us in Pub. Several times he must ask Bolton if he and I can have permission to attend the Sunday meeting of the safety committee. As we leave Pub, Bolton says offhandedly that he'll have to ask the committee itself, of which he is chairman. And then he makes Davie wait outside the Welfare Hall while, ostensibly, he slips inside to 'consult' with his committee. I wonder if he does this sort of thing to Davie all the time, or only when I am around.

While we're waiting in the draughty corridor, Carl Fish. the Home Coal Chairman who replaced Alf Johnson, looks in and winks. "Have they done me in yet, Davie?" he grins. "They haven't had tahm yet, Carl," replies Davie. Carl goes out, and Davie promises that today's meeting will be exceptionally interesting.

Next to the executive board of the branch union, the most prestigious body in Dinlock is the safety committee, election to which is of some importance (and often a step to higher office). Most of the village notables are on it.

Davie says that a cabal has formed to resist Carl Fish's attempt to unseat the present vice-chairman of the committee, led by, what could be more natural, the vice-chairman of the committee. It is all due to be hammered out today. The pro-Fish forces, of which Davie is ex-officio member, believe the tactic of the opposition will be to argue Carl's nomination papers out of order on some obscure technicality. It will then be up to Bolton, as chairman of the committee, to rule. For all sorts of reasons, having to do with union politics and impending elections for the branch executive and therefore the all-important assignment of status in the village, a great deal is riding on Bolton's ruling. Bolton is a good friend of Carl's. But Bolton is also a politician and not above waiting to see which way the wind will blow.

"Don't get me wrong," says Davie, "Bolton is lahk a father to me. But his tendencies worry me. They seem to be goin' in two different directions. For one thing, he lahks too much to be on first-name terms with the pit manager and such people. Whenever ah speak to him of it he can get to be very arrogant. He thinks he can outsmart everybody.

And then there's this other tendency I was tellin' tha' about. It's straight Stalinism, the way he talks about revolution and puttin' the capitalists up against a wall and shootin' them and the way he admires what the Russians did in Hungary, it's enough to make tha' sick. And it's got me worried."

I tell Davie that in my experience when militant union officials begin to equip themselves with the talents for accommodation to management, they often cover their retreat with a demagogic brand of insurrectionary radicalism. Davie shakes his head and hastens to say that I am off the mark. I mustn't misinterpret what is happening to Bolton, he says. As of now, Bolton is still doing an A-1 job for the men. With a frown he says, "It's only tendencies. He thinks he's the union. He thinks he's Dinlock."

I remember the talks I have had with Bolton, how he's been doing a lot more prefacing his remarks with "Tha' have to remember, lad, Ah'm not one of thy educated blokes", demonstrating the classic symptoms of a man becoming deeply convinced that he was meant for better things than Dinlock, no more so than when he insists the village is at the centre of the universe. In certain circumstances, I think, Bolton could be dangerous, by giving articulate expression to the inchoate and endemic suspicion of some of the miners towards those who are not, especially anyone "wi' education." For the present, however, the opposite is true. He goes out of his way, particularly in his formal relations with the men, to urge them towards a greater tolerance for the artist and intellectual. But for how long?

A door in the corridor opens and Bolton pops his head out. "The safety committee has given the two of you permission to attend this meeting," he says solemnly.

The eight or nine men of the safety committee are dwarfed by the high-vaulted oak-dark mahogany room, almost as

127

large as the auditorium in the same building. The walls are decorated with photographs of union outings and past executive boards and a number of plaques dedicated to the memory of those who fell in the wars and to those branch union officials who gave long service in Dinlock. "Ah once did a paintin' of this room," Davie whispers as we take our seats at the end of a great table, "but nobody lahked it."

It is a formal, dignified meeting, a set-piece of a meeting. Thirty minutes ago they were laughing over their ales, and in another hour they will be again, but now the men seated around the table are on their official, portentous behaviour. Carl Fish comes in last and takes his seat with a wink at Davie and me.

One of the men leans across the table and says, "Is it tomorrow tha're goin' down to pit," but before I can reply Bolton opens the meeting with a light tap of his blond ash-wood gavel. Usual procedure, reading of minutes. Usual business, allocation of moneys, arrangement for outing, donation to victims of recent mine accident in Nottingham-shire. Then Bolton speaks up, introducing me. To me: "The committee has been kahnd enoof to grant tha' permission to remain in this room during deliberations. It is understood that tha' will write nothing of what tha' hears and sees for the newspapers." I thank Bolton.

Every man at the table is self-consciously calm and un-concerned. A few more items of business are transacted with excruciating deliberateness by Bolton while the tension mounts in the room, marked only by those who were dood-ling on scraps of paper now leaving off. Bolton is enjoying himself, savouring something. The one who is enjoying it least is a sour-faced, fancily dressed man at Bolton's side who twirls a pencil around and around between his hands and spasmodically reaches up to smooth his thin black moustache. Who's that one? I ask. "Vice-chairman of committee," Davie whispers back, "the one Carl's out for." The vice-chairman is an obviously unhappy man. I look over at Carl. I know that grin. That's a UAW-CIO grin. He must have the votes in his pocket.

We're on the subject with deceptive smoothness, Bolton drones into it before we know it. The form of this particular *corrida* is that the safety committee must pass on the validity of nomination papers. Davie leans over, about to whisper something, but desists on a glare shot from Bolton.

Only the post of vice-chairman is in contest. The cork is pulled. A committee member, a shoe-faced man with bulging eyes, bluntly proposes that Carl Fish withdraw because if he does the vice-chairmanship will go by acclamation and the branch union will thereby be saved the cost of printing ballots. Bolton looks at Carl across the dark-wood beautifully finished table. "Carl, tha' feel lahk pullin' out?" Carl stares straight at the vice-chairman and says, "No, Bolton." I can't help grinning. Davie, Bolton and the others had primed me for an exercise in the subtleties of union politics. Subtlety hell. This is a brawl.

It doesn't seem possible, but Bolton actually makes a slow ceremony out of reading the candidates' names, all two of them. The vice-chairman nervously strokes his moustache when the shoe-faced miner seconds his nomination, making a slow short speech as he does so. The vice-chairman almost yelps with impatience. Finally, Carl Fish's nomination, duly seconded by someone at the table. The bulge-eyed miner is about to ask a question, probably the question, but the vice-chairman just can't wait that long. Aloud, he wonders if Carl Fish's nomination is in order.

A moment of vast silence. There is much clearing of throats at the table: it is the preliminary flourish of trumpets for the *paseo*. But not Bolton. He is in control. The pics have done their work, and now he unsheathes, calmly, the bandilleras.

All eyes are on the vice-chairman who seems a little horrified that he jumped the gun. Though he is not chewing, he is swallowing. He has no alternative but to plough straight in.

Acting by instinct more than plan, he generates a dispute about committee rules which I find difficult to follow. The gist of it is that a safety committeeman must have served a number of months on the committee before becoming eligible for the executive board. "That's the rule," he insists.

Bolton, who has been listening stone-faced, now breaks in sharply. The bandilleras flash in the gloom, find their mark and hook there. He slaps the rule book on the table. "You find me that rule in this little book," he demands.

"Eh, what's that?" says the vice-chairman, rearing back, bug-eyed and knocked off balance by Bolton's abruptly hostile tone after almost an hour of patient, neutral monotone.

"Ah said, you find me that rule in this little book. The rule that says Carl can't be nominated."

The vice-chairman squirms. "Ah didn't say Carl couldn't be nominated. Ah was talkin' about rules. Rules. Not Carl."

Bolton gives himself another set of bandilleras. "Aye," he says unruffled and stern, "Ah didn't say tha' wasn't talkin' about rules. There's the book. Now show me where it says a man has to sit on this committee a certain number of months before bein' eligible for election to vice-chairman. There it is. Open it up and show me."

The other miners around the table are deadly still, and the grin is even wiped off Carl Fish's face. The vice-chairman as though hypnotised, picks up Bolton's rule book and begins numbly to go through it. We all know that no such rule exists. The ancient, octangular clock on the wall ticks loudly in the heavy silence. The vice-chairman has Bolton's shafts hanging down from his flanks, is boxed in with no way of getting out, and knows it. He flips through the pages, looks up, but no one speaks up for him, not even the man who seconded his nomination, then down again quickly to go through the rule book page by page. Nobody speaks. His ally starts to say something and is interrupted by Bolton, "Tha' can have thy say after he's found the rule which says Carl cannot be nominated."

130

The victim fumbles with the book, discovers a paragraph. "Here, section 1-D," he says, then sighs, "ah, no, that's soomthing else." A moment later he reads out an entire two paragraphs before he realises his goose is cooked. He puts down the book and appeals to the men around the table. "Well, uh, Ah remember joost after the war we had a rule lahk that. It must've been changed. But that don't make no difference. We've done it for so long that it's the same as a rule."

Bolton snatches his rule book away triumphantly. Slowly, savouringly, he opens his coat, seeks out the precise location of his vest pocket and, going in straight and true over the shoulder, drops the rule book in. The vice-chairman is finished. Everyone is trying to talk at once.

"As chairman of the safety committee Ah declare Carl Fish's nomination paper legal and binding." Bang goes Bolton's gavel. One of the men at the table winks at Carl Fish and Carl Fish winks at me. The vice-chairman (for how much longer?) winks at nobody. The tension slackens. Davie leans over and whispers, "How about that."

With great etiquette everyone rises and files out of the committee room, heading for East Clu' where Bolton stands drinks all round, including the vice-chairman who looks sick. Tommy Hunter, the ex-commando, wanders in from watching television in the other room and announces that some American congressman has suggested moving troops into Cuba if the new land-reform law goes into effect. The miners of the safety committee, in the bar of Old Clu', accept this news with equanimity. "Aye," says Bolton without enthusiasm, "that's thy American imperialism for tha'." There are a few comments passed about how the United States left Britain in the lurch during the Suez crisis and then look what she herself did in the Lebanon. Davie says, "Why don't they let the people in those countries settle it for themselves? Why do they always have to be sendin' in troops?" Tommy Hunter says, "Because every few months if we don't give the fookin' wogs a clip on the nose they'll be tryin' to take our oil away from us, that's why," belligerently, "Ah know, Ah was a commando in Egypt in the war." The raised eyebrows say that this is one story Tommy hasn't told. Carl Fish says, "Nasser, joost lahk Hitler."

One more drink and the men scatter to their homes. Davie takes off to help Loretta and to get in an afternoon's painting even though the light is misty. Several times I have asked him when we are going to visit Len, the man who was caught in the Beckley explosion yesterday, but we never do go. When a man is eight-balled in Dinlock, it doesn't always help even when his wife has done yours favours.

I walk around alone. Dinlock on a grey Sunday afternoon is like a cemetery at dusk. A heavy quiet, unbroken by the chugging noises of the colliery, has settled on the mining village. All the houses look the same sodden wet colour, something between slate grey and Olde Englande brown, the most dispiriting colour in the world. Why don't the local councils simply paint all the cottages black and have done with it? The streets, as always, are almost deserted.

"Hello there, Yank!"

"Bless me, Sophie Tucker . . ."

"That's my boy!" she roars with delighted laughter. I fall in step beside her, and we walk along the street, the fat beautiful be-rouged woman who sang in Pub last night and me. She doesn't open with any of the usual Dinlock jive—how do I like the place, what part of America do I come from, etc. But immediately, without knowing who I am except that I am Davie's friend up from London, "Queer bunch, ain't we?"

Oh, I don't know, I say.

"Oh yes you do know." She belches a gargantuan laugh. "Crackers, every man jack of us! You would be too if you had to live here." We turn the corner into a smaller, tidier street.

"Now I have two choices," she announces. "I can take you home with me. Or we can talk for a few minutes, just like this. If I take you home my husband—he's on haulage—will see his duty as not to let you and me talk together. That's a custom here between men and women. Oh my, the customs here!" She holds her colossal sides and laughs and laughs. Behind us a curtain moves, a pinched face peeks out, then hurriedly disappears. "Next time she looks out," she grins from ear to ear, "I'll heave a brick through her glass. . . . Uh uh. My man. In the garden up there. Seen us, he has. See, now he's going in. That's my signal to follow him. Well, in a few minutes." We retreat back down the street to sit on a low stone wall.

"Did you enjoy yourself last night, love," she asks. She does not have the northern accent, more London. When I ask she says, "Aye, London. Heaven." She glances at me sideways. "Aye, you heard correct. *Heaven*. Wish to God I was there now." She waves a hand in the general direction of everyone she knows in Dinlock. "And if they knew what they was missing they'd feel the way I do. Poor wretches."

I tell her that I enjoyed her singing at the pub. "Aye, if I didn't do that I'd come apart. Twice a week at Pub I get up and yowl like a butchered calf and believe it or not, honey, if it weren't for those two nights I wouldn't last the course." She even talks like Sophie Tucker.

"Perhaps," she goes on, "you've noticed others can't. That little girl sitting next to me, the one the drummer was trying on for size. He does it every week, every week with a different woman, smiling that way. Last year me. He's not a bad sort, I suppose you can't really blame him, the way he travels round. I don't envy him his life. But Christ, I hope he doesn't envy ours. At least he can always leave. Like you. They tell

133

me you'll be going down the pit tomorrow and good luck. You go down, you come up and you go away. That poor little girl sitting next to me, she has one night with the drummer man and it has to last her a year, maybe two. Before it happens again. Men are pigs. Present company," she grins, "excepted of course. Aye, I know how the men have been talking to you. You think it's so sweet and smooth waters and respectable. But you'll not be writing a blessed damn' good thing if you listen to the line shot at you by Harold Bolton and Ray Sweet and all the rest of those strutting little union emper-r-r-ors, I can tell you. Why don't you talk to some of the wives? Not as though they'd talk to you. What a place. Customs! The whole village. But where could I go? Man, kids, life. Make do, make do." She turns on me fiercely.

"But don't you let Harold Bolton and those others shoot you a line. The people in this village are human, flesh and blood, they've got faults. Not married? Well, stay that way. It's like a life sentence, take it from me. Married 14 years and haven't had a week's decent kissing since. Man's all right, I don't hate him the way some women here do their husbands. But what kind of kissing can there be when your man is down in pit all day. I don't think I've ever seen him when he's not been tired. So tired he can't play with the kids. What kind of kissing can there be? Days he doesn't work, we fight. They say money doesn't bring happiness. Let them try me. Just let them try. So we get our kissing wherever we can. How long are you going to be in village? I'm only making a joke. I hope. Dinlock, it's like the Army. If the men yearn for the Army I wish they'd go already and leave us in peace.

"Peace. Look at it. The village. Quiet. Quiet and war. Quiet on the outside and war on the inside. It's not natural for a woman to go without kissing. So everybody gets their kissing from somebody else, somebody different, in the front door, out the back door, like games we used to play in school. Take my word for it, you've got to have a sense of humour to live in a place like this. Women married to husbands

134

come up from pit too dead to know black from white, so they go to another man, surface worker if they're lucky. He isn't so tired, except that the face men are the best, and the tiredest, except maybe just a little less tired than your own man. Hardly a woman I know isn't going with another man or hasn't done. Going from door to door of tired men and come back to give tea to your own still more tired man. Oh that Harold Bolton, president of the union and all that, he'll charm your ears off. The bastard." She catches my look and nods despairingly. "That's right . . ."

"Well," she gets up from the stone wall and smooths her dress, "coom on, luv, and Ah'll fix tha' up with a north-country tea. Luv, luv," she parodies. Where to? I ask. "My home. Where else? Did you expect me to be taking you to the Dorchester? I used to work there. Come on, now. Don't be hanging back just because of the way I talk. There's barely a woman in village who couldn't—but won't—tell you the same as me, only busier perhaps. I'm only average. Your mate Davie said you were interested in meeting the average British people. Well, I'm an average British wife. Tea now."

We stroll down the street, past some stares and to her home, a brown brick cottage sporting an oversize television antenna. Her husband is working in the garden. He gets up, a huge, raw-muscled miner with a stark, black moustache and dull, watchful eyes. She says, "Peter, I want you to meet a friend of Davie's from the States, a writer. By the way, my name is Louise." The moustachioed giant leads the way in to tea, stoically registering that I had been talking to his wife without knowing her name. When he turns I see a ragged red scar splitting his cheek and running down his neck. Louise points to it. "Happened a few years ago, three, four. NCB was testing a new kind of support. It didn't work." She giggles unhappily and then quickly falls silent.

Even with Louise, it is a Dinlock house. The same small parlour with the ever-burning fire and drying clothes and the chips in the grate, two small armchairs, two stiff-backed

135

wooden chairs, a small couch, a varnished table, yellow wall-paper with swimming green curleycues and a large-screen television set. The telly is on. Louise's two boys, ages 11 and 7, and a dour brawny neighbour woman are watching the set. "We've both ITV and BBC," says Peter, the husband. "Twice the curse," says Louise.

While Louise, Peter and I have tea at the table in the small, overheated room, the two boys and the neighbour woman sit unsmilingly through the final moments of "I Married Joan". Nobody makes a move to turn off the set because a visitor is present. Peter shifts his bulk uneasily. "Aye, and do tha' lahk our village?" Louise's eye glints humorously as, without another word, she moves her chair around to study the telly. Peter fiddles with his tea. I fiddle with mine. He says, "Funny woman, that Joan Davis of yours." I nod and mumble. Simultaneously, we both shift our chairs around to watch how Joan Davis even scores with her next-door neighbour for throwing dead leaves on the Davis back lawn. After several minutes of twitching double-takes and convulsive pratfalls, Joan walks into the enemy house for a heart-to-heart talk with the neighbour's wife. Joan points out that it is unneighbourly and, by gosh, un-American to bear grudges. The wife breaks down in tears. Joan puts her arm around the woman, who confesses that the feud was all the idea of her husband, who was angry over losing a case in Judge Davis's court. The story ends happily with Joan crashing into the side of a door. And, in Louise's house, we watch, without a jog of our eyelids as the BBC newscaster comes on to announce details of a Queen's honour for the superintendent of the Hola death camp and to prophesy that the Comet will soon be ready to cross the Atlantic in less than eight hours.

As far as I can tell, nobody's expression changes from Joan Davis to the news telecast to the National Youth Orchestra of Great Britain. We all sit absolutely unflickering before the set. The neighbour woman turns in her chair and says glumly, "There's a Hollywood film on ITV." Louise's

136

older boy gets up and is told sharply by his mother to sit down and listen. "When there's something decent, Mick, you sit there and lump it!" Nobody looks very happy at this including Louise. For ten minutes we listen to a Haydn symphony. The neighbour woman gets up and exits with a curt nod and no word. "There, that did it," says Louise. She switches to ITV, which is showing an old film in which Charles Boyer and Jean Arthur fall in love in Paris. But Jean is married to a cruel businessman, and the lovers must part, only to meet again in New York on the eve of Jean's return to Paris in order to save Charles from the guillotine.

Louise grimaces. "Do you know how this ends? Davie says you used to work there in Hollywood." I tell her that it ends when Jean and her husband come in for a last dinner at a swank Manhattan restaurant. Charles, contrary to what Jean was led to believe by a husband who wanted to keep her at any cost, is not under sentence of death in Paris, but is the head-waiter of the restaurant. Jean laughs from sheer relief that she has re-discovered her one true love. But Charles thinks she is laughing at him. He is bitter. But later that evening Jean returns to tell him she laughed because she loves him and that in reality she herself is only a mannequin and not a rich heiress.

While I tell the story Peter looks on in a sort of amazed hostility. When I finish Louise looks at me and says, "Is that what you did in Hollywood?" Things like that, I say. She gives me a look as if to say, You ought to be ashamed, and switches back to BBC in time the Brains Trust. "Oh, no" says the younger boy. He gets up and looks at his mother. "Okay," she says, "but take your mac." Peter looks as if he'd like to go out too.

One of the first questions on the programme is: "If Britain were to be destroyed by an atomic war what three most valuable and representative things would you consider saving?" One of the brains, in a fury, refuses to reply. It

137

should be everyone's job, he says, to struggle against the possibility of atomic war and not to engage in ghastly frivolities on TV. Louise says to me, "Those hydrogen bombs. Notice what's happening to the climate. Wetter."

We continue to sit absolutely without expression before the set. One of the last questions put to the Brains Trust is: "Do you consider hire purchase a good or bad thing?" Now, as an economic pundit, a left-wing art critic, a popular scientist and an abstract painter give their opinions, for the first time the faces of Louise and Peter change. They grin over at each other; indulgently. The more the brains talk, the broader grow the grins of Louise and Peter. After the economist makes a particularly pontifical remark, referring to the saving habits of the working class, Peter mutters, "He ought to go down to pit for a day. Fix him."

A moment later, Louise suddenly breaks in. "What would you save, Peter?"

"Ah?"

"That question back then, about the atomic war, what would you save?" Peter stirs his tea and looks down into it. "Ah dunno. Fool question if you ask me." Louise says, "You know what I'd save? Me."

When the Brains Trust is over it is time for me to go. Peter apologises. "Sunday," he explains, "is not such a good time for telly." Louise takes me to the door, from which I can see the neighbour woman moodily surveying us. Peter follows. "So tha're going down pit tomorrow." I tell him yes. Like all prisons, Dinlock has a fast grapevine.

So long, Louise, I say, and she and I shake hands. She looks sharply at her husband, who immediately does his duty by telling me how nice it was I dropped by. I walk to the gate. Louise runs down the path after me. Yes, Louise, I say. She looks at me and once again tries her arch, lusty grin, but it emerges a little crooked. She makes a vague, helpless gesture. Then she turns back and goes into the house.

When I get back to Davie's it is visibly tenser. What has happened in the parlour with the kids I don't know, but he and Loretta in the kitchen are studiously not speaking to each other. Not angry, just resigned again. As soon as I come in Davie asks me to come up to the bedroom with him, and disregarding Loretta's single sharp look he takes me up there and shuts the door.

He goes to a corner of the room, denoted as his studio by the presence of brushes and tubes of paint on an old white kitchen table, and uncovers his easel. I must tell him, he says, what I think of the picture. It is entitled "The Dying Miner". I can tell from the way he squints that his head is starting to bother him again. He grins and says he's taken a dozen codeine so far today, which is a record. What, he insists, do I think of the painting?

It is like all of Davie's work I have seen: simple, bold and terrifically emotional. Using a restricted palette, mainly browns, dark blues and yellows (self-taught, there are some colours he has yet to handle), he has somehow managed to overcome his deficiencies of drawing and design to produce an effect of startling power and even beauty. Done from an eye-level side view, the miner is seen lying under a great patched-up coverlet on a large bed in a cold upstairs bedroom somewhere. There is no perspective, no attempt to dramatise by foreshortening or literary analogy. He is not a Christ, not a symbol, but an old, dying man staring at the ceiling as though trying to read some message there. Through a window in a far corner of the room we can see a file of young miners trooping off to the colliery in the distance, but the old man is not looking at them.

After a while I tell Davie that the picture moves me very

much. He is learning how to use his knife as well as brushes. The only thing that really disturbs me are those young miners through the window. The comment, I say, is too obvious. It is the sort of thing the Soviet 'socialist realists' of the Gerasimov school do to ruin and render acceptable their work. Davie listens and then sits down on the bed and stares at his shoes. He asks me, in a low voice, if I am serious about helping him try to get out of the village. "It's so hard to paint when all tha' can think of is where the food money is going to coom from." Has he inquired about national assistance? An evasive reply, and I don't press the point. For a young collier to go on to national assistance would be a shame too burning to bear in Dinlock; it is the one thing he could never live down in the village.

"Ah don't think tha' understand, lad. Ah'm not *fit* for face work any more. Ah don't *want* to go back down to pit. That's a part of mah lahf that is over. Raht now it's a rope around mah neck. But what can Ah do? Loretta asks where the rent money is coomin' from an' all Ah can say is 'Wait until Ah sell a painting'. Now Ah ask tha': what kahnd of answer is that to give a wahf?" I agree, it's a hell of an answer.

And then, right now, there doesn't seem anything else to say. I stand at the window and look out on the sloping moor which is receiving rain again. Davie rolls over on the bed and stares up at the ceiling like "The Dying Miner". I say a few words, and he replies, and we fall silent. Desultorily, we talk about politics. Cuba, Berlin, Lennox-Boyd's whitewash of the Hola atrocity. He says the villagers are not very concerned about Kenya. "Trouble is, many of the boys served in the Army in Africa in the war and they don't have much of a good word to say about the niggers." With my mind elsewhere, I say it's about time he dropped that word from his vocabulary.

Suddenly Davie leaps off the bed in a fury. "You goddam Londoners, tha're joost lahk them, lad. Payin' attention to the small things and lettin' the big things slide." I shut my mouth or else I know there'll be a fight. "Why do you

Londoners always object to us bein' different up here," he says angrily. "Don't always be tryin' to change us. Ah've got coloured friends in Sheffield and they never mind bein' called nigger. And why are tha' always tryin' to get me to change my paintings?" He walks over to "The Dying Miner" and swiftly drapes it with part of an old torn sheet. "Ah don't paint fancy lahk they do in London. Ah paint the truth Ah know. The whole point of this picture is those young miners goin' to work, and if tha' can't see that Ah feel sorry for tha'." And just as abruptly he falls silent, morosely. We both stand at the window looking out at the rain pelting down on the little pre-war stone cottages on the near side of the moor. Davie wrenches his face into his artificial, charming smile and says, "What are we arguin' about anyway? If it makes tha' unhappy Ah'll never say nigger again in thy presence."

We leave the bedroom to go down to tea. At the top of the landing he turns and says, "Y'know, last naht, the boys, Bolton and Allan, the way they needled me, Ah hope tha' didn't take them too seriously. They'd had a few. Ah didn't mind."

Downstairs, and just before he opens the parlour door, he says, stubbornly, half to himself, "But Ah'm not goin' back down to pit. *Never*."

After tea, Davie announces to Loretta that we'll be going out for a few hours. She nods grimly and begins clearing up the dishes. We put on our jackets, and he tells me to wait a minute while he runs upstairs. When he comes down his face is dark and tight, and he tells Loretta he wants to see her in the hallway. I go outside and wait in the street. He emerges from the house ready to break something. We set out for Pub.

141

Davie is furious. He had gone upstairs to take ten bob out of the small porcelain piggy bank in his and Loretta's bedroom, only to discover Loretta had beaten him to it by several minutes. "She knew Ah wanted to go out with tha'. Why does she have to do things lahk that." He picks up a stone and flings it viciously into a field. I say that Loretta doesn't have it easy. "But," says Davie, "tha' saw for thyself. She went to Pub last naht. Why does she have to go *tonaht*?" Why do you? I ask. God damn it, he says, "Ah work all day down in pit. . . . Ah mean," he hesitates, flounders, seems almost to reach out physically for a point of standing, of justification, without finding it, ". . . or painting . . ." He doesn't finish the sentence, but bursts out, "But why did she have to do it? Tha' don't know her. She's spiteful. She's always doin' things lahk that. Joost to spite me." He seems almost ready to cry. "It's the hypocrisy of it that gets me. She doesn't really lahk Pub." His hatred is fierce and pure. Last night might just as well have never happened.

At the bar in West Clu' we run into Len, the Beckley miner, and his wife, a cheerful, shrewd-eyed mannish-faced woman who looks like her husband. Davie is friendly with her; Len is uneasy with us. I ask Len about the explosion. He lapses into the sullen monosyllables which Dinlockers use not to talk, like back-country Mississippi Negroes. He looks past me, around me, over me, at his drink. Wasn't much of an explosion, he mutters. Nobody was hurt. What about his arm? Just a scratch. And that's all he will say. Later, Davie says, "The story's already around that nothing serious happened. Last naht he was prepared to make a gigantic tale out of it."

Over by the wall a young miner sitting with his girl signals for us to join him. It is the bull-necked hand-getter Johnny. The girl is the quiet, immobile one we saw him with yesterday. Johnny has called Davie over to thank him for recommending a novel on mining life by the Yorkshire novelist, Len Doherty. He says, "Ah really did enjoy that book, Davie.

142

It was truthful, tha' know what Ah mean. It tells our sahd of the story." Johnny urges me to read the novel. Davie concurs. Doherty, the collier-author who works in a pit near Rotherham, is one of his idols. For two years, ever since he read one of Doherty's books, Davie has been trying to work up the courage to write a letter to Doherty asking to meet him. "Y'know, lad," Davie says to me, "knowin' Len Doherty is writin', that helps keep me goin'. I can't exactly explain it."

Even though Davie is no longer down to pit, he and young Johnny find themselves, naturally and compulsively, in talk of—wage rates.

Wages is what the miner says he goes down to pit for. It is, rightly, his obsession. Here, generally, is what I found out:

A large number of miners are well up in the wage-scale by British standards. A five-day week should mean £16 to £18 a week for a face worker *if* he works the five shifts. Absenteeism, by all accounts, is sloping off, and the general opinion among the men is that the work is growing steadily 'easier' due to mechanisation. In Dinlock pit, the men say, the effects of mechanisation are being felt for the first time.

Haulage workers make between £9 10s. and £11 a week, although it is difficult for me to compute their money because it comes under at least five different grades according to job.

Opinion is divided about whether many miners are saving more money. Davie and Johnny say definitely yes, but Bolton says this is for things like the all-important yearly holiday, for which every miner, almost literally, lives. It doesn't take long to discover that more miners than ever are taking holidays away from home and even—mark the *even*— abroad. There are few signs of nest-eggs being stored away for the future. It may not be polite, but the Dinlock collier still lives for today.

Both Davie and Johnny say that in the past year there has been a sobering down from the old free-wheeling attitude towards drinking; that there are more cars and a staggering amount of hire-purchase which all agree has vastly affected the appearance of their homes. And, as Bolton says, the pit men have their holidays 'in style' except for the old characters who couldn't be dragged away from Clu' and whose numbers are dwindling.

Davie says now that he is out of pit he can see that the sense of insecurity, which is very much present and brooding, is due to everyone's awareness of the industry's declining position. All whom I speak to seem subdued about it, and Davie says the village is becoming quieter and quieter even at weekends. Mid-week drinking is steady and increasingly confined to a few. The old-timers complain that Pub and Clu' are often half-empty. Community sense, they suggest, is weaker, with fewer and smaller cliques—and much quieter ones at that. They blame tombola, television and the motor-car. "Bread and circuses," mutters Bolton, disconsolately.

The general situation in the industry has Bolton troubled and baffled, but he will not be tied down to specific points. He will not, in fact, talk about it at all. But it is obvious that he is deeply uncertain about where he would fit in during the next chancy few years. The local issues aren't big enough to keep up the old stature of the union officials, and the national issues are too big for (at least it is felt) individual crusades.

To the social services, the Dinlock miner pays staunch, grumbling and unanimous allegiance. They have helped him a lot and he will say so. But if the services come in for much praise, the individuals who staff the welfare apparatus are paid something considerably less. Arrogance and indifference on the part of lower and middle-echelon officialdom are particularly slated. It is not immediately evident that the onset of comprehensive welfare servicing has seriously

144

altered the miners' social and medical prejudices—except, perhaps towards the welfare services.

Maternity benefits, family allowances and free hospital treatment *have* to mean a lot to the miner. Many tell me proudly how much their last baby or the treatment of their diseased hip-bone would have cost in America or Canada. Davie says he has often heard the British standard of social services presented as one argument against emigration in the clubs. The older ones knew the lack of even the rudiments pre-war and haven't forgotten. The young miners, such as Johnny, take the present set-up for granted but not in a cynical way. There is stronger feeling, however, on points such as the inadequacy in old age pensions—an increasing cause for concern—and industrial compensation benefits.

Carl Fish comes by to sell us copies of *Tribune*. Everyone Carl approaches in West Clu' buys a copy. Davie says it is because Carl knows his clientèle and doesn't try selling to anyone else. *Tribune* has a small but very loyal readership in Dinlock, and the miners are generally favourably disposed towards it, more so than to any other publication, despite their laziness in subscribing and reading it. "It's a fightin' paper," says young Johnny who is non-political. "It tells those fookers in Transport House where to head in." An old miner at the next table leans over and taps my knee. "Mark him, lad," he says. "*Tribune's* only paper in Britain never sold us out." "And never will," adds Davie.

I ask Davie if he will take me to a meeting of the local Labour Party, and he says there is no point. "It's just a bunch of old ladies," he says. Everyone except the shop-keepers in the village, he says, votes solid Labour, "but tha' couldn't drag them to a meetin'."

What about church attendance? Davie and Johnny laugh. Johnny says the only people in Dinlock who go to church are again, the shopkeepers. Then, when some young men

145

enter the club, without excusing himself Johnny jumps up to go and talk with them. Davie tries to make it up to the girl. "Where tha' from?" "Hamthorpe." End of conversation. She is utterly composed, completely inscrutable. Davie turns his face towards the stage and whispers, "Johnny can get away with it. Girls lahk him." Then Johnny comes back and fits himself in on the bench beside the girl, and soon, winking, he has pulled out his wallet and shown us a photograph of a girl in a bikini. The girl from Hamthorpe neither looks at the photograph nor at Johnny, nor even away. "Ain't she soomthin'?" asks Johnny. He flicks the photograph so that the girl from Hamthorpe can see. She gazes at it stolidly. "Ah, Johnny," says Davie, "tha' shouldn't do things lahk that." "Why not?" asks Johnny. Davie turns to the girl and says, "Tha'll have to excuse him. He's young and foolish." The girl says, "Aye, Ah know." Johnny grins at her with an open heart and asks her very politely if she would like another drink. She says no, and Johnny gets up. We say good night to them. As they leave the club, Johnny hastens to open the door for the girl from Hamthorpe. I shake my head. Men and women here, I say. They kill me. Davie says, Kill each other too.

East Clu'; tombola; "Heads down, everyone."

We join Bolton and his gang in the billiard room. Bolton, though obviously wanting to comment, heavily skirts the subject of the committee meeting earlier in the day. When I suggest that he had perhaps slightly too broadly interpreted his power as chairman, Bolton claps a big, nicotined hand on my shoulder. "There's a limit to impartiality, lad," he says. "There are some men who build up the union, others who tear it down. Job of chairman to decide which is which."

"Next," says Davie, "tha'll be puttin' 'em up against a wall."

"Some buggers," replies Bolton, "it's the only language they understand."

"But that's Stalinism, Bolton," protests Davie.

"Aye, so it may be, Davie. But Stalin wasn't so bad as he was painted. Tha' and thy friends in London keep forgettin' that." The rest of the men stop talking to listen to Bolton. "Tha' wait," says Bolton, "that Kroochov fellow won't stick it. Too soft. Not lahk Stalin." Fat, bespectacled Ray Sweet chimes in, " 'Ard as nails that Stalin. He knew what was important." Somewhere along the line, I know, this is a show put on for me, but not everywhere.

"Once a man knows what's raht," says Bolton, "he's got to have the coorage to do what's necessary."

"Includin' killin' people, Bolton?"

"Aye, Davie. That too. Whatever's necessary for the emanicipation of the working class."

How about Nasser? someone asks. "A fooking brigand, that's all he is," says Ray Sweet. "He needs a good clip, he does," says Tommy Hunter. A quick poll of the eight men around us shows a unanimous loathing of Nasser, hesitant support of the Suez adventure and perhaps another like it. I say that this goes against the announced policy of their chosen political arm, the Labour Party, and they look at me, and Bolton changes the subject.

"Tha' take this here village," he says. "Where do tha' think we'd be today if all we did was talked. Stalinism, is it? Well, Stalinism gets things done."

"Tha're a Chicago gangster," grins Davie uneasily.

"They got things done too in Chicago," says Bolton. "But where Stalin went wrong was, he was an Asiatic, and he didn't know how to be fair. Yesterday, some of the boys down in Sleythorpe seam they wanted me to push a claim for overtahm. Now, and Ray and Allan can back me up on this, Ah knew those boys didn't deserve any overtahm. Remember, Davie, 76 where they hit rock last year? So Ah refused to push their claim. Fair. That's where Stalin went wrong." He

147

fingers his CCCP badge, then turns to me and says sharply, "Six o'clock tomorrow morning in Tooley's office. Have Davie fit tha' with the proper clothes. If he can't"—a pause which everyone can interpret; Davie flushes—"Ah will."

The men solemnly listen. The subject of my going down to pit is now officially open. "Who's goin' with tha'?" asks Allan. Bolton says that Tooley has assigned as guide an overman named MacLane. "The soon of a bitch," observes Tommy Hunter. "No, don't tha' be sayin' that," says Bolton, "Ah want the lad here to make up his own mahnd. MacLane is not a soon of a bitch."

Between now, and closing time, half a dozen men casually drop by simply to observe that they have heard I will be going down to pit tomorrow. They are extremely careful to show neither interest nor disinterest. It makes Davie nervous. Johnny, the young collier, comes in, having sent his girl back to Hamthorpe, and we all start out in a hurry. For some reason, Davie wants to keep me away from Bolton tonight. He says, "Let's get out of here. Bolton'll chew your ear off if he comes home with us." But before we can get through the door Bolton comes up and takes Davie and me by the arm. "Well," he says, "shall we call on Loretta?" Davie says, "Sure, Bolton. Sure."

Loretta is sitting up with *True Romances* which she lays aside just long enough to make us a perfunctory tea and take the magazine up with her to bed. Bolton settles into his favourite chair, asks Davie to build up the fire, and does most of the talking. Johnny, who is a little drunk, listens with a cynical grin which Bolton affects not to notice. Davie is sitting tensely on the edge of his chair, dead sober and miserably dropping hints about how late it is. Johnny smiling slightly, says, "No, Davie. Still early, still early."

We stay up until two in the morning listening to Bolton's

148

stories of his early days in Dinlock. Depression stories, lock-out stories, without a crust of bread in the house. When he was awarded a scholarship he had to refuse it in order to go down into the pit. Several times, he insists that he feels no resentment against those with a higher education, such as myself.

As the fire dies down, and the drink settles in him, Bolton is moved to affirm that the British soldier is the best fighting man in the world, and that the Yorkshire-Lancashireman is the best of the best. When he speaks of the Empire it is with rotund pride. Davie, after a long silence, says, "Tha' know what tha' are, Bolton. A monarchist Stalinist." Bolton nods sleepily. "Aye, but Ah'll never leave the workin' class. Never." Johnny sits back comfortably and laughs outright. Bolton eyes him gloomily, then sits up and says briskly to me, "Ah'll meet tha' at the bottom of Theresa Road six sharp," collects his coat and stalks out of the house.

Davie carefully shuts the door and we all sit around the table, sipping ale. Davie doesn't say anything. It is up to young Johnny to break the silence. He says to me, "He was lyin', tha' know that, don't tha', lad? Lyin' in his teeth. Ought to be a movie actor, our Bolton. All those stories about the Depression. They happened to other men but not him. He went down in pit when he was 13, stayed for four years, then he emigrated to Australia and stayed there until he joined up the Navy. He's only been back in Dinlock since end of war." Davie rests his head in his hands and refuses to intervene.

Johnny shakes his head. "He was lyin'. Ah know Davie doesn't lahk me to say a thing lahk that about Bolton. Soom day ask Davie to show tha' the picture he made of Bolton. Smashin'. Ah don't lahk to say a thing lahk that. Bolton was lahk a father to me when Ah first went down. But why does he have to lie lahk that? Do tha' know the answer to that one?"

Both Davie and I remain silent. Davie is rubbing his

149

temples contemplatively. Johnny looks at both of us and for the first time I see him uneasy. Quickly he lifts his bottle, drains it and stands up to say good night. "Good naht, Davie," he says. Davie lifts his head tiredly and says good night. Johnny runs his hands through his hair. "Davie," he says, "tha' know . . . Ah just couldn't let thy friend leave thinkin' Bolton was tellin' the truth." Davie nods and lays his head on his arm. Johnny smiles tentatively at me, tips his hand and is gone.

Davie's voice is distant, as half-lying across the table, he murmurs abstractedly, "The men were trying to draw tha' tonaht." He says he doesn't know why. His mind is elsewhere. When I start making up my bed on the couch, he stands up and goes to stare at himself in the mirror.

Slowly and thoughtfully, as if to himself in the mirror, and dropping his Yorkshire accent, he says quietly. "There are no two ways about it, if I return down to pit I'm finished. I'll not paint any more. I'll never get out. I'll be with my friends who love me for coming back to them. But if I go back—I'm finished for good and all." Then without another word, looking very tired, he leaves the room. I can hear him trudge up to the bedroom. A couple of minutes later he is back again, slumped against the door-frame. He advances and takes me by the shoulder. "Thanks for stayin' with me tonaht," he says. Then he goes off to bed. I snap off the light and arrange myself on the couch and chairs. Once again the house is quiet. Not still. Quiet.

Monday morning. The clock says 5.30. Nobody is up yet. I dress quietly and quickly and slip out of the house.

It is the first clear, cloudless morning I have seen in Dinlock. The sun is low and brilliant. I walk around the village in the early morning, alone. On Theresa Road I pass throngs of men going to the pit, carrying bundles and lunch pails.

150

I nod to several I know. Nobody speaks in the morning. Just individuals and small groups moving off towards the colliery, their faces set like stone. There are no women in the street, and none of the wives come to the door with their husbands. I pass Allan and he gives me a short nod; Carl Fish gives the thumbs-up sign. They are like men full of fear long ago forgotten moving into battle. They are only faintly recognisable as the men I drank with last night.

Bolton is waiting for me at the top of Theresa Road. He has a look of surprise. He glances over my borrowed old clothes—Davie's pit trousers and shirt and torn black jacket and quietly says, "Aye, lad. For a second, tha' looked lahk *him*, Davie. Soomtahms we 'ud meet on this street corner and go to shift together." Just for this passing, unguarded moment he lets himself be seen, an ageing and vulnerable man. But then, curtly, he swings into the throng moving up colliery hill, Bolton the Fixer once again.

"Bolton." "Morning, Pat." "Bolton." "Morning George." "How tha' go, Bolton." "John." In low voices. A strange swarm of wildly chirruping birds sweeps overhead and the men, for a moment, turn their faces to the sky, then plod onward up the narrow cobbled road. The thin stream of men is now a throng, its pace imperceptibly slower. I notice that I am doing, without meaning to, what most of the other men do: my eyes are on the ground. Although it is a bright, clear day, and the approach to the colliery affords a chance for an unexampled view, I do not care to look at it. Nor do many of the others. Near me, two miners, in old torn trousers and shirts and jackets, keep their eyes on the ground while mumbling to each other. Nobody looks up at the several cows in the field just outside the colliery. As we climb the short slope to the gates it is only when we are almost there, because of a vagary of the wind, that we hear the full assortment of colliery noises. We seem to be drawn on an invisible escalator of the chug-chug of escaping steam towards the big black buildings beyond the gate. My legs feel stiff, and

151

my stomach is tight. I am nervous. Nobody I have known has spoken to me. Men I drank with eight hours before stare stonily at me.

A river of men pours through the gates. Bolton pulls me out of the stream and we walk up the steps of the red-brick headquarters building. It is very busy in the pit manager's office. The manager himself, whom I have never met, is in Barnsley attending a regional conference. His secretary, an unctuous and cow-like young man with a Presley haircut, bids us wait in the inner office. Bolton places himself on a chair, I take one opposite, and we do not talk to each other. He will not forgive himself for revealing that he had, at the top of Theresa Road, mistaken me for Davie. Nor will he forgive me.

While we're waiting, a couple of miners show up on the corridor side of the window and ask the manager's secretary to delete their names from a voluntary welfare fund devoted to the old people. Bolton doesn't even look at them. He lights a cigarette and holds it between his legs, seemingly asleep, his veined, battered face a study in repose. I know that expression. He is listening to every word.

On a nearby desk, the phone rings. It's Tooley, already down in one of the shafts, to say that MacLane, an overman, will be waiting for us at the air locks in fifteen minutes.

I follow Bolton out of the office and across the colliery yard to the wash-up building. Bolton's attitude towards me in front of the men in the supply room is one of formality and badly disguised irritation. When the supply clerk says that he doesn't have pit boots my size immediately available, but could do in a few minutes, Bolton tells him to fit me out with the next best size, which turns out to be nines, a size too small.

The supply clerk and Bolton smile as they watch me squeeze into the boots. When I stand up in them, I say that I'd just as soon wait around for some larger boots, but Bolton says I've already kept MacLane waiting too long. As I go out of the door the supply clerk winks at Bolton.

In the small hollow of concrete known as the lamp room I am handed my metal tag and lamp which I drape around my neck the way I see Bolton do. The administrative workers in both the wash-up and lamp rooms are a garrulous and chipper lot, but when Bolton speaks to them it is in brief, noncommital grunts.

After Bolton briefly explains the safety regulations to me in the lamp building, we make for the pit-head. Most of the men on the shift are already down. As I hurry past a string of coal cars braked under the bright sun, the lamp of my battery slams rhythmically against my hip and I have to keep one hand on my helmet to keep it from falling off. We cross the railroad tracks, and Bolton breaks the silence. Again, he asks me where I want to go, to Brierly seam which is mechanised, or Sleythorpe where it's still done the old, hand-getting way.

I thought we settled that last night, I tell him.

Just before he pulls open the large wooden door to the air chamber Bolton turns a slow, hard gaze on me. If I expected approval from him I was mistaken. He is smiling contemptuously, throwing down some sort of gauntlet.

So I'm on my own? I say.

You wouldn't want it any other way, Bolton says, swinging open the air-lock doors.

My ears crackle in the wood-slatted pressure chamber, and my stomach grows tighter. This is the sensation I had when I went up in my first airplane. For a wild instant I think of several excuses to get out of there and walk back down to Dinlock; suddenly I want a little time to think, to prepare myself.

Too late. Bolton pulls open the inner door, and we are blown out by a whoosh of cold air. At the lift cage hanging motionless at the top of the shaft we are met by the overman appointed to conduct me around. He is a plump little Yorkshireman with a virile black moustache and a firm,

153

unexcited way. He does not speak more than he has to, but he is friendly. His name is MacLane. It's quite formal when he and Bolton say hello to each other. They were once coal-getters in the same pit, many years ago.

Though it is not good politics for them to admit it, Bolton and MacLane obviously do not dislike each other. Later, in East Clu', I am to hear many conflicting opinions on Mac-Lane. Davie says, "MacLane, he's a real gentleman." Tommy Hunter says, "High and mahty ways, he has." Ray Sweet says, "He lahks to poot himself above the men. Talks different." In discussing MacLane, the men always emphasise his once having been a face worker and then having gone to a technical college on scholarship, after which he returned to Dinlock speaking and living 'differently'. The men unanimously, if not always explicitly, condemn MacLane for living in a more expensive house apart and for softening his mode of speech. On the other hand, there seems to be general recognition that he is fair in his dealings with them. If MacLane is aware of these attitudes towards him, I do not see him give any outward sign. Down in the pit he is completely in authority and always distant.

While we're standing in the echoing wind-whipped white-washed room which houses the top of the lift shaft, Bolton explains that I want to see the entire operation in Sleythorpe 78, with special attention to the face workers. MacLane narrows his eyes but does not otherwise alter expression. "Everything, Bolton? That's a big order for someone who hasn't been down to mines before." Bolton turns to me. "Mr. MacLane thinks that perhaps tha' maht not wish to spend the entire day down in pit. We do not want to wear tha' down."

So that's the way he wants it. I tell MacLane I will see everything and spend the entire day doing it; wherever he goes I want to be taken. MacLane shifts an uneasy glance at Bolton, who is all innocence. The cage comes up with a rush of air and a bump. We get in.

The cage sways and rattles in its moorings when the

154

operator slams the gate shut. Instinctively, I grab the side for support. Bolton grins broadly. I let go and stand straight, vowing to do nothing which I have not seen MacLane and Bolton do first. I stuff my shirt into my trousers and hope my London-bought belt won't snap under the weight of the lamp battery clipped to it. Suddenly we are plunging down at a dizzying, terrifying pace, into sheer, impossible blackness. Without my willing it my head jerks up, my eyes implore for the last sign of daylight. We appear to be dropping at rate too fast to let us stop short of disaster. Ssst. Ssst. Dropping down, down and down, past seams whose lights blink at us several seconds after the cage has plunged past. Nobody in the cage speaks. I yawn to ease the pressure on my eardrums. I am stricken speechless. Then the cage slows and bounces to a stop as precipitately as it was lowered. The folding metal gate is pushed back. I walk into the pit.

The first thing is the smell. Warm, oppressive, like a rank swamp into which cooking gas has seeped. We are standing in an enormous vault-like place, the walls curved and white-washed, bricked in. A small group of technicians and maintenance men squatting on a stone stage at a large black dynamo watch us. It's hot. I remove my jacket and carry it over my arm.

A well-lit, whitewashed tunnel leads down from the bottom of the cage head and we start walking along it. My senses are quite disarranged; I am dizzy at my stomach and in my head. Both MacLane and Bolton are looking at me. I ask how far down we are. MacLane says about 1800 feet. The figure means nothing to me. I come from southern California where the jet fighters habitually romp at 50,000, the present fiscal budget of the US Government is something in billions, and how many were killed on the Eastern Front in the last war? Only 1800 feet?

I tail after MacLane and Bolton down the darkening, deepening tunnel, and I discover that, with the different levels of oxygen down here, I can keep up steadily only by keeping up behind.

We pass a large ventilator blowing out used air and the stench is powerful and putrid. Past the ventilator, I take a few breaths of air which only seconds before I had found heavy and offensive, and already it smells sweet and light to me.

This tunnel, well brightened, is twice as tall as me. I relax and begin to enjoy myself, observing, making mental notes. This isn't half so bad as I expected. It is, except for the artificial air which I cannot seem to get used to, fairly easy going, and I find myself hoping it will all be like this.

At a junction of tunnels Bolton tells MacLane he wants to turn off to show me something. In the next tunnel tracks are laid and the whitewashed bricks and wooden beams bolted into the walls and ceilings are constructed with extreme precision. It is all brilliantly lighted. Bolton says, "Ah built this. Raht after the war. Craftsman's work." He nods again, proudly. "Bluidy damn' good work it is, too," belligerently.

We turn back into the main feed tunnel and now we are picking our way along narrow-gauge tracks. There is a sharp decline and we are among several miners carrying tools. They are waiting to get into the paddy train, a string of small man-cars. Bolton, MacLane and I take a seat in one, facing the whitewashed wall. The operator, in the front car, rises and leans over to touch with a spatulate metal device the double strand of electrical wire which runs along the tunnel wall. A ring of bells, and the string of tiny coaches sets off down hill.

Almost immediately the whitewash fades and is replaced by a greyish cement finish, and then bare rock, and we leave the lights behind and rattle into darkness. Along with the other men, I flick on the lamp hanging around my neck and adjust its beam. We seem to be bumping along each other's

156

beams as we sweep into warm, hot, humid gritty air. The man sitting on the other side of the board partition says to me, "A miner's lahf's an easy one if he can keep ridin' these contraptions, eh lad?" I turn about and peer into the rushing void. I know the man but I just can't think of his name. It's something that happens down here. I cannot remember their names. The string of cars slows down, and he and two other miners jump off into the darkness. They all carry picks, and one of them drags a burlap bag behind him.

We ride on for a long time. Then the paddy train slows up, the man in front leans out to touch the wires, the bells go off again, we stop. I get out with MacLane and Bolton. We pass miners totally unrecognisable, their faces black with coal dust. The tunnel becomes shallower. Walking and talking becomes more of an effort; it's not easy any more. We stop at the low-ceilinged intersection of several tunnels. Our voices do not echo; they carry but do not resound, like pebbles dropped into warm porridge, in and quickly covered over.

"Sleythorpe, Bolton?" asks MacLane.

"Sleythorpe," says Bolton.

I dive into one of the tunnel roadways, after them, totally lost, bereft of compass points. This shaft too goes down, ever down, and is pitch dark. Miners coming up, picks on their shoulders, are illuminated by our torches and then disappear, mysterious black slow-moving pieces of sludge. Breathing comes harder.

Suddenly we are in an even lower tunnelway, dimly lit by far-spaced electric bulbs in small wire cages. The walls on both sides consist of four to five feet of stone 'packing' built on each side of the road after the coal was removed. To walk is to walk stooped. I follow the sound of footsteps. After a hundred yards I find myself looking for the opening where I can straighten up again; instead, the tunnel narrows. This is the main highway for workers to get to the Sleythorpe seam, and it is necessary for us to walk doubled over completely. Sweat is pouring from me. I try to watch how

MacLane and Bolton do it but can detect no discernible style. It seems to me they are racing ahead, stepping skillfully and surely between the wooden ties of the narrow-gauge tracks which constantly trip me up, and every time I stumble my head jerks up and slams my skull against the roof, sending my helmet either flying or jamming it painfully down over my ears. To avoid the tracks I adopt a kind of crouching, rolling gait, wasteful motion, but it helps me keep up.

Doubled over in the hot darkness, sweating, barely able to see my hand in front of my face, my ears humming with the depth (1800 feet plus what? I keep asking myself) and the ventilators and dynamo thrum, I stumble on. It seems hours since we left the luxury of the paddy train. My back is killing me, my legs are beginning to tremble, I have skinned my arms and face, and MacLane says, over his shoulder, "As you can see, this is the easiest part. We're just taking the way the ordinary miner does to get to his face. Later on, you'll see some of the work."

Sections of hard grey rock, men's faces, flashing bulbs, damp blackened trousers contribute to sense reception, but nothing mixes. The single point of reference I have is the completely assured manner of my conductors, MacLane and Bolton, who, though hunched over double as I am, maintain a steady walking pace while MacLane briefs me. I grunt unintelligently from time to time and wonder how it was for them when they first went down to the mines, Bolton at 13, MacLane at 14, and how long it took for this to become their way of life.

For ten minutes, quarter of an hour, twenty minutes we walk along in this way while the air becomes closer, hotter, darker. The men we pass no longer wear their outer shirts but are down, some of them, to shorts and under-vests. I happen upon my first landmark: the smiling and brawny giant, Frank, no longer in his coloured nylon shirt sent him by a cousin in Philadelphia, but in grime-encrusted canvas shorts, bare chest and knee pads. Frank sees to it that

158

MacLane and Bolton can't see him, and he mock-presents arms with his pick.

Now we're coming into knee-pad territory. Crack! Off spins my helmet. Bolton cannot resist turning and grinning full into my face. On and on we go. Even MacLane has to turn back and smile. I have discovered that the most efficient way, for me, to do the roadway is a sort of duck-squat, harder on the legs but easier on the back. I remember something Davie once said to me: "A face worker can spend his whole life down in pit without once straightening up to his full height." I also remember he said that at Beckley pit he had to walk one mile along planks on his hands and knees, which is virtually what we're doing now, just to get to his place of work. "But Dinlock pit," he promised, "is better."

Now, as we get down deeper and deeper, towards what must be (I am thinking) some sort of molten core, it becomes intermittently possible, in short patches, to walk upright, only to be forced to stoop down again for another hundred or two hundred yards. Bolton drops back and says, "Was a tahm, not too far back, when the men had to walk all the way from cage head. No paddy cars." Then he rejoins MacLane with whom he seems to be having some sort of reunion. They point out various things to each other. It is all I can do to see I don't fall on my face. My legs stop; I can't go any further. Something has grabbed them. I start; I tug frantically, not wanting to know what has overtaken me and not surprised, only wanting to escape its clutches. "Hello, lad! Heard tha' were coomin' down today!" It is fat Eddie Bullen, his paunch hanging pendulously over his shorts made of old trousers scissored down. He is guarding a small dynamo. Eddie isn't a face worker and so it is easy to recognise him. "Ah told tha' Ah had an easy job," he says. Right here the air is like a thick gas whistling past us in gusts. I say hello to Eddie, and we give each other the thumbs-up sign.

159

And stumble on, keeping my eyes strained to the floor of the roadway, one hand latched around the bulb-housing of the lamp, the thumb of the other hand hitched securely to my belt to ease the weight of the battery on it. My torch picks out the ties, the rails, the sudden holes and bumps in the rock floor. I curse having refused Bolton's offer of a rope belt on the surface. The surface. It does not exist. It never did. I feel grim and tired, my mind clicking into a dreary, monotonous but not unrestful bitterness, what I taught myself to do after the first five miles of an infantry speed march. Oblivious.

Crashing continually against the protruding ledges and rock kinks, I feel nothing. Dizzyness comes and goes; I force it away with deep breaths. My feet are on fire, clawed and crushed. Size nine on size ten feet. I curse Bolton's canny maliciousness; there is murder in my heart; I curse my own vanity for allowing myself to play the game Bolton's way, Dinlock's way. I am furious, wholeheartedly delivering myself into a fury that I should be here, shambling so clumsily about in these fetid dungeons of coal, instead of having a coffee in Torino's in London. That any human being should have to make his living wage down in this well-wired, blackly populous hell. It is plain bloody ridiculous. I jerk up my head. Something was said. That was me. "It's plain ridiculous." Did MacLane and Bolton hear me? Where are they anyway? I lift the beam of my torch and play it down the thick-smelling blackish grey roadway.

I have fallen too far back. There is nobody in the tunnel, it is deserted. Hunched over, I run forward to what must be a turning. But no, it keeps going on, smaller and shallower, my feet kicking up small fluorescent fluffs of dry coal dust flat yellow in the cloud of my lamp. The car tracks end. Now it is just dust and rock and coal on all sides. I see and hear nothing. I kneel down and my eyes follow the pencil of light. No. Nobody here. Slowly, careful not to let certain thoughts intrude, I kneel around and flash the beam back of me. Nobody there either. I am alone. I drop down on my haunches. I swish my hand on the carpet of coal dust. All of a sudden, I do not dislike being down here by myself.

After a few moments I hear some noises, and I pick myself up and make my way back. At the junction MacLane is patiently waiting. "It's not always a good idea to go off on your own, sir," he says politely. I apologise. We go on.

The tunnelled roadway grows progressively more shallow and cramped. The going is tougher because squarely down the middle, raised up to about the level of our bent heads, on a series of metal struts, is a moving conveyor belt, V-shaped, carrying pieces of coal. The conveyor moves with a clackle and a hiss, and the space we move through is only just wide enough for a man with narrow shoulders. The conveyor stops. Another seated fat man in underwear says to MacLane that it has been stopping and starting since the beginning of the shift. MacLane reaches into a cleft in the rock and pulls out a field telephone, winds it up and speaks to someone, asking what the trouble is. He nods a few times and replaces the phone. He is concerned but still has time for his guest, pointing out in the same cleft a small locked metal case. He opens it to show me syringes of morphine. "A great help, that," he says. Are there many accidents requiring morphine? "Enough," he says. I remember that on the surface I have often heard the men talk about rock slides in this seam. Later, Davie tells me that MacLane himself, many years ago, was caught in one slide accident which put him in the hospital for six months and left him with a permanently crooked leg.

The conveyor belt starts moving again and so do we. From time to time, as we scramble along, MacLane reaches over and takes a piece of coal off the conveyor belt to examine it. Bolton sees this and says firmly, "Damn' good coal that." MacLane nods coolly.

We continue to encounter small gangs of black men, black all over them, coal dust on every inch of them including the eye-lids, making the whites of their eyes seem protruding and disembodied. We pass the mouths of other roadways,

161

and I can see tiny points of moving light at the far ends of them. "Face men," says Bolton.

"Here's Sleythorpe," says MacLane quietly.

We turn off into one of the tunnel roadways. For several moments we grope along without seeing anything. MacLane explains that this is a short-cut. Soon we can stand up straight and then, marvellously, we're in a shaft without conveyor belts and with space for our bodies on both sides. The lighting grows better, and we follow the ubiquitous tracks until we come to some heavy wooden doors at which a youth is waiting beside a string of grey-green coal cars. We pull the door open to a rush of cool wind and let it slam hollowly behind us and then go through another set of door locks. The wind dies down and the heat settles back in. Drawn by the sound of machinery, we move along the roadway, well-lighted and permanently timbered. A gang of workers with their picks and shovels brushes past, their eyes darting with curious brightness on us. I think I see Carl Fish and Peter Nolan. But I cannot be sure. I look back. One of the men, the new Home Coal Chairman Carl Fish or the one I think is, is looking back too. Our eyes meet. His eyes are hard and cold and unfriendly. Then he is swallowed up in the darkness of the roadway.

A run of tubs clatters by on the sloping tracks. MacLane and Bolton give the cars plenty of breathing space, not nimbly but getting out of the way deliberately and with time to spare. They are men supremely conscious of what causes accidents in the mine, and neither has time for jokers or show-offs such as they claim, with real bitterness, some of the younger miners are. Repeatedly, they warn me to stay out of the way of the coal tubs, exposed wires and such. I think of the statistics: a man killed for every day in the week, a man seriously injured for every hour in the day, and not once have

162

I heard a Dinlock wife openly express worry that her man one day might either not return, or come back, like so many men now on haulage and surface work, disabled.

Frequently MacLane disappears down one of the headings of the main roadway, and once I go with him, and find him testing, constantly testing for gas. Wherever he goes he takes his gas lamp with him.

Somewhere behind us, a muffled roar. "Blowin' a shot down," says Bolton. The echo dies away. I notice something. Bolton's attitude to the men. Down here, there is a dignified distance between them. There is some of this on the surface, but with an important difference. In East Clu', for example, it is the men who pay Bolton a certain deference. But down in pit, since he is not actually working at the face any longer, it is Bolton who—by retaining the distance—defers to them. Down here, he is careful not to speak unless spoken to, and he is careful not to get in the way of the workers. Harold Bolton, the reigning governor of Dinlock. A methodical skilful, wary governor.

A junction of conveyor belts rumbles along at right-angles to each other in a hacked-out hollow. Up above us, complicated machinery whirrs and jerks; though we have moved into a pocket of heightened activity all around us, it is blacker, darker, hotter than ever. But at least we can stand straight up again. Not for long. I blink. For a moment we stand in the centre of a dim cloud of coal dust, enveloped in it, its inner skin flashing puffs illuminated by our lamps, the outer layer surely billowing out to some kind of thermonuclear infinity. And then MacLane and Bolton are out of the envelope and into infinity. They are gone. I flash my lamp where they were. They must be crazy. Like Chester Conklin in Modern Times, they have dived into what seems the beating, clashing heart of the machinery and are entwined in its gears. A man stands nearby operating levers; he stares at me. I, too, crawl in into a black nothing full of ominous crunching noises and hope it doesn't squeeze me to death or that I drop into a

163

bottomless pit. Suddenly I am being tigerishly clawed by a rapidly revolving beast, its fangs ripping into my shirt, its scaly body heaving under me and then pushing me off into the dirt. I plunge forward blindly and dive on to another congeries of conveyor belts and this time roll quickly over it, and sweating and trembling, crouch in the shadowy darkness with Bolton and MacLane. "We're approaching coal face," says MacLane.

"Mr. MacLane has been kahnd enoof to show us a few short cuts," says Bolton with a straight face.

In the opening to a new heading lights bob and weave far ahead and I hear the faint chip of picks against stone. All around us bare coal gleams in the flicker of our torches, shining black coal in which are embedded patches of dull, colourless shale. The air is suffocatingly fetid; it is like breathing in an active, obsolete furnace; covertly, I pinch myself to keep from passing out. Bolton is sweating a lot too; MacLane hardly at all.

Bolton, breathing hard, points and says, "The lads are in there. Shall we go in to join them?"

In we go, clambering over rough rock and coal juts, duck squatting forward towards the tiny pin-points of light against a muffled dullness of bad hot air. I realise we are in a face. It is half my height, about ten feet wide across. And all pure black gleaming coal. Slim riveted metal supports slip past our beams, and thick wooden ones. Every foot of this passage hewn out of coal is shored up with wood or metal or mounds of stone. The sound of the picks comes louder, sharper.

We are amongst them.

I don't feel like fainting any more. My flesh crawls. Once, a long time ago, even before I got to high school, I was shown a history of Welsh miners by my father. The centre-piece of the book was a photograph, printed lengthwise. It was an early flash-lamp plate and it had been taken down in some mine. I never forgot that photograph. The miners, posing formally in three tiers, looked like starving paleolithic hunters caught in a coal jungle; they wore nothing but breech-clouts and crude pit helmets. I remember many of the miners in the photograph were smiling, and two or three had even assumed grandiose poses leaning on their pick-axes.

The several men nearest me, selected by our torches, are hacking away at the coal face, the wall of which seems to extend indefinitely in a sombre perspective composed of small teams of men, spaced several yards apart, working in a murky forest of steel and timber supports. This is the coal face, the work room. At no point is it higher than four feet nor wider than twelve. Life here conducts itself on the horizontal. The men move about on knee-pads with the agility of war amputees. Their bodies are smeared with a mixture of sweat and coal dust, their faces are flat black except for the startling, almost accusatory whites of their eyes which move about like captured moths in the dimness, and the unexpected sensuality of the redness of their lips and rims of their eyes. Every single one of them is naked except for a wide leather belt strapped across his waist from which hangs the box-like battery of his lamp and a strip of cloth across his private parts. Some wear jockey shorts. Jockey shorts, pit helmet and pit boots, and knee pads.

The only way to work in this confined space is on the knees, and they are all on their knees. In teams of two or three they act in short, concentrated movements, one man with a pick, his mate shovelling away the loose coal into piles or on to the small conveyor belt which rolls on castors along the floor of the face. Most of this normal long-wall coal-getting, with men in a long line working at the previously cut and blasted coal. The picks are used to back down stubborn coal clinging to the 'cut' and the roof, but it is the shovel which is primarily used here; most of the men are shovelling very monotonously. In some of the other headings I heard pneumatic picks being used, but none here.

Squatting, we watch the men at their work. MacLane says a few helloes, Bolton gives a diffident nod or two. Mostly these hand-getting colliers are young and in good shape; they look like dirty heroes. I watch the operation, as specifically as the light allows. Sometimes on their knees, sometimes haunching, these men have developed a technique of slamming away with picks at the long wall of coal in short, sharp bursts which explode deeply into the face and when wrenched away brings coal, coal ripped and tumbling and shooting out of the wall. This is not coal that crumbles easily; it is compressed vegetation that must be jarred loose by the sheer explosive energy of the pick.

All sounds are drowned by the monotonous, regular, almost metronomic crash and shove of the pick and shovel. On my left the hand-getters advance the wall of coal, four feet six inches a shift; on my right the packers slash away at the roof and build their buttresses of stone. Just in front of me a team of back-rippers are working in the roadway, dropping stone and packing it, driving another roadway into the face as it advances. Bolton tells me it's unorthodox to have all these operations going on at the same time, and that it only happens when ripping or packing work has been left undone by the previous shift.

MacLane and Bolton and I sit on the coal. When MacLane addresses the men it is in a different tone than he used with the surface and maintenance men. "How's it doin', lads," he says quietly. Several of the men knock off work for a moment, wiping their faces and foreheads with their forearms and reaching for the canteens of water which hang from nails driven into the timber joists. "Here tha' go, lad," says a gangly, thin miner who isn't even wearing his breech clout and is breathing heavily.

166

I drink some warm, brackish-tasting water from his Army-type canteen and remember Davie's warning not to allow my lamp to shine directly into a man's eyes because it will infuriate him. I direct the beam of my light to the floor and thank the thin miner for the water. Still breathing hard, he winks one wide thin eye. Good Christ, it's Walter! Walter, Sally's husband, Davie's friend. He looks criminally frail down here, the ribs stick out from his flesh almost surgically, but still he has his hand on the pick.

I say, What are you doing down here, Walter? The other miners, squatting around us in a temporary work break, crack the congealed coal dust on their faces with grins. "Oh," says Walter, "joost havin' a cuppa char." We all laugh.

"What's wrong, lad," Walter says, "did tha' believe Ah spend all my tahm winnin' away poor workin' men's wages at snooker?" "He wins," says the miner next to him, sceptically, a broad fleshy man with a shovel. I peer into the darkness. Who's that? I ask. "Lock Eastman," he says. "Hello, Lock." "Hello, lad." "How's it comin', lads?" says MacLane, the overman. "It's coomin'," replies one of the other miners. I dare not ask who it is for fear of discovering he is someone I know well. They do not understand why I cannot recognise them. Walter looks like an undernourished 11-year-old boy in an illustration out of Dickens.

MacLane starts to crawl ahead. Bolton, who has been silent, says sharply for me to come along. I tell him I will be along in a minute. Bolton tells me to suit myself in a way that warns I should not get in the way of the men shifting their yardage. Then I crawl right up to the wall face and examine the coal, using my lamp.

Hard, shiny, jagged stuff. I ask Walter for the loan of his pick. Lock laughs, "Will tha' be doin' a shift now, lad?" I smile and grab the pick and let go. It strikes the face squarely and dislodges practically no coal. I swing again, much harder. A little more coal this time. Walter and the other naked miners crouch in the coal dust and silently

167

watch me. I space my hands wider apart on the pick handle lean back and let go with all my might. That does it. The iron point of the pick sinks in deep; when I wrench it loose the coal comes with it. I hand the pick back to Walter. "Well, lad, what do tha' think?" asks Lock. I tell them that I think it is a hard job at the face They look at each other as though what I am saying is only good sense. Then they move back into positions for work.

The thing that impresses me, again and again, down here at the face, is the sinewy humour of these men. They are neither grim nor bitter nor angry. The point is, a visitor from the surface does feel all these things. These men are, however, tired; bone tired. You can see it in the way they start to work again, with pick and shovel; each man has his own little personal trick of conserving strength. Lock does it by letting a pile of loose coal accumulate and then shovelling it away in spaced bursts. Walter, by going into the coal deep, regularly and with strict rhythm. The back-ripper nearest me by humming, or rather droning an unmelodious and unearthly tune as he piles rock.

I thank the men formally for the use of their heading and the pick, and they say, Any time.

Then I scramble forward—and run head on into an overhanging wall of stone which almost tears my face off. I roll back and then try it again, squeezing ahead through a slit not much larger than I am. On the reverse slope a lamp shines like moonlight through the mist of dust, and I crawl towards it. I shine my lamp. There, in a crypt of coal not big enough for one man to stand erect but still small enough for a two-man team to work it, a naked miner is lying on his side swinging a pick. There cannot be two feet of height there: he lies absolutely supine and still uses the pick in short, slow efforts, lying there in muck and dirt and heat, with his mate, a few feet further back, near me, able to kneel and scoop away the coal. " 'Ave a visitor, Barney," says the shovel man. But the space is too confined for the man in the recess to turn his

168

head. He lies still and grunts, "G'mornin', whoever in hell tha' are."

"Tha' have to excuse him," says the shovel man whose raw-muscled coal-caked body is adorned (as are so many of the others) with a blooming beer belly, " 'e ain't 'is proper self till half past eleven." The man lying down laughs. I ask them how long they work like that. The man with the shovel says, "Full shift." But he warns me not to worry because they always take their own rest periods. I back down from the slit and return to what I now regard as a veritable spacious arbor, the heading which is four feet high. I make for the fuzzy lights up ahead, moving past a couple of loin-clothed teams chipping away at the side walls. The photograph in the book my father showed me was taken in the 1880's.

By now I've lost all sense of time. Have I been down an hour or half a day? How long did it take to get to the face? My guess is an hour. Does it take all the others that long?

Another thing I notice is that the miners who do not know me topside are the ones who are the friendliest down here, friendly in a straight and gentle way, very careful to see that their guest does not come to harm. It is they, and not Bolton, nor even MacLane, who warn me about the pot holes and sharp edges. I cannot get Carl Fish's look out of my mind, if Carl it was. This mixture of resentment and unsmiling watchfulness. True, Walter hadn't been like that. But then Walter is a special case in the village; something of an outcast himself. By unanimous agreement he is not fitted for face work but it is the only thing he has to hang on to, considering all his other failures of prestige. But even in this his instinct may be askew. Contrary to what Walter may believe, his mates may not respect him for persisting at a job which is clearly beyond his physical limit. But who is to gainsay him? Staying at the face at least gives him the right, undisputed by even those who think him a foolish little man, to blend his voice with the élite chorus of colliers in Dinlock. Poor bastard.

I come upon a couple of men sitting in the tiny roadway taking a breather. They grin at me with that characteristic wink and quick nod of the head with which the miners greet each other to save words and breath. One of them hands me his water flask. We just sit there, without saying anything, breathing heavily. And then I am up and away, duck walking, until I hear the sound of pick-axes and the spasmodic clatter of a conveyor belt. I slip down a shallow incline and find MacLane and Bolton waiting for me. MacLane is consulting with one of the miners about a recurrent failure in the conveyor system this morning. "Seein' owt tha' want to, lad," says Bolton coldly.

We are at the far wall of this heading, a slightly wider but not taller space. Four or five teams are working here, amidst wooden struts, rusty metal supports and one or two shinier pneumatic stilts which Davie has told me so much about. Leading off from this face seems to be a tunnel, through which the conveyor is moving into a special darkness of its own, to join up with other conveyors from other seams.

Here, sitting against the props, I listen to MacLane explain just exactly what is happening. The flattish, unwieldly chunk of rusted metal I am resting my feet on is a cutting machine which is used, on the shift previous, to saw deep slits in the coal face wall the better to enable the colliers to break the yardage off for the conveyors. Bolton listens with increasing impatience, then wanders off to another heading because "Ah want to see how some of the other lads are doin'." Bolton is not a man to be upstaged; and certainly not by an overman.

As MacLane is interpreting the use of the cutting machine, there is a slight sharp rumble. All the men around us stop

170

what they are doing to lower their tools and listen, freezing. MacLane hollers, "What happened?" Swiftly he crawls along the face and squeezes over the hump where I scraped my face. The miner nearest me says, "Rock fall." Some of the men wait, others examine the roof and supports with their eyes. Slowly, a little cautiously, they begin once again to cut at the coal. I wait.

MacLane comes back and is followed by two men. One of them has a black bloody gash on his shoulder, the red blood mixing darkly with the coal dust on his chest and stomach. MacLane says to the uninjured man, a deputy, "Take him out this way." The miner who is hurt holds his shoulder as he crawls after the deputy to the larger tunnel which houses the main conveyor belts. MacLane asks him, "Do you want a stretcher?" and is answered, "Ah'd rather have a mild and bitter." As they pass, the injured man gives me a nod and a wink.

MacLane goes back to make certain the deputy in charge of the site is making out a report and is checking the area for faults. Then he returns to continue explaining the long-wall hand-getting process to me. The men in the heading watch the injured miner disappear around a bend, and then work resumes, quietly, steadily. Because MacLane is an overman, the eight or ten men at this end of the heading are on their best behaviour; not in any way genuflective but not too talkative. However, after the first five minutes the men become accustomed to my presence, and work mounts to its accustomed rhythm and intensity. Bang . . . crack . . . *chick chick chick.* Bang . . . crack . . . *chick chick chick.*

At first, it seems the work of pick-and-shovel at coal face is painfully simple, almost too simple when you consider the many operations backstopping the coal face man which involve highly technical skills. A man, on his knees, hacking away at a face of coal, and another man, bent double, shovelling away the product; that's it. To be a coal face worker all you need is a strong back and the ability, or the

171

insensitivity, to take the profoundly miserable conditions down here. ("But no water, we've no water down here to cope with," says MacLane. "Thank God no water.") But the more I watch the more I see that to be a *competent* collier requires a substantial degree of both intelligence and skill. For one thing, the collier, unlike most industrial workers, actually plans his own work; it is he and he alone who is the ultimate judge of how a particular wall or shelf shall be attacked. At the face he is designer, organiser and executor in a task which must involve all the imperatives of production schedule, personal idiosyncrasies and mood, the ever-changing grain of the face itself and the nuances of safety for himself and his comrades. The need to know how to handle his pick in such a way as to reduce a wall of coal four feet six inches deep by four feet six inches high by eight yards, the structure and consistency of whose mass can change from hour to hour, to a pile of coal rubble, of the required chunk sizes, weighing 17 tons in such a way as not to endanger the safety of himself and his mates nor impede the production total of his or the following shift, having in many cases to allow for the failures of the previous shift to properly prepare the coal face, and doing this on shifts of seven hours or more each day in team combinations which can change from week to week so that he may never be able to plan a sane personal existence, and knowing that this is the way it will be for the duration of his natural working life, this requires a fine and well-paced paying out of sheer brain power unmatched by almost any industrial operation I know. For, in the last resort, the collier at the face knows that he, and he alone, is responsible for his quota. No excuses, in his own or his mates' eyes, justifies less than his quota. He is uniquely responsible.

Not all this is observable at once. It takes the entire day of watching the colliers at work for it to dawn gradually on me. At first, as far as I can tell, the two most requisite skills are the willingness to endure at a consistently high level of

172

physical expenditure, and an inherent sensitivity in the arts of co-operation. Endurance and co-operation. If you don't have these qualities, you are done for, for even before the gaffer finds you out your work-mates will because they will have to carry you, but you never ride for very long the razor-sharp rail of their contempt unless perhaps, like Walter back yonder, you have developed an appetite for it.

In the conditions of terrific output of labour in darkness, coal dust and harrying heat—not to mention the un- conscious despair which assails and constantly threatens to overwhelm the senses because of the sheer fact, which I do not believe any degree of familiarity can completely erase, of the millions of tons of black coal, shale, rock and dirt which separate you from the sunlight and the village under the open sky—the slightest quirk, the smallest impediment to communication between the pick man and his mate can produce an unspoken roar of hatred. For the seven or more hours daily which the collier must spend down in pit, he is united to his mate by devilish bonds of occupational marriage. On the surface I have some opinions about the rights and wrongs of introducing Hungarians into the mines; but down here, if I were a face worker I think my stomach would not feel good about the idea. Yes, I know that the road to pro- gress is paved with improved stomachs. But still.

I have already been warned by MacLane that, for technical reasons, this seam contains headings which do not follow normal work practice. Usually, on a long-wall face, each man has his own stint. A shot is fired, the coal is cleared, props are set. Then another shot, clearing and trimming, move props and so on to the end. It is at each end of the face, called the corner, where you find, in its simplest form, these two- man teams of pick and shovel men.

Here, at this end, in this corner I watch the two nearest

173

black figures as they shift their yardage. Seemingly there is no co-ordination. Figure No. 1 swings his pick. Figure No. 2 shovels the coal away, sometimes more, sometimes less, in what seems like open disregard for the rhythm of his mate. But, after watching them for fifteen minutes, I begin to understand that a most subtle and close co-ordination does in fact exist between these two; not, it is true, if the actual exertions are timed, but if they are seen as a moving tableau over an extended period; then it makes sense. Each man has found for himself that latitude and that discipline which is least abrasive and at the same time most productive. More and more, as I watch the two men carving a shallow cave out of the wall, I am impressed by the tendrils of experience and perception that bind them to each other. And it has, I think, nothing to do with affection or possibly even comradeship. I don't think it has anything to do with questions that can be asked outright. That is why, and not necessarily because of a lack of easy articulation or experience at conceptualising, the miner of Dinlock finds it so difficult to describe his relationship with his mate, and therefore his work, in the pit. The surface workers can, and so can the haulage men and technicians; but the face workers always shrug off the question. Even Davie, usually so self-conscious for himself and the village, takes this relationship for granted and deals with it in terms of its own mystique. It cannot be. It is the emotional reactor of the entire colliery, the 'hot' core.

In the enveloping, misty blackness Figure No. 2, the shovel man, stops work and reaches for his canteen hanging on a wooden prop just over my head. His naked body is caked with a gritty layer of sweat-wet coal dust; he is smeared with it. He nods and winks. He is a big man who knows how to handle his shovel. He wipes his mouth, and says, "Would tha' lahk to take a hand, lad?" I say no, I'd just as soon sit this hand out but my friend Jim Bowman is coming along any minute and I'm sure he'd be glad to. All the men around me burst into laughter, the first and only time I am to hear this kind of animation down in pit. Sir James Bowman, KBE, chairman of the National Coal Board, is a much beloved figure in Dinlock pit.

I crouch among the miners in this dark, dank workshop and learn not to blind myself in the flash of the miners' lamps. All the men down here are powerful, big muscled. Over on my left, one of the colliers is burly and fat whenever he stops working; as soon as he begins using his pick the muscles rise to the surface of his skin and he looks like a black, trapped Hercules. The other man with the shovel, right in front of me, the one who asked me to take a turn, is ready to go back to work. He kneels and smiles at me. It's Glenn.

He knows that it is just now that I recognise him. Hello, Glenn, I say. He gives one of those quick diagonal nods and for an instant the red membrane below the whites of his eye is blacked out in a wink. "Do tha' lahk it to your suitin' down here, lad?" I say, You do the shifting, I like it fine. The other men laugh murmurously. MacLane isn't too comfortable. It is not for a gaffer to stop and pass the time of day with busy face men. He excuses himself by saying that he must look into a break in the conveyor system in another heading.

When MacLane is gone there is no noticeable change in the men. Down here is their province and when gaffer comes along he will bloody well adjust to their ways and not the other way around. I also think they make it something of a point not to be different when he is around. The feeling is too implanted in them, learnt from their own and their father's and their grandfather's experience, that if you give an inch you give a mile. I think that is why Harold Bolton can never become a true Caesar in Dinlock, and why the Dinlocks of England would never support one. Face work has its own self-regulating democracy. Once the machines come in all bets are off. But by then Bolton won't be young. And I'm not sure this makes me unhappy. Bolton is an honest,

175

forceful, clever tribune for the pit men. Years ago he could have opted for position by driving, for example, straight up to Area Board, or even higher and become in fact what he is rarely permitted to be in Dinlock (except when shooting off his mouth over a pint), a hard-knuckled and ruthless dictator. But to have aimed at high office would have meant cutting himself off from 'the lads', and more than anyone in Dinlock it is Bolton—despite the curious distance he puts between himself and the men, and the stone-faced way he keeps his own counsel—who derives his strength and confidence from his connection to the mass of pit workers. And so, somewhere along the line, and I think in his case it was a conscious personal decision, quite possibly taken in a moment of crisis of insight, Bolton elected to remain among them: to achieve recognised and even pre-eminent authority in a small pond, but by doing so automatically limiting his potential for caesarism; for to remain in Dinlock is to involve oneself in the thick, electric web of village intrigue and to be cornered by the almost chloroforming odour of cautiousness lest basic susceptibilities be offended, which is anathema to the ambitions of any real tin-pot Bevin.

And Davie, the son Bolton never had, where is he right now? Is he still sleeping? Or does he sit in his bedroom, thinking on his high stool, staring at the easel?

Glenn peers up the other tunnel, leading off at a right-angle to where we are, to make certain that MacLane is out of hearing range, and then he and a couple of the other miners break off work, which they have been attacking with a kind of brutally regular energy, to come over and crouch with me. They are all smiling. "Lad," says Glenn, "why don't tha' leave a' that. Lunnon, fancy women, naht clubs an' all the rest. It's no good for tha', lad."

"It'll thin out thy bluid," says another of the smiling miners. I invite them all to come down to London and after a couple of nights we'll see whose blood thins out first. Glenn moves in closer. In a soft, confidential voice, he says, "Listen, lad. Don't let 'em shoot tha' a line." I say that as far as I can tell, so far, nobody is. "Okay then," he says, "but if they do tha' must coom back down an' ask us. Raht, lads?" The others nod assent. The two other teams working nearby, listening, look over at us from time to time, approvingly. All of a sudden I am happy. In this damned black hole, below 1800 feet plus of vegetation which someone has temporarily found useful, in a diabolically cramping underworld prison cell whose bars, ceiling and floor are raw coal, in the smudgy blackness whose air is almost impossible to breathe normally, amidst filthy, fatigued men whose humour is the spare, stark and generous humour of the front-line soldier, resting my back against a wooden board from which hang three canteens of warm water, I am happy. It's a disgusting reaction. But, the fact remains.

Glenn's mate lays off the pick for a moment to ask, "Anything about the job tha' want to know?" I tell him I can see some of it myself without asking, and the other parts would take six months of explaining. They all nod sober agreement. Glenn asks what it is I plan on doing, and one of the others asks if it is newspaper stuff or for the BBC? I tell them maybe all of that, but most probably a book. They are very satisfied. They like the idea of a book.

With a nod and a wink to excuse himself, Glenn goes back to the far wall where his mate is ripping into a shelf of coal. Glenn works steadily and efficiently, passing the chunks of coal from the feet of his pick-mate to the rubberised belt which moves ceaselessly and with a great ratcheting thrumming noise down the centre of the roadway of the heading. Sweat runs in globby rivulets down his streaked, blackened body. And I remember, Glenn has a bad reputation in the village as a slacker.

Now everybody is back at work, and this pocket in this heading in this seam resounds to the thud of metallic fracturing explosions of picks sunk into coal, of shovels ramming into piles of loose coal, of five teams of men moving wordlessly in damp semi-darkness, of picks and shovels clanking and plunging. Ten men in pit boots and leather belt and pit helmet and naked to the gods of the interior earth.

There is something about their nakedness. When I first crawled into this seam politeness required that my eyes take no special note of what was, in a stranger's eyes, a jarring sight: the simple nudity of men who, if they had the choice to make, would have their clothes on. Down here, these men reserve a special respect, almost a gentleness toward each other's nakedness. There is no horse-play, no punching around, and I do not think it is only because their energy must be conserved for the job. It is as though, in shucking off his clothes to stand revealed, and therefore in a large sense defenceless, the collier derives from the very nakedness of his coal-smeared flesh a unique self-respect, an unfleshly dignity which is both elemental and deep-driven. The fraternity of the naked worker need not be fierce.

Slouching for a spell against a timber support puts fire to my feet. Size nine boots on a size ten foot. Goddam Bolton, with a little effort he could have found the correct size, the storekeeper said as much. But no, Bolton couldn't be bothered to wait. "Coom on if tha're coomin'" and that's where I should have said I'm not going down without proper boots, that's when I should have stopped playing the Dinlock game. But no. I had to play the man. I can just hear Karen down in London mocking me for being so easily sucked into doing their game (which no stranger can ever win, by definition). And I agree with her. But not quite. I don't know all the things I've set in motion by coming down to pit, but I do know that I'm expected to pay for it. Everything they do

I must do; everywhere they go I must go, and not fall too far behind. It is the price they make me pay for my freedom never to go back down to pit. The size nine boots, perhaps, was gratuitous, a fine little extra touch for nothing, but it is also part of a price which I, too, feel it is proper and fitting I must pay. I don't think I could properly explain it to the people down in London, especially Karen, with her shrewd and ruthless unwillingness to romanticise the working class. There is no conceivable way I could make them understand except by perhaps shouting, angrily, as Davie does, It's not something you can put into words, man, you have to go and see for yourself. But there it is again, you can never remain above the village, to the extent you live in it you must choose between loyalties. An old, complicated and inscrutable game.

Those boots. I lean against the prop and loosen the laces. One of the shovellers, a tall wiry man named Mick, who works almost triply bent over, grins. "Did they fit tha' with the proper boots, lad?" he says. I tell him they're okay. I've gone this far. But, I vow, this is one thing I won't tell Karen when I go back down to London.

MacLane comes up and shines his lamp at me, suggesting it's time to go. He says Bolton is up ahead somewhere. He knows, of course, what's going on; he probably knows more.

Well, boys, I say, I'll see you around.

They all stop working to say goodbye. Mick calls out as I'm leaving, "Coom tha' back any tahm. Tha'll fahnd us in."

Picking my way among the props, I find myself in a dark round tunnel through which the conveyor belt is moving like a running brook of coal. Bolton is waiting. Glenn and the others are left behind. "Enjoy tha'self," Bolton says derisively. MacLane, who would just as soon not have Bolton and me stand around jawing, walks up the tunnel, stopping every so often to inspect a piece of girder, check a lock or inspect a chunk of coal off the conveyor. He stops. We can, he says, walk this tunnel for about half a mile, or we can ride the conveyor, which is against regulations. He looks at Bolton and me. Then he trots along the conveyor and agilely leaps on, balancing himself and riding it erect. Bolton easily rolls on and sits down. I heave aboard. Bolton looks back at me and says, "Scoop out a place for tha'self." So I move the coal around with my hands and sit like a passenger, hunched up. I decide to stand. It takes some balancing but it's not difficult once you remember the coal shifts under your feet. After squatting and bending and kneeling for so long, this is fun. Crash! I'm almost knocked off by an over-hanging girder. Up ahead in the moving darkness Bolton chuckles. "Aye, Ah forgot t' tell tha' about certain things lahk that." You old bastard, I say, I ought to bust you. "What's wrong," and I can almost see that cat-grin of Bolton's, "bein' down in pit frayin' on thy nerves." Oh no, my goat won't be got that way. So I do what I've often seen the men in the clubs do, cover over temper. I tell him not on his nelly, I'm having the time of my life. I can feel nothing below the ankles. Thank good Christ.

We roll past a couple of miners leaning against the rock wall, resting and talking. And then, riding upright on the conveyor, it strikes me, for no particular reason, that not once down in pit, and seldom on surface, have I heard the speech of the Dinlockers laced with phrases culled out of the newspapers or television or the cinema. The mode of con-versation in Dinlock is stylised and not subject to much change from year to year, and is strikingly resistant to the impact of the 'mass media', unlike similar communities in America, and even in the south of England. Tradition, and isolation, is still so strong that even the teenagers, in and out of the pit, rarely attempt to breeze up their language which, for example, my teenage friends in Hammersmith constantly toy and experiment with. I wonder how soon that will change.

As we sail along through the dark tunnel numb feet, a sort

of racketing silence and the sense of forward, smooth movement combine to produce a temporary feeling of—of all things—euphoric timelessness. Just for a moment I think that MacLane, Bolton and I will remain on the belt and conclude our journey on some coal-strewn planet somewhere between Earth and the Moon which has not yet been discovered by Jodrell Bank. "Watch it lively!" calls out MacLane, rolling off, then Bolton, then myself. We duck into another tunnel, through a couple of those huge wooden doors through which the ventilation whistles. It's more spacious now, easier to walk, but the memory of Glenn, and the men at the face, lingers.

Now, far from the face, we are into the sprawling and complex machinery of transporting and processing the raw coal. The work here is still hard, but it is something which does not shear and scrape at the conscience. Here, in this part of the mine, there are stationary lights and cemented surfaces and conversation and also, paradoxically, an atmosphere of human gloominess. Here, the workers seem dour and hang-dog by comparison with the face men.

What mechanisation there is in this part of the mine both MacLane and Bolton are extremely proud of. We pass dynamos and MacLane explains their function and workings; a string of tubs stopped on an uphill slope and Bolton explains, coldly, how the automatic brake is notched. We enter a beehive of activity; it is actually shaped like a beehive. Men, now clothed, assist the tubs coming down from the seams along the rails. The scene is lit with long fluorescent tubes. At the base of the beehive is a shaft cage which operates automatically. The moment the cage gate opens, a tub of coal is bumped in, the gate slams shut, and the cage rises swiftly, tips its tub somewhere on an upper floor, and plummets down for another load.

While MacLane goes off to consult the man who watches the timing on the cage gates, Bolton and I go behind the cage, downslope, and stand on the 'empties' tracks to watch the tubs come off the lift. It is an extraordinary swift, abruptly clattering operation. When the cage comes down, an empty tub presses against the gate, opening it, and then roars down the track towards us and whips around the corner to bang and latch on to a string of motionless empties. Bolton knows I am strange to this operation. He knows I am standing on the track engrossed in watching how the cage mechanism works. He also knows that I do not know an empty will come barrelling through here just as soon as the cage next comes back down to our level.

He is over by the wall. I squat down in the track, like a fool, fifty feet down from the moving cage. Meanwhile, Bolton proudly speaks of the speed of loading and unloading. I am interested and ask questions. The next cage, bearing an empty tub, plummets down, blasting us with a wall of fresher air from the upper levels. For some reason, I think that the gate on the opposite side will open to disgorge the empty, and that in any event the track I'm on is disused. Instead, and I continue to look on as though it had nothing to do with me, the gate on my side zips up, which trips an automatic brake, and an empty steel tub roars down. Bolton, leaning against the wall with his arms folded, calls out lazily, "Better watch it." And I leap out of the way, feeling the breeze on my leg as the tub speeds rattling past me and disappears around the corner. Bolton unfolds his arms and strolls down the track, careful to keep an eye out for himself. "Mining's a dangerous occupation, eh, lad?" he says.

For the next few hours MacLane, with Bolton brooding along, takes me over the entire operation, from start to finish. He is formal, precise, knowledgeable and gracious. At each and every point safety is harped upon. Time and again he says that the easiest thing to do down in pit is get yourself hurt. All along the walls are tacked stretchers and locked strongboxes of morphia. It must be hell to bring an

182

injured man out of a mile of shallow seam. "They'd bring a man out of hell," growls Bolton. In 1949, Bolton was caught in a cave-in in which one man was crushed to death. Except for the surface men, and often including them, I have not seen a single miner in the pit who is without bruises and cuts and scars all over him. I wonder again if Bolton's ear was knocked off in pit or in war.

Wandering amongst the haulage men and itinerant back-rippers, the tub men and prop men, I believe anew that which Davie and Bolton have always insisted on: down in pit there is really no such thing as an easy job. Away from the face, the men, grimy and clothed, work grimly and humourlessly. Occasionally we encounter, around a tunnel bend, or near the cage, a cluster of miners squatting on their haunches, resting or waiting to be taken up, and these never greet us with a word or a smile or a nod or wink. They simply lift up their heads slowly to gaze at us, blankly. These are the only ones who could fairly be compared to animals; these are the ones who are through with their shift; these are the ones too fatigued to be even sullen.

From the tub terminus, a sprawl of trackage and inert strings of empties, past the gangs of silent waiting miners at the bottom of the shaft, on to a loud, splattering chamber. Again, a mechanical pride. Two sets of rails mounted on a huge concrete stage on which are pushed interminable strings of tubs loaded brimfull of coal. High above the tubs, in a caboose screwed to a metal platform, a young man controls the speed of the tubs and the flow of watery spray which gushes from limp, overhanging canvas nozzles. Here to keep down dust, the coal is sprayed, virtually an entire shift's output, by one man, operating levers in a railroad-type control box. This spray room, together with the automatic tub-supplier to the lift cage back there, are the prides of MacLane and Bolton who out-do each other, lovingly, taking turns, to describe how it works. MacLane climbs up a long, greasy metal ladder to the control platform and beckons for us to follow. Bolton glances up the slippery ladder and says he will forego the pleasure; his leg is acting up. I have been watching him, and I believe him; in order to put me through the paces he has put himself through a special pain also. But the ladder in this wash-room he will not try. Revenge at last. I shout at MacLane to wait for me and scamper up. I make it and look back down at Bolton. He is staring up at me. Then he cannot help but grin. One up for the visitors.

It is almost my downfall. Looking triumphantly down at Bolton I take a step forward and it is only empty space under my feet, below me a moving tub of wet coal. I grab on to the side rails and pull myself up. I quickly look down. Fortunately, Bolton's attention is diverted elsewhere. Still one up for the visitors.

After the controls operator explains his operation, MacLane climbs down the ladder, and I start to. Then I notice a greased pole running alongside the ladder, and for the hell of it I lean out and slide down. MacLane frowns in disapproval and I decide to do nothing of the sort for the remainder of the day. Bolton says, "Still feelin' spunky, eh lad?" He knows it was a mistake to say 'still'; now it is out in the open. My legs are like to fall off, my chest feels as if a ton of stone were laying on it, and I've got the king of headaches. A piece of cake, I say to Bolton. He knows it is a bloody lie too.

For the next hour we tunnel in and out of various evil-smelling, dark and low-hanging seams, with not so much as a backward glance from Bolton. Everywhere we go, especially those pockets which are not being worked in by men, MacLane lifts his gas lamp to test. Except when they encounter a piece of machinery, he and Bolton continue through the day to maintain their distance and their circumspection towards each other. Each is careful and self-conscious replying to my questions in the presence of the other, they are like two boxers circling incessantly without landing, or indeed wanting to land, a blow. Bolton, surprisingly, does not needle MacLane, as he does mercilessly the other under-managers like Tooley; nor does he take advantage of the many opportunities to get one in for the union, at least not verbally. Perhaps with a sceptical grunt here, or a low growl there, or by walking off indifferently he may imply dissent with MacLane's narrative, but that's all. But—as the day wears on their relationship enlarges upon itself and turns up a slightly new face. Increasingly, Bolton deepens his Yorkshire accent, and is more aloof, while MacLane, for his part, more and more steers clear of anything which might involve Bolton or the union, to concentrate exclusively on the technical aspect of pit work. This is about as far as either is prepared to go by way of personal criticism or comment. At the end of the day there is no doubt whatever that, however much each may respect the other, Bolton will never forgive MacLane his scholarship, and MacLane will always have to control his contempt for Bolton's glory-hunting.

For another half-hour we ride the conveyor belts through dark and dusty seams.

"Well," says MacLane, "that's it. You've seen the lot." Suddenly we are standing in front of the main lift cage waiting along with a group of haulage men to be taken up. There's something wrong. I feel uneasy, unrelieved, drawn somewhere. I apologise to MacLane for taking up more of his time, but could I please go back to that last heading in 78, on the face? MacLane and Bolton exchange looks. "What for, lad?" says Bolton, "you've already been." I tell them I know but I'd like to go again, just once more. I'll probably not have the chance again. MacLane frowns, and Bolton grumbles openly. Then MacLane says he can't see where it will do any harm. Bolton curtly says he'll take the cage up; he's got work to do.

This time MacLane takes me by a different short cut, a tight-squeeze of a tunnel strewn with twisted girders, where the air is even hotter and fouler than usual. We crawl for fifteen minutes, cross over a conveyor which has stopped and MacLane reaches for a wall telephone. When it is apparent he will be a long time reaming out hides for the constant stop-and-go of the system, I wordlessly ask if I can go ahead. He has already told me that the heading I am looking for is just around the next turn. He nods and begins to speak sharply into the blower, "I've told you twice already if it comes to that don't be afraid to cut into the auxiliary generator——"

I crawl on ahead, alone, using my face as a probe into the moist darkness, listening for the tell-tale clink and scrape of working tools. When it comes it sounds familiar and harsh. I let myself down a crevice and then I am, once again, amidst darkness and shadowy props. I hold on to organise myself, and up ahead there are the tiny pin-points of bobbing light. Here, again, at the face, the black air is choking to the nose and mouth, the heat bites into the throat, there is an inescapable, pressing loginess all about, a smouldering, sour-smelling torpor stinking of millions of years of stagnation.

I crawl past one of two teams and from the way they turn to stare at me I think they are men of a new and different shift from the morning. They stare furiously but not in fury, wondering, I suppose, what in hell I am do-ing down here alone. (There is that *New Yorker* cartoon depicting Pennsylvania miners saying, "Hey, it's Mrs Roosevelt!")

Actually, I don't know what I came down here for. For the first time I feel useless and in the way. And, for the first time, a little ashamed. Some of the men turn to stare and then turn back to the coal face. Others don't pay much mind at all; I have come at a time, early on in the new shift, when they are swinging away hard to make the yardage.

I scrunch down in the dirt, wishing I knew what I came

here for. The men I watch have a mass rhythm all their own. Each team seems to work disconnectedly in the pocket, both the pick and shovel man, and the teams; the clinking, chipping, scraping and shovelling sounds provide a rough but persistent metronome by which they do, in fact, time themselves. I look for Glenn. But I don't think he's here any more.

Beyond those rusty steel props, right up against the far face, two shadowy figures engage in a brute struggle with the coal. I came back to see or say something; I wish I knew what. I flick my lamp up towards the wall of the face and then down again. For a moment a naked miner was caught in my beam, as he knelt on his knee pads and drew back on his pick, like some mad frieze-like figure in a coalfield Elgin marble. There was something familiar about him. Glenn? I crawl past a couple of miners who nod and wink and continue to chip away. To get where I want I have to go on my belly. I haul myself over the coal floor. Glenn . . . ?

The shovel man, bent over double and dripping blackened sweat, glances at me. His pick man, back to me, keeps at it, a slim lithe man with a hard, easy swing. The shovel man is wearing a cut-down pair of khaki trousers over his pit boots, the pick man not even jockey shorts, just the leather belt by which to hang his lamp battery. No, I can see it isn't Glenn. Glenn is much bigger. Still he looked familiar. I start to back out of the coal nook, and my beam strikes the pick man arching his back. I tumble forward, past the shovel man.

It is Davie.

He sinks his pick into the wall, worries it back and forth and rips it out. I lift my torch. Davie, his body and face and thick fair hair blackened with coal dust, turns and puts down his pick. "What ah tell tha' about shinin' thy lamp in a miner's face," he says quietly. Slowly I lower the lamp. The shovel man is watching us, the light from his helmet flashing on the coal floor between us. Davie's large blue eyes gaze under dust-blackened lids and rest on me squarely, steadily.

187

I blink a couple of times. Then I start to crawl out, backwards, my face to the coal floor.

By the time I am in the roadway all I know of Davie is the chipping of his pick.

In the conveyor tunnel I meet MacLane and tell him that I have seen all that I want to today. We ride the belt to a large, well-lighted roadway which takes us to the bottom of the lift cage, and wait for it quietly to come, and when it does we shake hands. I thank him for taking me around, and he says it was a pleasure. Then the lift cage slams shut, and together with four or five miners I am winded upwards.

Outside the air doors, Bolton is waiting for me in the fresh, clean wind- and sun-filled world of the surface. I walk down the ramp, my boots sounding loud and military on the wood, and unbuckle my pit lamp which I turn in with my metal check tag in the lamp cabin. Then we head across the grass lawn and railroad tracks for the shower building. In the supply room I strip and hand back the helmet. Bolton is on a chair taking off his boots when I take off mine. I am very careful with myself about this. My feet have swelled. The gnarled old man behind the supply counter eyes me slyly. When I finally get the boots off, I sprawl in my chair, and feel terrific. It is like shucking off a hundred-pound ball and chain. Bolton looks across at me. I say, it sure is good to get out of those shoes. Bolton rares back and bursts into a roar of hearty laughter, and the man at the supply counter chuckles appreciatively, as if I had just told a good joke. I wiggle my toes and Bolton whoops. I say, with a smile, Some day, Bolton, it would give me real pleasure to kick you in the balls. He says, "You know, lad, Ah think tha' mean that."

The shower room is partitioned off into fifty or sixty small cubicles. Except for Bolton and myself nobody is in it, and

I stand under the alternately hot and cold spray and let the water soak in. A few moments later a shift, coming off work, clatters into the shower room and fills the other cubicles.

These men shower quietly. There are no echoes or horseplay and shouting. After five minutes of just standing under the water I use another five minutes rubbing soap all over myself. The black coal dust runs off in rivulets. Then I rinse and step out of the shower. A red-head in the cubicle opposite grins and says, "Mate, tha' don't want to go out lookin' lahk that." I turn quickly to a full-length mirror nailed to the wall in the corridor. I am nude, and except for a strip around my middle and below my ankles, after ten minutes of intensive showering, my body is coated in a glistening film of heavy blackish grey, and parts of it are still soot black. My face is a dull even grey. I borrow a wash rag from the red-headed man and spend another quarter of an hour rubbing myself. Even then, when I step out, there is a greyish ring around my neck, coal dust on my eyelids and in my ears. Two weeks later, in London, I am still to find coal dust in my ears and under my eyes.

Bolton is waiting impatiently in the supply room, wanting to know what took so long. It took him only two or three minutes to shower. A miner, he tells me, learns that bathing himself after pit is a science. There are hair cream machines all along the walls of the locker room adjoining the showers. After I dress I say goodbye to the man behind the supply counter and tell him to save the pit boots for the next midget that comes along. He thinks that is funny.

In the canteen next to the shower room I insist we stop for some bottles of pop, which I drink greedily sprawled in a chair. Bolton asks me what's wrong, am I tired, grinning hard. Does he know about Davie? I don't know, and suddenly I don't care if he knows. I tell Bolton I don't give a damn for him or his village, and suddenly I am shivering. Bolton asks me if I am all right. I tell him I am okay, and then we make our way back across the lawn to the colliery office, along the tiled corridor to Tooley's office. He is not there, so Bolton tells the manager's secretary to leave our thanks. We have a cup of syrup coffee with the secretary, on invitation, and Bolton asks him about the two men who came in earlier to get off the old people's fund, and the secretary repeats their names.

As we walk down the asphalt roadway, under the bright polished-blue sky, we pass gangs of miners coming to work. It is three or four in the afternoon, and the shift system at Dinlock is complicated. In silence Bolton and I follow the hedges and low stone wall down The Hill away from the colliery to the bottom of Theresa Road. At the corner I thank Bolton for showing me around the pit, and he tells me to think nothing of it at all, he only wanted to help. He hopes I will write a truthful story about Dinlock. I tell him I will do my best. He says the Dinlock lads are the finest in the world. Among the best, I amend. Do I feel too tired? he asks. Christ no, I say, I could go down again, right now in fact if he's game. Do my feet hurt? They pinch a bit, I say. He says he'll see me later. On the corner of Theresa Road, under the sun, we separate.

I don't feel much like going back to Davie's. He isn't going to be there anyway, so I drop in at East Club.

There is an afternoon stillness about the Club. The rays of the sun glint through the glasses of ale being drunk by the few off-shift miners around. Most of the men in Dinlock are either on shift or sleeping. A miner is playing a desultory game of snooker with himself, and over by a long oak-wood table under the clock sit Tommy Hunter, Carl Fish, the young pneumonocosis-stricken miner Dick and another one I have drunk with, a big lumpy blear-eyed ripper, Robert, who is the spitten image of that old pre-war left-hander in the Chicago Cubs bullpen, Big Bill Lee.

190

Now that we're both on top of pit, Carl seems friendly enough. Tommy Hunter puts his arm around me and asks me where he can find Bolton, he's just had another row with an under-manager about finding him alternate work to his old job. Dick, who hasn't worked for over a year, wishes Tommy would shut up, but I suppose it's better than having to listen to the commando stories again.

None of them asks me how it was down in pit. Carl, especially, does not mention it. Last time I was in Dinlock they told me Dick didn't spend much time at all in East Clu' with the old, disused or disabled miners; this trip, every time I've come in he's been here. Yesterday Bolton said, "Dick keeps tellin' himself that in another month or two he'll be fit to go back down to face. But none of us have the heart to tell him to stop kiddin' himself."

At the table under the clock they are talking about what they always talk about: the pit. Robert and Carl are bone dead weary after their shift, and are arguing over yardage rates. Soon, the frail, tall old codger who sweeps East Clu' comes by. Nobody much ever pays attention to him. I don't even know his name. He sweeps around our feet, waiting to be invited to join the table, and when no invitation is uttered, sits down at the end of the bench. As the minutes pass, he edges closer and closer to Tommy who at first studiously ignores him. Carl and Robert are drinking very fast, and Carl is pie-eyed a little. Robert, who is about 40 and thinning on top, is thick-tongued and glassy-eyed, sitting with a silly smile and a half lean. They talk just to be talking, to have something to do while they drink and wash away some of the coal and tiredness. The more Carl drinks the more he withdraws into a stoical dignified silence; Robert becomes loose-tongued. "Ah'm gloomy," he says. Tommy asks Robert why he is gloomy. Slowly the afternoon shadows lengthen in the almost deserted bar of East Clu'.

"How in Christ's name do Ah know why Ah'm gloomy," says Robert. Dick, the sick young miner, smiles slightly and

191

tries to cheer up Robert who won't talk about anything but the details of shifting yardage which he has heard they use up in Bumley. Carl jerks awake. "Bumley's got stockpiles," he says. Robert says, "That don't make a fookin' difference." They argue about whether it makes a difference. Then they dispute about how yardage is measured in a seam in Dinlock which they have both worked. Tommy Hunter tries to get a word in but they do not have much time for Tommy now that he is no longer working down in pit. Finally he blurts out, "Aye, Ah knows a lad over at Bumley. Soldiered together. 'E was a commando wi' me when we stormed Cassino." Carl, drunk, swings his square thick head over to take a good strong look at Tommy, and Dick and Robert grin to themselves. But Tommy is a man in trouble, ageing and out of work, so nobody remarks his having fought in Italy and Burma and Egypt in the same year, besides being landed in the Suma Straits by submarine. The trouble is, Tommy always has an out: that damned submarine of his.

Now Dick and Robert and Carl juggle production techniques and statistics, and leave Tommy out. Tommy has nobody to talk to. Seeing his chance, the old caretaker slides along the bench and says quickly, "Aye, Tommy, were tha' truly at Cassino?" And because Tommy has no one else to talk to he starts, at first indifferently and then with mounting enthusiasm, to tell a story to the man who sweeps the floor, something which six months ago he would not have been caught dead doing. But that was when he was down in pit. Tommy hasn't quite understood all this yet, because if he did he would not be talking so eagerly and so rapidly to the man who nobody notices or talks to but who wanders East Clu' mumbling to himself, a broom in his hand, keeping an eagle eye out for those who fall by the wayside, like Tommy, the only ones who will talk to him.

Robert is really drunk now. Dick is morose and sober. Carl sits erect and says nothing. Tommy drivels away to the open-mouthed caretaker. The lone miner plays snooker with himself in the afternoon, and in the other room five or six men, not sitting together, brood into their beer through which the sunlight no longer glints. Somehow Carl Fish finds himself saying, pursuing a line of thought withheld from us until now, "The fookin' German Army is t' best fookin' soldiers in the world."

Robert lets his spine slam into the back of his chair, as he sprawls drunkenly and eyes Carl, and Dick says, "Aw now, Carl." Robert leans forward, cupping his chin in both hands, and says, "How can tha' say a thing lahk that? How can tha'? Y'know as well as Ah do, the British tommy is t' best foot soldier in the world." Then he adds, "And next to the tommy it's the Israel boy. The Jew soldier. Second best." Carl stubbornly repeats that the German Army is, or at least was, the best in the world. "Fookin' Jews," he says, "all they can do is trade. No fookin' good as fahters." Robert slaps his brow and asks Carl how he can say a thing like that. Look what the Israeli Army did to Nasser. "Ah stand by mah claim that the Jew soldier is second only to one other."

Carl, normally imperturbable, slams his fists down on the table and overturns Dick's glass. He points his finger at Robert. "Too goddam many Jews in the world," he says with placid anger. "All over the place. Them is mostly Jews, or influenced by them. Fookin' Labour Party guvnors, half of 'em JEWS!"

Robert's reply is to insist that Carl take another look at what the Israelis did to Nasser and what they will probably do again. He tells Carl to use his head. Carl says, Aye, he'll use Robert's head in another minute. Robert tells Carl not to talk to him like that, the Jews are the best soldiers in the world. Dick points out that a moment ago Robert was only claiming the Jews as second best. Robert says that on thinking it over he has decided they are the best, and if necessary, soldier for soldier, they could conquer Britain. Carl takes no umbrage at this, and seems to be thinking it over. Robert offers to fight him. Carl thinks this over too. Tommy continues telling his story about storming Mount Cassino to the caretaker who wishes he could find a polite way to dislodge himself from the torrent of Tommy's flamboyant lies in order to see what will develop at our end of the table. Dick asks Robert what he wants to fight for. Robert says it is because Carl Fish denied that the British tommy was the best fighting soldier in the world. Then he glances up at the clock on the wall and lumbers to his feet. He says to Carl, "See tha' in the club tonaht." After he goes, Tommy calls over, "Cheer up, Carl. Tha' can faht him another tahm." Carl turns a level glazed stare to me and smiles broadly. "Robert," he says, "he is a good chap. Tha' mustn't pay him no mahnd. 'E gets drunk like. 'E treats his kids proper." "Aye," adds Dick with a muffled, covert spasm of coughing, "Robert's got principle. He is good to his kids. He's a widower lahk. He ain't married."

Half an hour later, in the shadowy club, all the conversation has dribbled out of us. The caretaker has gone off somewhere to his duties, leaving Tommy slumped against the wall, staring at the floor and waiting to deliver his complaints to Bolton when he shows up. Carl and Dick, at opposite ends of the table, drink steadily and morosely. I play a game of snooker with the lone miner. Then I buy a final drink all around and bid goodbye to the boys and walk out of East Club leaving behind ten or eleven miners off shift who are not saying very much to each other. At the door Tommy Hunter runs after me to ask if I'm coming back. I tell him I don't know.

Outside, across the streets, near the Pub I run into three young miners, Dick's age but healthy, who call out to me. I don't recognise them. They say they were down in Sleythorpe on morning shift and I had spoken to them. They insist on taking me back to East Club where we stand around in the tombola room and where, through the doorway, I can see Dick and Carl, still worldless and wordless with drinks in their hands, and Tommy now again chewing the ear off

194

the caretaker. The boys from morning shift in Sleythorpe and I lift a ceremonial drink, and then another one for luck. I tell them I have to go now and they say, Come back down any time. Then we scatter.

On the way back to Davie's from the Club Bolton mysteriously materialises out of a side street and falls in step as we climb Theresa Road below the colliery. He asks me if I enjoyed myself down in pit today and I reply, I had a fine time. He says I must come back some day. Unexpectedly, he stops walking and jumps up on a low stone fence and invites me to sit with him. He starts to say something and trails off. I don't help. We get off the fence and go on up to the top of The Hill where we must go separate ways. Bolton turns to me.

"Those lads. Grand lads. This village, it's summat to be proud of, eh boy? Soomtahm Ah think it will be here, Dinlock, when London is in flames. The key is to stick together. And when the men won't, tha've got to make them. Those two who came by in mornin', to strahk names off old people's list. It took me two years to get that list goin'. Now what kahnd of man would deny old people a shilling a week. No, they've had it, those two. Ah will make lahf a livin' hell for them in the village. They're traitors, that's what they are."

I suggest that the two men had a right to remove their names from a voluntary roll. "Democracy is it?" says Bolton. "That kahnd of democracy c'n ruin the village. Kill it. Nay, when they do a thing lahk that, they put themselves beyond the pale. As far as Ah'm concerned, they have ruined themselves in this village. Ah will see to that."

He puts his hand on my shoulder. "It's been good havin' tha', lad. Tha' must send me a copy of thy book." And with that he turns on his heel and walks away, his hard burly body leaning forward as if into a stiff wind.

When I open the garden gate Loretta is out in the yard

195

hanging wash, which flaps about her in the warm summer breeze. I pass her and go into the house. Baby Michael is asleep in the kitchen and the kids are in school. The twin sisters who also live in the house are not due back in Dinlock until I go, that much I can tell without being told. There is a fire going in the parlour. I drop down in the easy chair, tired. Loretta comes in after a while and asks if she can wash anything for me.

I sit up straighter. Loretta bustles around the house, smiling nervously at me, and then she goes into the hallway. She is carrying my kit bag when she comes back. She sets them down and says, "Davie said as how tha'd be wantin' to make the early train."

I stare at Loretta. Her plump arms folded, looking at me, there is something hesitantly defiant, doubtfully triumphant about her. She seems to want to locate expression for several conflicting emotions. She giggles, and then because there was no reason for it, flushes. She touches her hair, having to explain.

"Ah," she says, "it's been a day. That kahnd, y'know."

It is as if, having won a victory, she were fearful of handling it because in winning she has opened up so much that may be new and terrible to her.

I go upstairs to change. My body in the bedroom mirror is still grey with coal dust. The sheet is off "The Dying Miner". Davie was looking at it before he went to the pit. The brushes on the table are untouched. I finish dressing and go downstairs.

I thank Loretta for packing my suitcase.

"Oh that's nothin'. Davie said as how tha'd be wantin' to make the early train. Oh, Ah told tha' that, didn't Ah?" She giggles, covers her mouth like a schoolgirl. Then she says, "Mus' be a Purpose or we wouldn't be here."

She looks utterly amazed, stunned, by what she has said. She smiles tentatively and claps her hands in front of her, as though to say, Whatever in the world caused me to say a thing like that. Instead she says, "Ah was sure to pack all thy things. Are tha' sure tha wouldn't lahk some tea 'afore tha' go?"

I don't think I'll have any tea.

So it's a last look around, at the chips frying in the grate, at baby Michael in the pram in the kitchen, at the yellow-and-green wallpaper, at all the accoutrements of the fantastically intense life which is had in this tiny, cluttered redolent room.

The weather, I say, seems to be holding up, and she says she hopes it continues to do so. When will Davie be coming home? I ask.

She replies complacently, "The usual tahm."

I ask her to forward any mail. Then we stand in the middle of the room. I say, So long. Thanks for having me.

"Oh, it was real nice havin' tha'. Tha' moos' coom again."

Say goodbye to Davie for me. Tell him I'll write.

"Oh yes, Ah'll be sure to do that."

And say goodbye to the kids.

"Oh yes . . ."

What more is there to say? I pick up my kit bag and walk out of the house, past the garden gate, up Davie's street to Theresa Road. There is some sort of idea in my mind about having a last look at the colliery. But from here, on the deserted street-corner, I can see the head-stocks and spinning wheels, and I don't want to see any more.

And then the bus comes.